GW00470412

RETRIBUTION

A DI SCOTT BAKER CRIME NOVEL: THREE

JAY NADAL

PROLOGUE

hristopher Johnson gazed through his study window as the darkness of the night enveloped him. The warmth of the summer sun still hung in the air long after its global orb of light disappeared below the rolling hills of the Sussex Downs. A tall brass, antique nightstand towards the back of his room illuminated the darkness. The soft glow from a lamp cast a faint shadow across the hundreds of books that filled the built-in book-case. Row upon row of worn volumes displayed on wooden shelves that extended the full width and height of one wall.

As the evening wore on, he found it increasingly harder to concentrate. His thoughts whisked him away at every opportunity, far from the countless hours he'd already spent reviewing the books. *How many bloody ways were there to explain the impact of conflict and change in the Middle East c.1914–1995 on modern-day society in the region? So very dull*, he'd decided.

Many hours at his desk had left him tight and knotted. He leant back in his vintage chesterfield dark red leather captain's chair. The leather squeaked beneath him as he shifted, the 1940s wooden frame creaked like the timbers of an old sailing ship from a bygone era. His back and shoulders cracked as the tension eased. It was the least of his worries. His weak arthritic hip locked, forcing him to lean to his right to release the seized joint. He rubbed the tender area as it clicked. To the left on his desk, stood a tall pile of books that he still needed to work through. To his right, a half glass of Merlot, his third tonight which helped to numb the monotony of his work and melt away the stress of the day.

For company tonight it was just him, his books and the relaxing sounds of *Tristesse* by Chopin, wafting from his well-worn mini-CD player positioned on a small mahogany coffee table. The energetic and atmospheric tones of the music left his senses sated. The dramatic rise and fall in tempo stirring the air and taking his mind on an intoxicating journey.

The music was just loud enough to mask the sound of the intruder. His footsteps softened as he walked on the thick plush red hallway carpet that led to the study. He'd chosen his footwear carefully. The bare wooden parquet floors of the hallways and walkways of the main building magnified sound, making it impossible for a silent approach.

Johnson was deeply engrossed in his work, flicking through pages, humming along to the music, whilst tapping the end of his pen on the dark mahogany desk. The overpowering smell of mellow Virginia pipe tobacco clung like a mist in the air. Faint clouds of smoke floated gracefully as they swirled and danced around the room in no particular direction, their trails illuminated in the glow of the light.

The ornate brass handle on the old mahogany door turned

millimetre by millimetre. The intruder opened the door just wide enough to peer around the edge. From his vantage point, he could see Johnson at the far end of the room in front of the window. The fool hadn't heard him coming, dozy sod. *You've made this far too easy. A bus could have driven past you and you wouldn't have noticed it.*

The intruder crept forward one step at a time, his body moving in perfect synchronisation with each slow steady breath. He was just a few inches behind his target as he raised his left hand, the thin blade of the knife glinting in the light.

Johnson froze as the feeling of the cold steel blade pressed against his neck. Terror gripped him; his drowsy senses loosened by the wine willed him to fight back. He swallowed hard as he stared ahead, his eyes wide open in fear. From his seated position, he could see the reflection of the intruder standing behind him in the darkened window, his face masked in a balaclava.

"Get up," the intruder said in a calm and measured tone.

"What is it that you want?" Johnson's voice quivered.

"Retribution."

The intruder repeated his demands again as he pressed the blade against Johnson's neck, his right hand yanking the man's collar from behind, pulling him out of the chair.

"You're coming with me."

"Retribution? I don't understand," Johnson asked in abject terror. Sweat trickled down between his shoulder blades as he tried to keep his body from shaking. "My wallet is in my jacket. Take it. There's fifty pounds in there. Here, you can take my watch. Take anything you want. Just don't hurt me," he said holding out his wrist.

"Come with me," he repeated more forcefully this time, yanking Johnson who stumbled and almost fell. But only almost.

He marched Johnson through the hallway and downstairs, leading him out of the back door into the darkness of the night. Johnson squinted hard, desperately trying to adjust to the blackness. Confusion and panic forced bile to sour his throat.

The intruder had waited for this moment. He'd planned this for many years. He'd chosen his spot in the forest, a place isolated enough where no one would disturb them, or hear the man's screams.

The masked intruder pushed Johnson. The half crescent of the moon provided enough brightness in the blackness of the night to illuminate the edge of the forest. Johnson struggled to keep pace as he was pushed and shoved along, forcing him to stumble on the uneven ground, a mixture of heather and gorse tangling in his feet.

The two men arrived at a small clearing. All along Johnson had been insistent, his bravado surfacing occasionally, demanding an explanation. He'd receive none. He was thrust down to the ground, the intruder now looming above him, holding the knife just inches away from Johnson's face.

"It's your fault. You're to blame. You let it happen and you did nothing," the intruder said reciting the Latin phrase *Ignavus iners timidius tu mori debes*. Johnson being well versed in Latin challenged the intruder. "I'm not a coward. I don't deserve to die. What the hell is this all about?" he shouted in fear, bucking upwards in a futile attempt to throw the intruder from his prone body.

"I want you to admit your guilt. I want you to beg for forgiveness."

Johnson started to cry, his frustration boiling over as he pleaded for his safety. "I can't. I don't know what you're talking about."

"You're going to die anyway. You don't recognise me, do you?" the intruder said through gritted teeth as he unmasked his face.

Despite the darkness, Johnson studied the man's exposed features. "You?…but you're…"

The steel blade pressed further into Johnson's neck.

"No, think back…much further back," the intruder insisted.

Johnson studied the man hard. Certain features bore a resemblance, a striking resemblance in fact, to someone he once knew. The realisation hit him, his eyes widening into shocked orbs. Johnson's jaw dropped as if it had become unhinged, the magnitude of his situation sinking in bone-deep. As deep as the cold, unyielding earth below his own face. Tears started to well in his eyes, fear turning his stomach into knots. "I can't say anything. They'll kill me. I swore I'd never say anything."

The intruder waved the knife in the man's face with wicked intent, pressing the tip into Johnson's cheek causing a small nick, the first signs of precious lifeblood glistened in the night sky.

"You have a choice. You die by the sword or you hang," he

said looking towards the noose that hung from a strong branch.

Panic consumed Johnson. His head spun, his chest heaved and he struggled to breathe as bile raced up his throat once again. He was old now. Once he'd been a junior wrestling champion afraid of no one and fought opponents older and bigger. Now he was a former shell of his past virility. He had very little chance of overpowering the man, and an even slimmer chance of outrunning him.

The desperate plight of his situation spun his mind like a tornado, his thoughts colliding into each other. He found himself submerged in a dire hole, and tried to rationalise it. Perhaps he could talk his way out of this, but the wine had dulled his ability to think clearly. Or the fear. He fought back.

"This can't be. No. This is ridiculous, but…but…no you won't get away with this." The words tumbled out as he struggled to draw ragged breaths. Even though he wasn't making sense, he continued to plead. To poke a hole in a psychopath's twisted logic. "You can't make me do anything. You're just trying to scare the shit out of me!"

"You're right. I can't make you do anything so I'll make the decision for you."

The intruder flung the knife down on the ground, before leaning down and punching Johnson hard in the face, dazing him in the process. He grabbed him by both collars and hauled him up, before delivering several more blows to the man's stomach, forcing him to double up in agony and crumple to his knees.

Offering Johnson no compassion or mercy, he dragged him

along on his knees. He pushed and pulled him in the direction of the noose, forced the noose over his head and yanked up the slack before Johnson could wriggle out of it. Johnson fought hard to remove the rope from his neck, but he was a fraction too late. The intruder started to pull hard on the rope as it tightened around Johnson's neck. Johnson screamed, as both of his hands gripped either side of the rope. He struggled, thrashing and kicking in a desperate attempt to release the pressure from around his neck. Ragged inhales racked his torso as his lungs fought to take in oxygen.

The intruder used all his strength to haul the rope up just high enough to lift Johnson's feet off the ground. His muscles tensed, forcing him to grit his teeth and use every last drop of energy to lean back into the pull. The forest floor offered little grip as the overgrown grass and dead vegetation robbed his shoes of any firm footing.

Johnson fought with every drop of energy that hadn't been sucked out by fear; desperate to pull down on the rope so that his feet could still remain in contact with the ground, affording him precious seconds to take a few more gasps of air. Spittle tumbled out of his mouth; his eyes bulged as the pressure increased, crushing the veins in his neck and starving his body of oxygen. His mind swirled like a dark vortex as confusion took hold, the light-headedness blurring his vision.

His body thrashed as the pain intensified, every sinew of his being fighting to stay alive. The intruder proved far too strong for him; he was fast losing the battle to live. With one final pull of the rope, Johnson was now suspended from the ground, his legs flailing in an imaginary running action. His eyes bulged as the pressure built in his neck.

His final few gasps of breath came small and sharp, his arms scratching and clawing at his neck.

In the space of a heartbeat, he stilled. His body hung there with his head bowed forward, his arms and legs hanging lifelessly. His body swayed gently and melodically in the stillness of the night much like a human wind chime, the only sound, the creaking of rope as it pulled tighter, slowly coming to a stop.

1

The undulating slopes proved a challenge for the most competent of runners. To the group of fifteen-year-old boys, the hills presented the ultimate test in endurance, pace and strength. They'd been running for twenty minutes. The reputation of the house was at stake and the risk of facing the wrath of the sports teacher and housemaster, proved enough of an incentive to spur them on.

Even though the summer heat loomed only a few hours away, the cooler conditions of the morning offered them a light breeze and a refreshing chill that prevented them overheating.

Their route led them east towards the hamlet of Westmeston. They travelled along single lane tracks barely wide enough for a car, and certainly not accommodating enough for the farm vehicles that criss-crossed this landscape as they headed from one field to another. The lead runner frequently shouted a word of warning about oncoming vehicles to those behind. The message was relayed in sequence down the line, as they puffed out their cheeks and carried on.

They barely had time to take in the beauty of the landscape, or the tall green hedges that skirted the road, and the traditional stone walls that enclosed the few dwellings that made up this small community. The 11th century parish church was a mere spectator as the runners passed. From there they headed north-west towards Ditchling across country. Their legs were fast being sapped of energy as the rough terrain and inclines forced the line of boys to thin out, the strongest taking the lead, the weakest beginning to trail.

Matthew Edrington was a trailer. Running had never been his forte; he was into reading spec fiction, creating music on his laptop, and keeping his Facebook fan page 'All Things Ginge' going. He'd spent most of his life being the butt of jokes about his bright ginger hair. A recent attempt to play it down by growing it longer and sporting the unkempt mop look, hadn't stopped the jibes and digs. Together with his bright blue piercing eyes, pale complexion and high cheekbones, many had taunted him about his soft boyish looks. "Poof," "gay boy," "you big girl," and "grow a pair of tits," were hurtful comments he took on the chin daily.

His Facebook page was an attempt to face his issues head-on, to embrace his traits. In reality, it was his alter ego running the page. He hid behind it and the smokescreen the page created. Matthew was weak; he knew it, often never feeling comfortable in his own skin and lacking in self-confidence. He never sought out attention. "Edrington, you're not a team player. You're a waste of space," were the words that crumbled his self-esteem each and every time his housemaster singled him out.

He puffed out his cheeks and stared at the ground as he plodded on. As each minute passed, his pace dropped off a fraction more. The heavy panting of the other stragglers loomed up behind him. They levelled with him briefly, throwing him exasperated looks that suggested he was once again going to be responsible for the house coming in last in the weekly cross-country competition.

Despite the sinking feeling that swelled in the pit of his stomach, his pencil-thin, pasty legs wouldn't carry him any faster. His mind willed him to speed up, to turn things around. *Come on you can do it.* But his body was fast failing him, his lungs were tight as he fought to take in deep lungfuls of air. His throat was dryer than a desert plain. The lactic acid in his thighs stung. They felt like two heavy concrete blocks that were stuck in a quagmire of mud.

Time seemed to stand still and the landscape remained the same. He was sure that he'd travelled a few hundred yards further, but his surroundings remained strangely familiar in his eyes. The other pupils were fast disappearing in the distance, as they looked like tiny dots on a radar jerking forward inch by inch.

He had to think fast. He couldn't come in last yet again and face the humiliation from those gathered at the finish line. He slowed to a walking pace, familiarising himself with the landscape. He had no choice; he'd have to find a shortcut. He looked in all directions desperate to find the fastest way back to school. He leant forward, his hands resting on his knees as he caught his breath. Sweat beaded on his forehead, stinging his eyes, causing him to squint.

He knew that if he had any chance of making it back in time, he would need to cut across the fields, climb the brow of the hill, and then head down in through the forest that surrounded the school on three sides. Urgency hastened his thoughts, coupled with doubt as to whether his body would carry him that far. He turned off the road and fought his way through the hedgerow. Sharp bramble bushes tore into his body. Stinging red scratches criss-crossed his legs. His shorts snagged as he fought his way through. In places, the hedgerow was as tall as Matthew and certainly not designed for easy transit through.

He pushed on, calling on every ounce of energy to carry him over the hill. He gritted his teeth. His mouth was parched. His feet barely able to trudge over the brow. The force of downward momentum carried him swiftly downhill and into the dense woodland that surrounded the perimeter of the school. The forest had an identity of its own, a thick tall canopy created a darkness that added to it ghostly, unwelcoming atmosphere.

There were a few paths that criss-crossed the forest, well-trodden ramblers routes. For Matthew, they offered him little relief. He had never ventured into this part of the woodland in the time that he had been at the school. He stopped for a moment to catch his breath, his eyes darting in all directions. But it all looked the same, brown, natural barriers that rose from the ground blocking his line of sight. Birdsong high up in the trees was drowned out by the sound of his heavy breathing. From the direction in which he had just travelled, he figured that if he continued to run forward, he was sure to find his way out.

Small beams of light broke through the heavy curtain of darkness above him. They looked like tiny glimmering stars in the night sky. It was enough to create small patches of illumination in the dense undergrowth. In the distance through the trees, he could see what appeared to be the edge of the forest, and the first signs that he was close to the school. A mixture of adolescent shouting, whistles and clapping heralded the finish line.

He struggled; his ribs tight, crushing the air out of him. His rasping breath was evidence of the asthma that caused his chest to heave violently. He had to stop; he couldn't carry on. He knew he was only just a few hundred yards away from safety, but the shortness of breath gripped him, cold fear spread through him, as the lining of his lungs burnt. Stopping for just a few seconds wouldn't harm his efforts, he decided.

He came to a grinding halt, falling to his knees, his hands reaching out in front of him, making contact with the ground to steady himself. His stomach heaved as he fought to take in oxygen. A whistle of breath and phlegm rattling in his throat, warned of an imminent asthma attack. He needed his Ventolin inhaler but he'd left it back in his room foolishly thinking he wouldn't need it. *Oh shit, I can't breathe. I need to move on. I have to move on.* Each exhale was accompanied by an eerie howling cry.

A foreign sound snapped his head to attention. His mind whirled as he tried to identify it. It was coming from behind him. He realised it was a sound of a branch creaking. A slow, hypnotic and rhythmic creaking. He turned to look over his shoulder. The sight that greeted his eyes caused him to spin around on his knees and recoil. His eyes widened in fear, on his lips a gasp, unable to comprehend what he'd found. He desperately hoped his mind played tricks on him, a hallucination, a consequence of the fatigue that racked his body. *This can't be. My mind is creating this horrible scene to scare my body so I can get up and run again, even faster than before.* But as the seconds passed, reality hit him straight between the eyes. It wasn't a dream. He was in a living nightmare.

In front of him was the outline of a man hanging from a rope, his face larger than it should be, with bulging eyeballs that stared off into the distance. The body slowly rotated like a musical ballerina in a jewellery box, the taut rope repeatedly rubbing on the branch.

Matthew fought the bile that crawled up the back of his throat, his breathing coming in shocked pants as cold fear raced through his veins sending shock waves through his body. He trembled violently as he clambered backwards, desperate to get away from the hideous scene in front of him. He glanced around, terror contorted his face, frightened whimpering screams escaping from him. He tried to get back up on his feet, but his mind moved faster than his body, causing him to stumble back several times on to the uneven, overgrown forest floor.

Each step increased his acceleration, providing him with enough momentum to spin on his heels and run. His feet caught exposed tree roots that were discreetly hidden by overgrown mosses and lichens that offered his trainers little grip. Stumbling once again, his arms took the full brunt of the impact, small trails of blood seeping from the multiple deep scratches.

As he cleared the forest and entered the grounds of the school, he was met with a cacophony of whistles, boos and the inevitable cries of "*loser.*" He didn't care on this occasion, he needed to get away fast, as far as he could from the scene he'd just witnessed.

"Edrington, get a bloody move on," rang in his ears, as his housemaster screamed at him.

He knew the welcoming party was going to be hostile. Some of his co-pupils glared at him with hate-filled eyes. Others leant on each other's shoulders, pointing at him, the spectacle giving them plenty to laugh at. He fell to his knees by his housemaster, who looked down at him in displeasure as he shook his head slowly, his brows pulled down in a stern stare.

A mixture of pain and fear plugged the words in his dry throat. He raised one arm jabbing in the direction of the forest. "Body," he mouthed, his slight voice drowned out by the barrage of abuse coming his way.

Drawing on all his reserves and taking one huge breath, his voice was just loud enough to be heard by those within a few feet of him. He shouted once more. "Body." Poking hard now in the direction of the forest he tried again. "There's a body in the forest."

2

Scott and Abby swept through the imposing black wrought-iron gates that fronted the school. It seemed inadequate to merely call this a school. A luxury hotel or retreat seemed more befitting, judging by what greeted them. A long sweeping drive took them along the left flank of this sprawling estate. To the left, a long line of tall, established oak trees offered a natural boundary.

Scott noticed how every twenty yards or so, the border of oaks was broken by ornate weeping willows, with long flowing branches that drooped and gently grazed across the grass. A light breeze rustled through the branches, breaking the silence. To the right, a row of small wooden stumps poked out of the ground at evenly spaced intervals. Thick boundary rope was draped in perfect symmetry from one stump to the next. Scott guessed that the lawns beyond them stretched for some distance as he couldn't make out the right-hand boundary.

A uniformed officer waved them off to the left of the main building, gesturing towards the rear. Coming around the back, they again were presented with even more open land that stretched off into the distance a few hundred yards where it met the edge of the forest that surrounded the school.

"Shit, this is a big place," Abby remarked as she whistled through her teeth. "Can you imagine how much it costs to send a child here?"

"I hate to imagine, way more than our salaries… combined…including overtime," Scott suggested.

"And the rest," Abby replied pointing ahead of them.

The presence of two white scientific services vans, several police cars, Cara's silver Ford Focus and an ambulance loomed up in the distance.

Scott looked back as they kitted up in the white paper overalls and couldn't help but admire how the main school building looked just as imposing and elegantly impressive from the back as it did from the front.

This was a completely different type of schooling. It wasn't your average comprehensive school found in the sprawling suburbs of every town and city across the country. This was a fine example of an institution, a way of life, a privileged, educational system reserved for the elite and wealthy dating back generations. Pupils who attended would have had their lives mapped out long before they were out of nappies.

You wouldn't find kids here from poor backgrounds, or unruly disruptive teenagers looking to start a fight at every opportunity. Places like this offered an honoured education and guaranteed route to success. Many would head to Oxbridge and then go on to be leaders and CEOs in industry, or one day be future politicians or ambassadors in far-flung countries, or upholders of justice in the courts of law.

"Why do I always end up in forests?" Abby said with a grimace as once again she found herself trampling through dense undergrowth in shoes far from appropriate, whilst adjusting her body cam to begin relaying footage back to the station. "You would have thought I'd learnt my lesson after the Newland's murder a few weeks ago. Lack of preparation on my part…again," she fumed.

"Stop whining. You're starting to sound like an old bag as each day passes. Seriously, what's up with you?" Scott asked.

"Nothing, I hate getting messy, and Lord knows what's beneath this undergrowth. I could be treading in animal shite or dead, decaying rodents and I'd never know," she said scrunching her features as if she'd sucked down a lemon.

"You need to lighten up, Abs, otherwise, your face will get stuck like that," he teased.

"Ha ha, very droll."

The forest offered a cooling shade from the heat that was building from the midday sun. July was shaping up to be a warm month, with temperatures regularly jumping into the mid-twenties. The crime scene was much deeper into the forest than Scott had anticipated. Scott wondered if this was deliberate, an attempt to hide the scene and the body for as long as possible from prying eyes. If that was the case, then that strategy had failed.

The officers puffed a bit by the time they reached the blue and white police cordon tape. Scott could clearly see the suspended body still in place whilst forensic officers logged and photographed the scene. Having signed in to the crime scene log earlier, Scott headed in the direction of the crime scene manager.

"Matt, how's things going?"

"We should be ready to cut him down any minute now. We don't want the poor sod up there any longer than is necessary. Cara can then get stuck in. Looks like a suicide on the face of it. It's going to be a lengthy job mapping out the scene, and gathering any evidence."

"Have we got an ID?"

"We understand he's the assistant principal of the school from what staff have told us," he said nodding over towards where they'd just come. "Poor lad in the ambulance found him. Gave the kid an asthma attack."

Scott glanced around trying to get a feel for the geography. It was a dense secluded spot, not the easiest to get to, but the spot where they stood offered a clearing of some sorts. He assumed that it had been chosen deliberately rather than randomly because of its inaccessibility.

"Okay, mate, keep me informed," Scott said as he headed off to track down Cara who was now engrossed in yet another cosy conversation with Abby, which left him decidedly nervous.

"Inspector," Cara called as he approached, a glint of affection in her eyes, as both Cara and Abby stopped to stare at him.

"What?"

"Nothing, my dear, just making sure you're all right," she replied, a hint of mischief in her tone.

"Yes, why wouldn't I be?"

"Just thought you might be tired from all these late nights you've been having?" Cara winked knowing Scott would be squirming from her loaded question.

Amusement danced across Abby's face as she watched the natural banter between them. She raised a questioning brow in Scott's direction.

Scott ignored her question. "Guess you've not had a chance to do much yet?"

"No, I'm on shortly. I can give you an initial assessment not long after. On first impression though, it does appear as if he's taken his own life. There's no evidence of other injuries other than a small nick on his cheek from what I could see, but then again, he's hanging from a rope at the moment."

"Abby and I will go and have a chat with the lad, there's nothing much for us to do around here at the moment."

———

ABBY BREATHED a sigh of relief as they stepped out into the warm sun once again. A smile returned to her face as she wrapped her golden blonde hair behind her ears, closed her eyes and raised her face upwards towards the blue sky, enjoying the warmth of the sun on her face.

"What do you make of that then?" Scott asked, breaking her moment of indulgence as he stepped out of his suit.

She remained motionless, enjoying the moment as she pondered the scene.

"Sounds like Cara keeps you busy at night!" She laughed.

"You know what I mean, you cheeky mare."

"It does look like he took his own life, and the fact that it's out here and not indoors suggests it was premeditated."

Scott nodded as he entertained his own theories, but Abby had a point. He certainly didn't want to be discovered.

***

MATTHEW EDRINGTON SAT in the back of the ambulance shaking, wrapped in a red hospital blanket. He sucked hard on a nebuliser as his chest heaved, his shoulders hunched tight on each inhale. His ginger hair was matted with sweat, his dirty arms and legs heavily scratched, scabbed with blood. His frightened eyes glared at the officers as they peered in the back. Whatever he'd witnessed had certainly shaken the boy to his core.

A woman in a two-piece matching grey check suit and white blouse comforted the boy. She had one arm around Matthew's shoulders, pulling him closer to her. She lightly dabbed her moist eyes with a tissue.

"I'm Mary Harrison the deputy principal," she announced.

Scott gave her a nod of acknowledgement, before turning his attention to the boy. "Hello, Matthew, I'm Scott, a police officer," Scott said gently as he held up his warrant card. "This is my colleague Abby," he offered nodding in her direction as Abby smiled. "How are you feeling?"

Matthew shrugged, his little frame looked helpless and weak beneath his red shroud.

"Can we ask you a few questions?"

The boy hesitated for a moment, unsure of his surroundings, before nodding once.

"Did you see anyone else when you found…erm, when you found the body?" Scott struggled to find the right words without upsetting or alarming the boy any further.

Matthew shook his head once.

"Did you notice anything out of the ordinary or odd as you approached the forest?"

Matthew shook his head again.

"How about when you came out of the forest, anything odd?"

"No," came a crackling, muffled reply from behind his plastic oxygen mask.

"Well, you've been very brave, and I know what you saw was very upsetting. We'll make sure you're looked after and that your parents are notified. I understand that it's the assistant principal of the school. Is that correct?" Scott asked looking at Mary Harrison.

"Yes," she replied with a weak nod.

"And his name is?…"

"Mr Johnson, Christopher Johnson," she replied.

"I've let the house down. I came in last again," Matthew interrupted through deep gasps, glancing apprehensively in the direction of the officers.

Mary Harrison gave him a sympathetic hug, as her red bloodshot eyes looked over the top of Matthew's head towards the police officers. She opened her mouth in readiness to say something, but then stopped herself, perhaps deciding that now was not the time to be talking about the tragic death of her colleague in front of the boy.

"You'll find Mr Collier, the principal, over in the main building."

Scott gave Matthew a reassuring smile. Despite discovering a body, the fact he'd come last in their cross-country run seemed to play on the boy's mind more than anything else, and that troubled Scott.

"Poor bugger, he's as white as a ghost." Abby sighed.

"That's going to stick with him for a long time; poor lad will need some counselling."

MATT ALLEN, the crime scene manager, pulled Scott and Abby to one side as they headed back to their car. "We've taken down the victim, there are no further visible injuries that we can see, other than some swelling to his face, and so cause of death looks like strangulation by hanging. We're still sweeping the floor for evidence. The ground has been disturbed quite a bit, so we're not sure if that's as a result of the boy, foxes or those who investigated it before calling it in. Cara will know more; I think the PM is for tomorrow.

"He had his school ID card on a lanyard in his trouser pocket. It says Christopher Johnson, and the photo looks like him."

"Well, at least we know who he is."

"There's something worth noting here, Scott. In one of his pockets, was a folded piece of paper with something that looks like a Latin inscription on it...and a white feather," Matt said raising a brow as he held up a clear plastic evidence bag.

Scott and Abby exchanged a look of curiosity, not sure what to make of it.

"Despite my many talents, I can't admit to being a professor of Latin, so the inscription would mean nothing to me," Scott said looking perplexed.

Abby looked equally blank. "Me neither."

"We'll look at that later. Let's head over to the main building to see what's what with the principal."

3

S cott couldn't help but admire the magnificent architecture and history that exuded from Edmunston-Hunt boarding school. An impressive 18th century Gothic-style grey stone design complemented the 19th century additions that had been added as the school grew. It was a well-proportioned building set over three floors. Directly above the main entrance, stood a fifty feet high steeple, topped off with a spire. A large black and gold clock with Roman numerals proudly dominated the front aspect of the steeple.

The splendour of the building was completed at both ends with two large extensions with elegant stained-glass windows. The effect was to create a horseshoe shape building. Its early Christian influences were clearly apparent to Scott as he admired its ornate stone features.

Scott and Abby exchanged glances as they entered one of the bastions of elite education. He glanced over his shoulder at the large green lawns that fronted the school. From what he could see, they were being used as cricket pitches. The lawns were perfectly cut and striped in true British fashion, the distinctive smell of freshly cut grass hung in the air. The setting, the school, the lawns and smell of grass all were quintessentially English in Scott's eyes.

Silence reigned supreme so the place took on a sense of isolation. For a school like this, there should have been a hive of activity, children hurrying from one class to another, various sports in action, laughing, and the sound of excited chatter...but nothing pierced his eardrums, just an eerie silence hanging in the air.

"Guv," Abby said, catching Scott's attention and nodding in the direction of the far right-hand side of the building.

A sliver of a man appeared, wearing dark blue overalls, a broom in his hand. He'd stopped cleaning and leant on the top of the broom handle just observing them. His face, devoid of expression, gave nothing away. Scott couldn't tell if the man was curious or concerned, even a cursory wave didn't prompt a reaction. He made a mental note to obtain his identity.

The school reception carried on the theme of style and history. Dark wood parquet floors stretched in all directions as far as the eye could see. A thin lady, in a tweed skirt, white blouse and choker chain greeted them. She peered over the top of half-rimmed glasses.

"I'm Mrs Hilary, *senior* receptionist," she said introducing herself in a plum voice.

Scott couldn't help but smile to himself as he noticed the intonation in her voice.

"Mr Collier has been expecting you for some time," she

uttered in a voice clear, crisp and sharp, with an undercurrent of dissatisfaction.

Scott hated being talked to like that. There was no need for sarcasm or the lack of diplomacy. He wondered if she was even capable of being pleasant or welcoming. Mrs Hilary either loved her job too much, or punched above her weight and thought she ran the school.

"I appreciate your concern, Mrs Hilary. As you can imagine, we needed to review the scene first, and I'm sure even *you* would want to make sure that Matthew, the little boy who found him, was safe and well before we spoke to *Mr Collier*," Scott replied through clenched teeth.

Suitably chastised and clearly annoyed, Mrs Hilary led them to the principal's office without further comment or eye contact. Her short, quick steps echoed through the old corridors. A pungent aroma clung in the air as ancient Asian spices wafted through from the school kitchen. It smelt more like an Indian takeaway than a school. The pupils would no doubt be tucking into a curry of some sort later today.

As Abby glanced around, the oak panelling on the walls had their fair share of old historic paintings and pieces of artwork, none of which she recognised. She wouldn't have been able to guess what century the paintings belonged to or who the artists were who'd created them. Scott found it strange that despite the death of a senior colleague, the principal was holed up in his office. He naturally assumed that following such a tragedy, he would have had a strong visible presence to reassure the pupils and teachers alike.

Mrs Hilary knocked firmly on the large oak door which had a gold plaque inscribed with *Mr Collier - Principal.*

"Please come in and take a seat. I'm Adrian Collier, the principal," he offered extending his hand.

Scott shook Mr Collier's hand. "I'm Detective Inspector Baker and this is Detective Sergeant Trent, we need to ask you a few questions."

"Yes, yes, of course," he said in a firm, deep booming voice more befitting of the military than education as he took his place behind a large leather-topped mahogany desk. "Yes, it's a terrible tragedy. It's shocked all of us. Unfortunately, I haven't got much to go on," he said shrugging his shoulders. "I'm hoping you will be able to shed some light on what's happened, Inspector. Can I assume he took his own life?"

"We're not at liberty to discuss that at the moment. We are still conducting our preliminary investigation."

"Yes, of course I understand," he replied nodding slowly.

He rested his elbows on the armrests of his chair, his fingers interlocked in a spire beneath his chin. Collier was a tall chap with a large frame. He had lost most of his hair through age and what little that remained was now grey-white and skirted around the edge of his head. His thick, frameless glasses were perched high up on his nose, and his thin lips held a straight line across his face. He was bland in appearance but smart at the same time. His grey, two-piece suit coordinated with a light blue shirt and matching blue tie.

Abby pulled a notepad and pen from her bag to begin taking notes.

"What can you tell us about Mr Johnson?"

Collier paused for a moment whilst he gathered his

thoughts. "He was a hard-working, likeable chap. A real grafter, and a stickler for rules and regulations."

"And how did he get on with other staff members?"

"Well, as I said, he was a likeable chap. In all my years here, he'd never really had a major spat with anyone. Of course, when you're working in such close proximity to others, you can sometimes grate on each other's nerves. But I've personally never seen anything that flagged up a cause for concern for me."

"Do you know of any worries that he had?" Abby asked, looking up from her notepad.

Collier shook his head as he reflected on that question. "Nothing I'm aware of. In my experience, I've never noticed any of the staff unburdening their troubles on each other. I guess it's mentality and upbringing…we remain strong and steadfast, and deal with our problems in private."

Scott leant in a bit closer. "Was Mr Johnson in a relationship?"

"He was single as far as I know. He lived on the grounds since we provide staff accommodation. We have a small row of cottages behind the main building. All staff members are entitled to bring back a partner, that's if they're not married of course. And I do know in the past that Christopher had brought back the odd lady here and there. But that's going back some time now."

"Did he have any financial problems?"

"I'm afraid I wouldn't know, Inspector. That's something you'd need to look into," he replied thoughtfully.

"How long had Mr Johnson been here?"

"What? In a teaching capacity?" Collier clarified.

His reply wasn't what Scott expected. "Yes."

"Off the top of my head, I think just over five years or so."

"Do you know of any reason why anyone would want to harm him?"

Collier sat up, his body rigid with curiosity. "Are you suggesting that something more untoward is going on here?"

"Not at all, Mr Collier. As part of our investigation, we need to explore all avenues, personal, professional, financial and even psychological."

"Well, then my answer is no. Let me make it perfectly clear, Inspector. I run a tight ship here," he replied firmly.

"Just one last question. What was his state of mind like in the last few days?"

"I'm not sure what you're implying, Inspector," Collier replied, furrowing his brow. "He wasn't weak-minded if that's what you're suggesting. None of my staff are."

"Okay, Mr Collier, you've been very helpful. We need access to his personal file, and a visit to his cottage whilst we're here."

"That goes without saying, Inspector; you will have our full cooperation. Mrs Hilary can see to that. I'll inform her. If you make your way back to reception, I'll arrange for her to meet you there," he offered as he stood up from behind his desk, signalling that their meeting was over. He showed them out of the door, shutting it swiftly behind them.

"Can't quite make him out, Guv. He seemed very matter-of-fact, and a bit blasé in places. Judging by his reaction, you wouldn't think that he'd just lost a member of staff. I'm not being funny but the deputy principal, Mrs Harrison, showed more emotion than that old codger in there."

"Mentality and upbringing…" Scott uttered. "What's all that about? Something doesn't sit quite right there. On the one hand he was helpful, but then he knew very little about a senior member of his management team. I think we've only touched the surface with Mr Collier, as I'm sure time will tell."

4

S cott's opinion of Mrs Hilary had fast descended from tolerable to a pain in the arse battleaxe after she'd left them waiting for fifteen minutes whilst she'd reluctantly gone in search of the spare keys to Johnson's house. She annoyed Scott even further by insisting on accompanying them, commenting that "I'd hate for anything to go missing," and "you just don't know who you can trust these days." A jobsworth seemed too nice a title for her.

Johnson's property was one of a series of two-bed, three-storey period cottages set back away from the main building on the sprawling estate. Accommodation had been provided for those members of staff who didn't live within easy commuting distance. Visually, the properties had a quaint look about them. An assorted row of potted plants with ornate Greek-style vases skirted the front of all the properties.

The owners had taken great care in maintaining their homes. The brown brick, weathered fronts were suitably maintained. Pristine, white sash window frames with matching windowsills added a symmetry that spanned the block. Each property had a matching stable door, all sporting a traditional racing green colour.

Scott had given Mrs Hilary strict instructions to stay outside of the property and under no circumstances enter, lest she disturb possible evidence. Obviously not used to being told what to do, the woman looked over the top of her glasses that sat low on her nose. With crossed arms, she shot Scott a scornful glare as he and Abby pulled on rubber gloves.

The inside of the property was just as impressive and cosy as the outside. It was rich in features, with exposed oak ceiling timbers, floors, doors and frames. Exposed brick fireplaces offered a contrasting accent feature to their adjoining plain white plastered walls. *A well-balanced mix of traditional and modern contemporary*, Scott thought.

Johnson appeared to live a clean, healthy life. The ground floor was tidy and functional if not perhaps a little impersonal. Absent were any family photos, flowers and ornaments. The theme continued throughout the first floor where they found the first bedroom, which had been converted into a study. A bathroom was situated to the right. The top floor of the property led to the second bedroom. Everything seemed to be packed away, neat and tidy.

Abby searched the ground floor as Scott explored the first floor. His feet sunk into the thick, red velvet carpet, a marked contrast to the firmness he felt walking around downstairs.

A faint smell of tobacco hung in the air, instantly transporting him back to when he was a boy. Every time he had visited his uncle who lived around the corner to their family home, he'd sat in fascination watching his uncle stuff tobacco in his pipe, taking short, sharp puffs whilst he lit the pipe with his Swan Vesta matches. He'd enjoyed the rugged smell, it was a grown-up smell that he'd fondly embraced as a child. Uncle Tom was a great storyteller; he'd entertained Scott for hours with stories that just seemed to ramble on as he chugged away on his pipe.

Scott was never sure how much of the content was truth and how much was embellishment, but at the time he accepted every word as the gospel truth because his uncle was a man's man. He was big, well-built, with a deep booming voice. Spending what seemed like hours in the study with Uncle Tom, made him feel like he was eighteen, and not eight. At the time, he thought his uncle was so cool, especially because he used magical matches that he'd strike on the sole of his shoe to ignite his pipe.

It was only in later life that Scott realised that his cool uncle had slowly been killing himself, the evil weed gradually robbing him of his breath, his life and well-being. That rasping cough that Scott didn't notice as he grew up had become louder and more painful through the years. The days of kicking a football around the garden with his favourite uncle becoming more infrequent. At the time, Scott had put it down to old age when Uncle Tom kept stopping because he was out of breath. Then one day it rocked him to the core when Uncle Tom had collapsed, the ambulance staff strapping an oxygen mask to his face to help him breathe easier. The mask became a permanent feature from that day onwards, until he passed away. Cause of death, emphysema.

The study in marked contrast appeared to be the hub of the house. An oversized desk piled high with student work-books, notes and random pieces of paper that left very little clear working space to admire the red leather surface. A well-worn metal ashtray was half-full, and an unfinished glass of red wine had somehow managed to find its rightful place on the table.

Scott cast his eye around the room looking for any evidence of something untoward that may have happened and been the precursor to Johnson taking his life. A laptop perched precariously towards the back of the desk, its screen now blank as it rested in sleep mode. A bright orange power light was the only indication of the laptop still being on.

"Nothing down there, Guv," Abby offered as she walked into the study. "I couldn't find a phone downstairs but there's the usual collection of bills and receipts on the kitchen table. I've just bagged them up to look at later. The back door is unlocked though. Perhaps he felt a degree of security and privacy here on the school grounds and didn't lock his doors?"

"I didn't think you'd find much down there. It looks like Johnson spent most of his time here," Scott added glancing around the room. "I need you to bag up that laptop, and the wine glass and bottle; we need to get them to forensics." Scott reached into the inside pockets of the suit jacket that had been left hanging on the back of the captain's chair. After fishing around for a few seconds, he pulled out Johnson's wallet. It contained an assortment of credit cards and bank cards, plus a driving licence.

As he peered into the notes section, other than two twenty-pound notes and a ten-pound note, he found three small white pieces of paper neatly folded. Taking them out, he inspected each one in turn.

"Looks like Johnson was in a relationship of some sorts," Scott said, passing the notes to Abby.

"You make me feel so alive and wanted. Can't wait to see you again. My body is aching for you. S xx," Abby read aloud, raising her brow.

"That's kind of you to say, Abby. I didn't know you felt that way about me," Scott grinned.

"In your dreams, mate," she fired back, sticking two fingers in her mouth as she pretended to gag.

"The other two notes are signed off in the same way," Scott added. He made a mental note to bring this up with the principal next time they met. "We could do with tracking down who this person is, they might be able to shed some light on his final few hours and his life in general," Scott suggested before placing the wallet and notes into a clear evidence bag, hoping that forensics might be able to lift a print off them.

"Can't see his phone anywhere," Scott pointed out before heading over towards the grand bookcase that filled one whole wall. It was obvious that the majority of his books hadn't been used in a long time; the spines of which were worn, tatty and cracked, with a thin layer of dust resting on their top faces. Scott ran his finger along one shelf, a pile of dust collecting before his finger, the way snow collected on the front face of a snowplough.

Abby started rooting through the various files that packed out the first drawer of a grey filing cabinet in the corner. Most of the files contained the performance records of various students he taught. A few other folders contained invoices from expenses incurred, but the rest of the filing cabinet was empty.

"Found it," Abby said as she knelt down in the small space between the filing cabinet and the wall. The phone had been left charging, in the wall socket. "That's handy. The phone's on, and there's no screen lock," she added scrolling through text messages selecting a few at random. "The mysterious S seems to have had the hots for our man. There are dozens of messages on here, and some of them are X-rated enough to make a vicar blush. Judging from some of them, she was a frequent visitor here, too."

"Even more reason to find her," Scott stressed as he pursed his lips.

"Back to the station, Guv?"

"Yes, let's get a briefing organised."

Just as Scott was about to drive off, he noticed the man they had seen earlier. Still standing in the same spot, the caretaker was slouched up against the wall slowly puffing on a cigarette. He hadn't moved, his eyes still firmly fixed on them. He watched as they turned the car around and headed back towards the main entrance. Scott looked in his rear-view mirror and saw the image of the man slowly fading into the distance.

5

The late afternoon sun poured through the windows making the briefing room decidedly uncomfortable. The air conditioning had broken down some time ago, and attempts to repair it were being delayed due to the station's refurbishment programme. The project management team had deemed it far more appropriate and cost-effective to replace the air conditioning system in that part of the building when the briefing room got its refit. In the meantime, it meant that any meetings were held in an atmosphere of stuffy heat and the pungent smell of human eau de BO.

The team had convened around the large oval table, Raj and Mike had both loosened their top buttons and their ties and had rolled up their sleeves. Mike seemed to be suffering the most, his face a tomato red, with small beads of sweat erupting on his forehead. Even though Abby and Sian also suffered in the stifling heat, they were still able to maintain a degree of decorum.

Raj had brought a packet of chocolate Bourbon biscuits,

which although welcomed by all gathered, seemed to cause everyone to slug on their water bottles more frequently, as they battled the dryness the aftertaste left in their mouths.

"Okay, the victim is a Christopher Johnson age forty-five," Scott started as he pinned a picture of Johnson to the briefing board, adding his name, age and title alongside it. "He was the assistant principal at Edmunston-Hunt boarding school and he had held that post for four years. You'll hopefully have seen the body cam images Abby relayed back to the office?" Scott asked looking for an agreement from those around the table. Whether the heat caused the lethargy, or the time of day, his team appeared a little flat and unengaged. He took the lack of response as a general agreement that they had seen the footage and pushed on.

"Did you glean anything from the school?" enquired Mike.

"Not as much as we would have liked, Mike. We spoke to Mr Collier, the principal, and he wasn't able to shed much light on Johnson. Sorry, let me rephrase that, he either wasn't able to shed much light, or wasn't willing to in my opinion. I got the impression he was being economical with the truth. That's my hunch anyway," Scott added. "According to Mr Collier, Johnson was well-liked by both pupils and staff alike. On the face of it, Johnson didn't have any pressing worries or concerns around his job, money or relationships. His mental health appeared good, he was a grafter and a well-trusted member of staff, so it's a bit of a mystery."

"I've checked his history, Guv. He had been with the school for five years, promoted after one year to assistant principal whilst also being the housemaster for Ditchling. I'm still doing a bit more digging around on him," Raj added.

Scott wrote the extra information on the whiteboard. "Abby and I will go and speak to the other teachers at the school to find out a bit more about our man. I've also got a few more questions to ask the principal. Sian and Mike, I want you to speak to the pupils in the Ditchling House, find out what type of man Johnson was. Kids sometimes have an uncanny knack of saying a lot more than they are supposed to."

Scott crossed his arms as he looked at the picture of Johnson staring back at him. It was a formal photograph obviously taken as part of the staff photos. He was standing side-on against a backdrop of an external brick wall. The formality of his grey suit, light blue shirt and yellow tie, were offset by a slight, but friendly smile. He still had a full head of dark hair, but with age it was slowly creeping backwards exposing a larger than normal forehead. *What was so bad that you needed to do this?*

"The forensic team found a Latin inscription on paper together with a white feather stuffed in his pocket. Now I'm no expert in Latin, but we need to find out what that inscription means. Raj, can you look into that for me? I'd suggest touching base with someone at Sussex University. Start with the languages department. We need to find someone who can decipher this for us."

Raj nodded in agreement as he brushed away biscuit crumbs from his notepad and wrote down Scott's instructions.

The low rumbling vibrations of Abby's phone as it bounced around on the table interrupted Scott's train of thought. Abby couldn't tell if Scott's glare was one of curiosity or of annoyance. The interruption and subsequent centre of attention caused her cheeks to blush as she looked at him apologetically, fumbling with her phone. Before she had time to do that, the phone signalled the arrival of another message. Scott raised an eyebrow in her direction to suggest *I'd expect better of you.*

She silently mouthed "sorry".

Scott turned towards Raj. "Check in with the high-tech unit. We need to pull off a list of all phone records from Johnson's phone and identify multiple callers. My guess is someone called S will be one of his most frequent callers. I found several messages in his wallet, and they weren't any old messages. They appeared to be love notes, which were pretty racy in places."

This revelation led Mike to whistle the way builders on a building site would when they saw a sexy woman walking past. Mike's response drew smiles from those around the table.

"Mike, grow up will you," Scott said sharply. "As much as you'd like the goings-on between Johnson and this myste-rious person to descend to a laddish level, whoever this person is could be vital to our investigation. Considering this seems to have tickled you so much, find out what you can about this mysterious S. See if there are any other teachers with a name beginning with S."

"I presume that could be male or female?" Mike replied sitting up straight having been suitably put back in his place.

"That's a fair assumption, but in this case it's female unless you know of any man who likes to wear heels and stock-ings whilst having sex, and has a *vagina that's wet at the thought of you!* See what you can dig up from Johnson's past. We know he was probably seeing someone, but what about relationships in the past? Was he married at one time? Any acrimonious splits?"

Sian raised her pen, a fixed concentration on her face. "What did the pathologist and forensic team conclude at the scene regarding the method of death?"

"Well, until the post-mortem is done tomorrow morning, we've been led to believe it was strangulation by hanging. The loose end of the rope had been tied around the base of the tree, and the way in which it had been positioned seems to suggest that he had gone to great lengths to have the noose accurately positioned so that when he fell off the branch he landed just a few inches above the ground."

"You'd have to be pretty determined to go through with something like that." Sian grimaced. "You'd have to have some pretty heavy shit going on in your life to string yourself up."

It's a thought that had crossed Scott's mind several times and no doubt the rest of the team's too. "That's what we need to find out. He could have had money worries, personal relationship issues, terminal illness or even a mental health illness." That last point caused Scott to research another avenue. "Sian, get banking details, job history and medical records. His doctor's records could help us to eliminate or determine whether something like a terminal illness or depression had a part to play in his death."

"We're going into a lot of detail for what could be a straightforward suicide?" Sian asked.

"We have to cover every possibility here, Sian. We don't know enough about him to conclude that it was just the taking of his own life. We've not found a suicide note either."

Abby could tell that Scott was mulling over another theory as his eyes darted around the room processing what he'd seen at the crime scene plus subsequent conversations. "Care to share what's on your mind, Guv?"

Scott thought for a moment, biting his bottom lip as he tapped his temple with two fingers. "The scene that we saw this morning was perfectly plausible, but…there was something about the way in which the rope was positioned that didn't sit right with me. Call it a gut feeling."

The vagueness of his reply seemed to stir up more curiosity in the minds of those sitting around the table.

"Okay, let's get to work first thing tomorrow. Get yourselves home and get an early night. I'm stopping in to brief Harvey now."

ABBY SWITCHED her phone on once they were back in the corridor. She hissed in a shocked breath as her phone went through a series of continuous bleeps that signalled the arrival of one message after another. She began scrolling through them, not paying much attention to the direction of her walking feet. Her concentration was interrupted as she collided with another officer coming out of an office. Her phone flew out of her hand. "I'm so sorry," she said, smiling as her face heated over her embarrassment.

Scott had been about two paces behind her, watching as she swayed along the corridor deeply engrossed in her phone.

"Seriously, what is it with you and your phone? You're up to something; I can tell."

She knew she couldn't hide it from Scott. He'd find out sooner or later. "Don't laugh, but I took your advice. I joined Match.com. Now my phone won't stop. The amount of email alerts I'm getting from guys on there is crazy."

Scott raised a brow. "Welcome to the 21st century. You've finally taken the plunge for the whole Internet dating thing?"

"Yeah, I've not met anyone yet, but I've been chatting to a few guys online. Just as I thought, I'm getting sent pictures of fucking knobs. Don't get me wrong, some guys have been really nice to chat with. But for some reason the male psyche seems to think that the way to open a conversation with someone is to send them a picture of their cock," she said, rolling her eyes. "No wonder they're bloody single."

Scott grimaced and pursed his lips. "Seriously, blokes do that?"

"Yep and I'll show you if you want?"

Scott turned and began walking off in the opposite direction, raising his hand in the air. "Erm…I'll pass on that. I'll leave you with that pleasure."

As Scott ducked through the back door towards his car, his phone pinged. It was Abby.

I've got a date tonight with Phil. He's an electrician. What happens if he doesn't like me? Wish me luck!

Scott shook his head. *Once again glass half-empty, Abby.*

6

Nocturnal life broke the silence of the night. The eerie and distinctive sound of an owl perched high up in the trees no doubt sent a wave of panic through the small rodents that called the overgrown forest floor their home. The predator watched and observed, on alert for any movement that could suggest a possible meal.

The sounds of a busy school, the energetic life of boys rushing between lessons and enjoying outdoor games of cricket had long faded, replaced with a calm stillness as tired bodies rested and recovered from their busy days.

In the Stanmer House dormitory, eight boys slept like logs. The only sound permeating the stillness was the occasional creak of a bed as one of them turned over to get more comfortable, or the escape of wind as another fart erupted from under the covers.

The bedroom door opened and the faint shadow of three boys came into view. Three pairs of menacing eyes locked in on their prey. They too preferred to hunt at night, taking their victim by surprise, using stealth to attack.

They circled the bed of Matthew Edrington, waiting for their moment. He was fast asleep, his bedding pulled tight up around his neck, cocooned to keep him warm and cosy. A luxury that was soon shattered. James Rollings gave the others a nod. Tobias Ford ripped the bedcovers away and Stephen Hunter plunged his hands around Matthew's neck, pinning the boy to the bed and muting any noise from his mouth as he jolted awake in terror from his deep slumber.

Fear gripped his body, his heart threatened to explode from his chest as he gasped for breath. His legs thrashed across the bed as he fought to rip the strong, powerful hands from his neck. Despite his bravest efforts, he couldn't free himself. He was weak; he'd always known that. His mind spun as oxygen deprivation blurred his vision and muddied his thoughts.

As his hopes of surviving slipped away, he was thrown a lifeline as the crushing weight on his windpipe eased off. Hunter and Ford unceremoniously dragged Matthew out of bed, each grabbing an arm, and forced him to the floor. Matthew lay in shock, not quite comprehending what had just happened to him, as his conscious mind fought to jolt him to his senses. Hunter pushed Matthew's face into the floor and sat down hard on the boy's back, pushing the air from his lungs. He pinned the frail boy down with a knee in his spine causing Matthew to wince as lightning bolts of pain raced up and down his back.

Ford threw a pillowcase over Matthew's face, robbing him of what little he could see in the blackness of the room. Rollings, who up until this point had been directing the assault, stepped forward and with a swing of leg, delivered a hard kick that buried itself deep into Matthew's stomach. The pain erupted through Matthew's torso, forcing him to draw his legs up into a foetal position, hoping his legs would offer some degree of protection.

His assailants remained silent as their punches and kicks rained down on his body from every angle. He winced in pain as he threw his arms up around his head to shield himself. He pulled his body as tight as he could into a protective ball like a hedgehog would if under attack. Unfortunately for Matthew, he wasn't as well armed to repel his attackers.

The attack only lasted a few seconds, but felt like minutes in Matthew's eyes as his body ached. Rollings knelt down pinning the boy's neck to the floor from behind. He leant in close, "You lost our house the race…you pussy," he hissed. "You're a waste of space. There's no room here for weak, pathetic girls like you. Man up or else…" he threatened, delivering his warning with a slap to Matthew's face.

Matthew fought the bile that crawled up his throat, his mouth watered and his jaws ached from being clenched tight. Now his cheek stung, burning red hot. There was silence around him, the boys had released him, but had not gone, that he was sure of. *But what now?* he thought. Dread filled his racing mind once again as he heard the familiar sound of trouser zips being undone.

His pyjamas clung to his body from the wetness that soaked his body as the three assailants stood over him enjoying the pleasure of urinating all over his small, thin, cowering body. As the strong smell invaded his nostrils, he gagged yet again. His fragile confidence and self-esteem ebbed away even further.

He paced nervously in the dark, waiting for the others to turn up. The gravel beneath his feet felt firm and uncomfortable. The ornamental gardens skirted the far right flank of the grounds, a place that offered elegance, quiet and solitude. It was a sanctuary he often escaped to when he felt the burning need to get away from everything and everyone. The gardens were the product of many years of dedicated care and attention from resident gardeners and groundsmen.

Watchful Istrian stone lions and the giant leaves of kiwi fruit framed the wrought-iron gates that marked the impressive entrance to the walled gardens. Over the years, the gardens had been designed and redesigned with a vast and colourful array of plants chosen for their aesthetic pleasure and appearance. A mix of flowering plants and bulbs in addition to foliage plants, ornamental grasses, shrubs and trees all combined to recreate the splendour and smells of yesteryear as they surrounded the central feature, a splendid lily pond. Yew hedges provided the final outer ring to the gardens before they nestled up against eight feet high weather brick walls.

The cloudless sky and natural light from the moon allowed his eyes to adjust easily to the semi-darkness that surrounded him. The rusty creaking wrought-iron gates drew his attention as they opened, followed by the sounds of footsteps, moving swiftly in the darkness even before the figures came into view.

"You took your bloody time, didn't you?" He barked at the men who joined him. "Now I know one or two of you, in particular, are concerned by what happened to Johnson," he began, staring in the direction of one particular man who seemed slightly inebriated. The smell of whiskey hung in the air. "But we have remained steadfast and resolute for many years. We all swore to keep this buried and keep our mouths shut," he stated, glancing at each man in turn. "At the moment, we have no evidence to suggest it was anything more than Johnson bottling out, and taking the easy route."

The men mumbled amongst themselves, shifting nervously, staring at the ground and flicking gravel with the ends of their shoes, rather than lock eyes with their leader.

The drunken visitor perhaps buoyed by the alcohol in his system chose to speak out. "I don't like this. I don't like this one bit. You made it very clear that this problem would go away," he growled through gritted teeth.

Stepping forward and now nose to nose with the drunken visitor, his jaws clenched tight, the leader seethed. *How dare he challenge my authority?* "Let me make it very clear to you. I will not tolerate dissent in the ranks. You listen to me and no one else. Do I make myself clear?"

The drunken visitor trembled, a combination of fear and a fuzzy head causing him to clench his fists and breathe rapidly. "Okay, I admit it. I admit I'm bloody scared. What happens if someone's found out?"

"No one is going to find out. No one is going to open their mouths. We are all going to act normal," he said, looking at the three men in turn, "and you are going to stop drinking," he said, jabbing his finger in the chest of the inebriated visitor. "Your tongue is far too loose, especially when you've had a drink. I will not tolerate that. If anyone steps out of line, they could wind up like Johnson. Do I make myself clear?"

The threat hung loosely like a heavy rain cloud hovering overhead, as the men turned and headed off in different directions. The three visitors knew that it wasn't bravado or a veiled threat but a consequence. And they'd do well to remember it.

7

L aurence Goddard unlocked his front door before stumbling in, coming to a rest against the wall in his hallway. His head pounded, spinning wildly. He fought hard to focus but his eyes wouldn't let him. Everything appeared blurred, hazy and off-balance. The sidelamp seemed to be defying gravity as it tilted to one side, and the bannister newel post lurched precariously as he reached out to steady himself. He needed another drink. Whether his body could tolerate another was a different matter.

He walked slowly, his feet dragging on the floor, weighed down with imaginary bags of sand. The drinks cabinet loomed into view. He jerked his head backwards in surprise as two cabinets seemed to be sitting in the corner of his lounge. *I'm sure I didn't have two*, he thought, as he grabbed a bottle of Jack Daniel's and ripped the stopper from its neck.

A hefty glug of whiskey shocked his taste buds and set his mouth alight. The harsh liquid raced down his throat burning a fire trail as it made its way down to his empty stomach. He couldn't remember the last time he'd eaten, *breakfast maybe?* Goddard scrunched up his face as his throat burnt, his eyes firmly shut tight as he waited for the soothing sensation to replace the bombardment of grittiness that he felt inside. He ran a hand through brown, receding hair. The warmth of the alcohol started to build from deep within, a burning ember that rippled out from his core, leaving a soothing sensation that washed over him.

Damn bitch.

His moment of contentment was short-lived as his thoughts turned to *her*. He despised her, hated the sight of her face. He looked upwards at the ceiling, his bedroom directly above. He wasn't even sure she'd heard him come in, her sleeping pills no doubt taking her to a land of bliss and ignorance. His face hardened. His eyes narrowed as his jaws clenched tight, his breath coming deep and hard as he took one more gulp before slamming the bottle down hard on the dining table.

The house was quiet, but in his mind the London Philharmonic Orchestra played Mahler Symphony No. 5 at maximum volume just to annoy him. He groaned as he took one step at a time, ascending the stairs into the darkness of the upstairs landing. His bedroom door was closed. *Fucking bitch, you fat fucking bitch.* Goddard swayed into the room, his eyes searching out the silhouette that lay under the duvet and in *his* bed. Anger seeped from every pore, his teeth ground as his temper reached fever pitch.

He tumbled onto the bed, grabbing his wife's hair. The assault of pain shocked her awake as she felt her hair being pulled out by its roots. Her senses fought hard to gain a bearing on what was happening. Her body's natural instinct was to minimise the pain by following the path of where she was being dragged.

"Get up you silly bitch!" he yelled, his eyes wide with aggression, his double chin shaking as he shook his head. "Please, Laurence," she pleaded. "Please stop, you're hurting me. I'm sorry, please." Desperation etched her voice, as her senses jolted her into survival mode. "You need help. You can't keep hurting me."

"Shut the fuck up, you filthy bitch. You make me want to puke. You don't think I know what you're up to," he sneered as he put his hand around the back of her neck and pulled her face within inches of his. His alcohol-infused breath forced her to look away. "Don't turn your face when I'm talking to you. You whore. Look at you, dressing up in short skirts, tight tops, flaunting yourself. You make me sick. Do you hear me?...Sick!" he screamed as his hand launched across her face sending her crashing to the floor.

Samantha Goddard held her stinging cheek, her head spinning, pain racing across her scalp. Holding herself up with one hand, she placed the other over her head to shield herself as Goddard stood over her.

"Please, Laurence, you've got the wrong idea. I'm your wife. Please stop hurting me," she implored.

"You're not my wife, do you hear me? You never have been," he replied, punching her in the face. "It's the biggest mistake I ever made, marrying you. I can't cope with you and that stuff; it's killing me!" he shouted as he gripped his head on both sides.

"Tell me. I can help," she offered, hoping to calm him.

"No one can help. Not you, not anyone," he seethed, before hitting her once again.

The blow sent her sprawling across the bedroom floor. He turned and staggered out of the room towards the stairs. Samantha Goddard dragged herself to the corner of her bedroom and wedged herself between the bed and wall. She cowered in fear, pressing her hand on her hot cheek, the sting still radiating heat across her face. Tears welled in her eyes as she pulled her legs in tight to her body and wrapped her arms around her shins. She rocked gently as the tears turned to a whimpering cry. She couldn't take much more of this. She craved a normal life, one where she didn't fear what fate awaited her every night.

Laurence collapsed into the armchair, his hand stung, his knuckles bruised. *Jack* was his friend. *Jack* was who he turned to when he felt darkness closing in. Knowing what he knew felt like a life sentence, an imaginary weight around his neck dragging him down. He repeatedly banged his head into the cushioned back of the armchair in frustration. *I can't do this anymore, I can't*, he silently screamed deep inside his dark, distorted mind. Jack would know what to do; Jack *always* knew how to take his pain away.

He took another large mouthful and let it burn a trail through him. He closed his eyes and leant back. Jack took over, taking him to a place where no one could hurt or blame him.

8

Abby pulled up alongside Scott's car in the mortuary car park. He greeted her with an exaggerated grin as he stepped out. The early morning sun was bright and warm, causing him to squint.

"Morning, how was Phil? Did sparks fly between you?" He winked, looking pleased with his attempt at humour.

Abby shot him a glance. "Really? Is that the best you can do?"

"Well come on, spill the beans. Did he manage to thaw the ice maiden?" he continued as they walked to the door.

"You make me sound like some frigid old woman," she replied, playfully punching him on the arm, before pointing a wagging finger at him. "Choose your next words carefully sonny Jim."

"Seriously, how did it go?"

Abby shrugged. "It was okay, a bit awkward to start, but a pleasant enough evening."

"The *excitement* is bubbling out of every pore, Abby." He laughed. "I used to date a female electrician...she was shocking in bed," Scott said and then roared.

Abby groaned. "Oh my word, they get worse. Don't give up the day job," she said, pressing the buzzer.

"Why did Mr Ohm marry Mrs Ohm?" Scott asked desperate to crack out another joke...not waiting for an answer, he carried on, "Because he couldn't resistor. Get it? Resist her?" Scott rocked his head back chuffed with his latest jokes, his shoulders shaking up and down.

"So pathetic, so, so pathetic," Abby replied shaking her head in disbelief.

THE OFFICERS KITTED up in robes, paper face masks and white wellies that were too big, before joining Cara, the pathologist, who was well advanced with the post-mortem examination of Christopher Johnson. Scott had only seen Cara a few hours ago after she'd spent the night at his, but nevertheless, he was pleased to see her once again. She was definitely having a positive effect on his life. The grief he'd experienced had taken him to dark places; he'd sunk to new lows and contemplated his own existence. Much of this he'd kept buried from others. It had been a lonely and desolate journey that appeared to have no final destination.

Cara had brought light back into his life. He welcomed her balancing influence; he cherished her support and energy that had rescued him from the precipice.

A distinct coldness enveloped the examination room. The faint whirring of the air conditioning kept the room on the decidedly chilly side to slow down body decomposition. That in itself sent cold shivers down Abby's back as the hairs on her neck stood up. The white and cream tiled floor and walls added to the blandness, lack of warmth and lack of emotion that made the room so unwelcoming. It was as if someone had taken the room and put it through Photoshop to bleed the colour from it.

It wasn't just the room either. Other than his face, Johnson's body looked like a pasty off-white rubber manikin that had been used for medical students to practise their dissection skills.

The cadaver lay on the first of three tables in the mortuary. Scott recognised Cara's assistant Neil from his last visit. Neil stood on one side of the table peering over the cadaver, holding a sliver specimen tray, whilst Cara undertook her detailed examination opposite him. Neil looked up as Scott and Abby approached, pushing his thick-framed glasses back up the bridge of his nose and acknowledging them with a friendly nod and smile.

Cara glanced up offering them a small smile which lingered on Scott for a few moments. "Morning…you got here a little late, unfortunately. I've got a lot on today, so started on Johnson earlier than I anticipated."

"That's not a problem. We've got a lot on too. We just need the summary points so far," Scott replied as he looked up and down the cadaver.

Johnson's body had been opened up in the formal Y formation, his internal organs had been removed for sizing, weighing and analysis, and some were sitting on the metal bench to the back of the examination room ready for closer inspection. His face was a shade of blotchy red from where blood had become trapped and tiny blood capillaries had burst. His face was slightly swollen, with thick puckering of the skin beneath his jaw.

"Well, at first I thought this was a straightforward suicide when I inspected the body at the scene, but there were a few discrepancies that concerned me."

"Really?" Abby asked.

"Yes," Cara replied, as she moved back towards the neck region. "Let me give you a bit of background to cases like this. When a body is suspended, like a short drop death in this case, the weight of the body tightens the rope around the trachea and neck structure. The person experiences some degree of struggle before they go limp and reach an unconscious state because their jugular vein and carotid arteries are blocked and blood flow to the brain is reduced. However, the person dies slowly of strangulation, usually over the course of several minutes, and in some cases up to fifteen minutes," she added with a shrug.

"This results in a considerably more elongated and painful death compared to what we call a long drop hanging, which is intended to kill by using the shock of the initial drop to fracture the spinal column at the neck. Normally in long drops, there'd be evidence of a dislocation of the C2 and C3 vertebrae that crush the spinal cord and or disrupts the vertebral arteries. There's no evidence of dislocation in this instance.

"If the airway is constricted, and full suspension achieved, by that I mean, their feet are fully off the floor, this method, at least initially, is likely to be very painful. The person struggles for air against the compression of the noose and against the weight of their own body, being supported entirely by the neck and jaw. It's a pretty horrible way to go to be honest."

"You said you felt there were discrepancies in this case?" Scott reminded her.

"Erm…yes. I'll get onto that in a bit. Let me finish my lesson, Scottie."

Abby bowed her head to stifle the laughter that threatened to escape.

Scott held up his hands in mock surrender.

"The neck of a hanging victim is usually marked with furrows where the ligature has constricted the neck. An inverted V mark is also often seen. And we have both in this case." Cara confirmed her words pointing to the thick red line beneath the jaw. "There's also some evidence of petechiae, which is purple spotting. This is clearly seen in places on his face from broken or burst capillary blood vessels." She pointed that out with a thin metal spike that resembled a metal toothpick.

"Coming back to your question, yes, we have ligature marks under the larynx, and the presence of significant injury to the skin of the neck. But my suspicions grew when I noticed under a magnifier, scratch marks on the ligature, and lots of scratch marks on the skin on either side of the ligature mark in various places around the neck."

"What does that mean?"

"If I had to make a more concrete assessment, it looks like he was frantically trying to pull the rope away from his neck."

"Do you reckon he started to go through with it, and then

had a last minute attempt to stop himself as panic set in?" Scott suggested.

"That's plausible. He may have intended to go through with it and then tried to stop, but it was too late."

"You said firstly, Cara…?" Abby interrupted. "You found something else, didn't you?"

"Yes. My suspicions grew because I also found bruising to the skin on his face, stomach and knees," Cara replied looking towards Abby.

"Recent?"

"In my opinion, yes. And something else I spotted whilst at the scene. There were distinct, long scuff marks on the ground beneath the victim. I asked forensics to look a bit closer at that. And there was a second disturbed area of ground a few feet away that Matt pointed out to me. The foliage had been scraped away exposing the earth beneath it."

"What do you think caused that? Foxes?" Scott suggested. "Like they were scratching on the surface of the forest floor?"

"Perhaps. Or scuff marks from shoes trying to touch the floor? Just a thought."

Scott and Abby shot each other a glance. There was a new angle to the case now.

SCOTT ORDERED the eggs royale and Abby ordered a coffee. Moksha Caffé was another favourite haunt of Scott's. He enjoyed going there on a Sunday morning and tucking into a cooked breakfast whilst leisurely enjoying a cup of their fresh locally sourced filter coffee.

He'd spent many hours people watching. He was fascinated by human interaction, and would try and figure out people's personalities and character traits simply by watching from a distance. Often he'd smile to himself as he challenged his internal dialogue, deciding who was the extrovert or introvert amongst couples, who was visual or kinaesthetic or who was confident or not.

Abby turned her nose up when Scott's food arrived. "How can you eat? You astound me every time. I can just about stomach the coffee," she added, sipping from her cup.

"As I said, a man's gotta eat," he replied shovelling in a large mouthful.

Abby had to look away and force the pictures from her mind of what they'd just observed that morning. "Cara's findings put the death in a new light, eh? More questions than answers?"

Wiping his mouth with a napkin, Scott replied, "Mmm, yes it does. We need to look into Johnson's background in a bit more detail. We need to find out what was going on in his life full stop, personally and professionally. I definitely think Collier knows more than he's letting on. As each minute passes, it becomes more of a suspicious death."

Abby nodded, cupping her coffee in both hands, and pulling her arms in close to her body.

"So, sparky…you going to see him again?"

Abby smiled. "I'm not sure. He text me this morning to say he'd had a nice time. He's got a son aged fourteen, so between his job and seeing his son, he doesn't get much time free. Besides, it's early days; I still might be brave enough to face a few more first dates if some of the other profiles turn out to be good." She shrugged. "Their pictures and what they look like in reality are two completely different things."

"They would probably think the same about you." He winked.

"You cheeky git," Abby objected, throwing her scrunched up napkin at him.

———

ON RETURNING TO THE STATION, Scott and Abby made a detour via the canteen to grab an extra couple of bottles of water. It had been a warm morning. Despite the mortuary offering a coolness and respite from the heat, the short journey back to the station had left them feeling decidedly hot and bothered. The tourist crowd was already starting to pack out the seafront. The roads around the Old Steine were coming to a standstill as parking spaces became rarer than rocking horse shit. Thankfully for them, they were able to circumnavigate the tourist traffic by taking the back roads to the station.

As they queued up now, Abby nudged Scott in the ribs and pointed over her shoulder. Scott turned to look in the direction of Abby's pointing finger. Tucked away in the corner of the canteen, he spotted Mike in deep conversation with a female officer. Scott could tell by the body language that Mike was either more than friends with her or wanted to be more than friends. He had his jacket slung over the back of the chair, his tie undone, his sleeves rolled-up. He was clearly on a charm offensive. The officer rocked back in her chair laughing as she held a hand over her mouth in embarrassment.

"Looks like Mike is eyeing up his next unsuspecting victim," Abby said, rolling her eyes. "He really does have his brains in his pants. He's such a lech. Even if you're in the middle of a conversation with him, he can't help looking at the backsides of every woman that walks past, *even* if you're looking him right in the eye. Worst still, he always talks to your boobs, especially if he's interested in you. And to top it off, if he's walking behind a woman, he's always staring at her arse."

On this occasion, he agreed with Abby. As far as he could recall, just in the past six months alone, Mike had dated, if you could call them dates, two female officers and a civilian support officer. For some reason, they seemed to fall for his charms. However, the novelty would fade within a few weeks. Mike could never keep up the pretence for too long and they got to see the real Mike. "Poor cow, you have to try and warn her," Scott said with a laugh.

Abby was just about to reply, when Scott's phone rang. He grabbed the phone from his pocket, and smiled as Cara's number came up. "Hey there, what's up?" His face became serious for a moment as he remained silent listening to Cara. "Listen, listen, calm down. Did you see or hear anything?" he asked before falling silent again.

Abby raised her hands in front of her, with palms up, an inquisitive look etched on her face.

Scott shook his head once and raised a hand to ask Abby to wait a minute.

"Just stay put. I'll pop back over. See you in a bit." Scott hung up. "Listen, Abby, can you hold the fort for half an hour? I just need to pop back to the mortuary."

"What's up? Development in the case?"

"No, Cara's car has been vandalised in the mortuary car park. She's in a right state."

9

Giles Rochester was home alone, quietly working through some new course notes. He'd had a usual run-of-the-mill day at school. Students had been a tad unruly for his liking, staff members had huddled in their small groups in the staff common room talking about England's result in the test series against their formidable enemy Australia. From his recollection, it had certainly provoked a heated debate about the whys and wherefores of the England team's tactics.

Despite being in close proximity to his colleagues most days, he preferred his own company. He paused for a moment to look back over his time there earlier. He'd sat in a solitary chair in the corner of the room closest to the ornate bookshelves that were set into the walls at right angles. They contained hundreds of books dating back years, and now stretched the full width and height of both walls.

Meanwhile, his colleagues had sat in a circle on low, high-back chairs, the fabric of which had been worn away many years ago to leave a dull shine and imprints of various sizes. Their incessant nattering and seemingly *professional* opinions had irritated him as he read.

In deep reflection, he was unaware of movement behind him. The intruder had entered through the back of the house via the kitchen before making his way up towards the study. Before leaving the kitchen, he'd left a length of rope on the kitchen table, whilst at the same time picking up Rochester's car keys knowing that they would come in handy later. Inch by inch, he'd slowly made his way through the house careful to avoid any creaking floorboards.

He peered in and could see his next target quietly sitting at his desk. Rochester was sitting side-on to him, which meant he couldn't creep up on his target from behind as he had done with his first victim. He'd have to rush this one, hoping the element of surprise would give him the upper hand.

The intruder burst through the door rushing towards his intended target, causing Rochester to jolt out of his semi-daydream, and reel back in his chair as the masked intruder bore down on him, pinning him back in his chair by his throat. The intruder's fingers felt like steel jaws as they gripped his neck, closing off his windpipe. Gasps of breath were mixed with spittle that exploded from his mouth. His face reddened, the veins in his neck bulging as the tourni-quet-like grip tightened.

His mind swirled in confusion as he fought hard to compre-hend what was happening. His eyes widened in fear as his pupils dilated. The hooded face of his assailant loomed closer to his own, dark brown eyes twisted in anger glared at him through tiny eyeholes. His eyes tracked the glint of the steel blade that came into his peripheral view. If his assailant was trying to terrify him, then he had achieved his goal. His stomach knotted in fear and his eyes bulged as the pressure built in his head, drowning out any noise around him.

"I…I…caaann't breeeaatthh," he managed to squeeze out, as both of his hands pulled hard against his assailant's in a desperate attempt to fight him off.

The intruder released his grip slightly, as he inched his head closer to his victim's. "I've been waiting for this for a long time," he said in a slow, deliberate voice.

"I…Don't know what you mean?" Rochester stuttered in reply. "Waiting for what? Who are you? Please…Please don't hurt me."

"It's too late for that. You're coming with me." And with that he grabbed Rochester's arm, and buried the tip of his blade under the man's jaw, being careful not to pierce the skin.

"Now listen here, I'm not going anywhere with you. I don't know what you think I've done. This has to stop right now," he demanded, his voice a mixture of fear and bravado.

"I'm not looking to hurt you. I just want a friendly chat, that's all," the intruder hissed enraged by Rochester's insistence. *You've got a cheek to think we can play by your rules.*

Rochester paused for a second; he stared at the hooded assailant, confusion in his eyes. "Hold on a moment, I'm sure I recognise that voice." His mind raced, desperate to make the connection and join the dots. His eyes widened

once again as he stared hard into his assailants eyes. "Yes...
Yes, it's you. Why?..."

Before he had time to finish the sentence his assailant
pushed him forward violently through the doorway of the
study, the knife firmly pressed between his shoulders. As
they marched down the stairs, his feet struggled to maintain a safe footing as he was repeatedly shoved through
the house and out of the kitchen door into the semi-
darkness.

"Don't mutter a word or I'll slice your innards out here on
the grass," the assailant whispered, being careful not to
attract unwanted attention.

He thrust the man up against the silver VW Golf, continuing to pin him in place with the knife whilst reaching in
his pocket for the car keys. Throwing the keys on the roof
of the car he demanded that Rochester drive.

"This isn't my car."

"Don't take me for an idiot. I want you to get in the car. I'm
going to sit right behind you in the back seat and you are
going to do everything I say...understand?" he demanded.

Giles Rochester nodded slowly as his shaking hand reached
out for the car keys. His thumb trembled as he tried hard to
press down on the unlock button in the dark, finally
releasing it, two pulses of orange lights confirming it.
Rochester was forcibly pushed into the driver's seat, and a
moment later, the assailant quickly got in behind him and in
a split second slung some white plastic packaging tape
around Rochester's neck. He pulled it tight, startling
Rochester and forcing the man's head back into the headrest, pinning him into position.

"Drive to Teville Gate car park in Worthing," the assailant instructed.

Rochester hesitated for a moment. "What?…Why?…" was all he had the opportunity to say before the assailant tugged a little harder on the plastic tape as a warning. The sharp edge of the tape cut hard into his skin, sending out a sharp stinging pain.

"Shut up and drive."

———

THEY HAD TRAVELLED in silence for the journey. Giles nervously glanced in his rear-view mirror, but at this time of night there were very few cars on the road as they made their way to Worthing. His grip on the steering had tightened as the fear churned inside him, turning his knuckles so white they resembled hail balls. His eyes had darted from left to right in terror hoping that he might see a police car. But what good would that have done? Falling short of driving straight into them, he had no other way of attracting attention. Each and every time he tried to drive erratically to attract attention, the assailant had tightened the plastic tape around his neck as a warning.

Teville Gate car park was an isolated spot close to Worthing rail station. Set behind industrial offices and nondescript small factory buildings, it was the last place Giles wanted to end up. An urban, grey concrete monument empty at night, the stomping ground for teenagers and drug addicts who left their calling cards. Graffiti tags lined the stairwells, discarded needles and condoms presented further health hazards, and the overpowering smell of urine hung in the air like the gents toilet in a pub.

He had been forced to drive to the third floor of the car park, before being dragged from the car and pushed hard against the white railings. His ribs stung as the metal dug into the base of his back. The tip of the knife was positioned beneath his jaw ensuring he remained firmly rooted to the spot as his hands reached out to his sides to grab the cold steel. His eyes were fixed wide in terror as his body shook violently in the low glow of the strip lights that gave off an eerie, excessively bright glow.

"I've waited a long time for this," the hooded man said in a slow drawl. "I've counted down the days, just waiting to finally say what I had to say."

The smell of stale breath assaulted Giles's nostrils, as his chest heaved. He shook his head in bewilderment. "I don't understand. What have I done wrong?"

"Everything. You let it happen. You knew about it for all these years but you've remained silent. You're nothing more than a coward," he hissed as he grabbed Giles's throat and pushed him backwards further over the barrier.

Giles shook his head violently, still unable to comprehend. His eyes bulged as the man's grip pressed down hard on his windpipe.

"Nancy boy," he uttered. "Remember that?"

It took Giles a few moments to process the statement as his mind tracked back over the years, recalling all the times, places and situations in his life. And then somewhere deep within the recesses of his dark mind, he latched onto the elusive memory. His eyes slowly tracked round to the hooded assailant. Their eyes connected, and in the silence that prevailed, silent words were spoken.

That's all the hooded man needed as his cue, and with a final push on Giles's neck, he tossed him over the railings. Giles frantically grabbed the edge in a vain attempt to save himself, his chilling screams echoed around the stillness of the car park as he fell to the ground, guttural screams silenced by a heavy, dull thud.

The hooded assailant didn't bother looking over the edge. He turned his back and made his way towards the stairwell taking one step at a time. He was in no hurry. The adrenaline still coursed through his veins as sweat beaded under his hood. He was pleased with his work.

He stood over the mangled body of Giles Rochester. The man's arms and legs were contorted in ways not humanly possible for a living body. A shiny pall of darkness grew around his head. It glinted in the moonlit night sky. He felt no remorse, he felt no anger. *This fucker had received what was coming to him.* He crouched down looking at the twisted body with a morbid curiosity, his eyes darting up and down the mangled mess. His silence was only accompanied with an assured nod, pleased with his end result.

Before walking away, he placed a small scrap of paper and white feather in the man's trouser pocket. Silent footsteps melted away into the dark night.

10

Scott groaned as he was awakened from a deep slumber by his phone rattling and vibrating as it bounced across his bedside cabinet. Today for some reason he was feeling particularly tired. Yesterday, everyone seemed to want a piece of his time. He'd spent several hours in the afternoon trying to reassure Cara after her Ford Focus had been vandalised.

Although the nature of the damage had raised some suspicion in Scott's mind, he hadn't told Cara. The last thing he wanted was her freaking out even more. Both her windscreen and driver's window had been smashed. What surprised Scott was that nothing had been taken. Her satnav was still firmly planted in its cradle stuck to the windscreen, several pounds in loose change were still sitting in the pocket in the centre console, and her pink CD case was on the passenger seat. Going from experience, these were typical items that opportunists would have stolen in the majority of car crime incidents.

DCI Harvey had been on his case for most of the evening.

She had wanted a progress report when the team didn't really have much to go on. Even though it was just the beginning of the investigation, the DCI was already giving Scott a hard time. It wasn't the way that the DCI operated, but something or someone was causing Harvey to be a little uptight and short with him. That alone was enough to stress him out.

Scott flung his head back on the pillow as he held his phone above his face allowing the screen to come into focus. "Baker…" he said in a course, gravelly voice.

"Sorry to disturb you, sir, Sergeant Trillo here. The DCI asked me to contact you immediately. Got a possible suspicious death." The sergeant paused.

"Go on…" Scott continued clearing his throat and rubbing his eyes in an effort to shake off his sleepiness. He tried hard to concentrate as Cara rolled over towards him, her ample, warm breasts tucked into his left arm, her hand travelled down to his groin as she groaned.

"We've got what looks like a jumper at the Teville Gate car park in Worthing. We've got uniform in attendance."

Scott paused for a moment allowing his brain to engage. Cara had already kept him up for what felt most of the night with her insatiable sexual appetite, and clearly was hungry for more. That warm fuzzy feeling of the night before was fast fading as the prospect of attending a messy incident loomed into view.

"Why is it *potentially* suspicious and not a straightforward jumper?"

"A vehicle was discovered in the car park, with its door open and the keys in the ignition."

"Sergeant, that still doesn't make it suspicious, and you're not helping." Scott sighed in frustration. He never understood why people waffled and never got to the point. And at that precise moment he had the patience of a gnat.

"The vehicle is registered to a Giles Rochester. The address of the registered keeper is...Edmunston-Hunt boarding school. He's a teacher there."

Scott's eyes widened. His mind furiously processed the information. *Was it stolen? Was the deceased the registered keeper?* This was more than a coincidence. He had no proof as yet, but more a hunch. "Okay I'll be there in forty-five minutes, make sure the scene is secure," he barked.

"Yes, that's all in hand. Shall I alert the rest of your team?"

"Yes, contact DS Trent and DC Wilson. Inform SOCO, we need the scene documented and photographed. Oh and contact the pathologist."

"I'll do that right away, sir. We have tried to contact the pathologist a couple of times already but she's not answering her phone, so we've left a few messages for her to contact us immediately."

After hanging up, Scott stroked Cara's dark hair that was spread across his chest. "Wake up, trouble," he said kissing the top of her head. "We've got a job on. Oh and check your phone. You're needed too. We've got forty-five minutes to get to Worthing," Scott announced, wiggling out from underneath Cara.

"Oh, can't we just have five more minutes in bed? I'll make it worth your while," she said in a slow, seductive, sleepy voice.

"Nope, so get your lazy ass out of bed," Scott replied as he searched around his room for something to wear.

"You're such a spoilsport, Scottie."

A SEA of curious faces greeted Scott by the time he arrived. He pushed his way through the growing crowd of morbid onlookers. The presence of a familiar white forensic tent was out of view around the back of the car park, so the scene offered little to see for those milling around. *Well at least that's something*, he thought hoping to keep the scene obscured from this lot.

He signed into the scene log, and paused to scan the surroundings, looking at entrances, exits, the type of buildings in the locality, their uses and CCTV, before proceeding around the back towards the tent. He hated jumpers, not because of what they did, they all had their own reasons, but because they created a bloody mess. It wouldn't be long before a council approved cleaning company was on scene washing away the remnants of someone's life.

Scott looked over his shoulder at the swelling crowd beyond the cordon. Various onlookers were recording images on their phones. Scott picked out two individuals who stood out from the crowd with their DSLRs and long lenses. *Bloody press.*

The car park was L-shaped in structure which afforded some degree of concealment as the incident had taken place at the inner corner of where the two sides of the car park met. The area looked out over a secondary open-air car park. The white forensic tent had been positioned close to the wall of the car park. A solitary scenes-of-crime officer was finalising their work outside of the tent as Scott walked up.

Scott acknowledged the SOCO with a nod, before he peered in through the flap in the side. He saw the twisted body of a man, one leg projected forward, the second bent at the knee and flexed backwards. He was lying on his side, with a dark, dried pool of blood framing his head. Even from this angle, Scott could clearly make out a large depression in the side of the man's head that had practically flattened the shape of his face.

"I've got this for you, sir," the SOCO offered Scott, holding a clear evidence bag. "This was the only evidence we found on him."

The moment Scott saw the contents of the bag, he knew that in some way the incident involving the jumper was connected to his ongoing murder investigation. Inside the bag were a white feather and a small note with a Latin inscription, which Scott vaguely recalled looked remarkably similar to the first inscription that had been found on the first body.

Scott scanned the scene once again. Clearly from the multitude of weeds that were breaking through the stones in the pavement and the white railings, which upon closer inspection were an off-white with large patches of brown rust, the car park and surrounding area indicated years of neglect. He glanced up to look at the side of the car park and the path that the body had followed. From where he was standing, it was a significant drop. With any luck, Scott hoped that the man had died on impact.

"Guv, up here." Mike was leaning over the railings on the third floor. "His car is up here."

Scott took to the stairwell, and instantly scrunched up his nose. The smell of urine was overpowering on certain floors. He trod carefully. He could make out dark stains from those who'd relieved themselves and worse. As he stepped out from the stairwell, he glanced around the deserted floor. Despite the brilliant sunshine outside, there was a darkness and chill inside. The only car visible was behind a police cordon. Scott ducked under the tape and walked over to the car. The door of the silver Golf was still open, the keys in the ignition.

"I guess we can assume it's his car, considering there's nowt else up here." Mike gesticulated, swinging his arm in an arc.

Scott hummed to himself. "More than likely. We'll get SOCO to do a sweep of the car and see if they can grab some prints."

Scott walked over to the dirty railings, and glanced over the edge. He wasn't a great one for heights, and from where he stood it seemed like a bloody long way down. From this elevated position, he could get a much clearer view of the surrounding area.

From his vantage point, there wasn't a lot to see except the back of low-rise office blocks. Some had their windows boarded up. Others less fortunate had various windows broken, no doubt from stone-throwing youths who had little else to do in what appeared to be a bit of a run-down area. Graffiti tags on brown brick walls had repeatedly been whitewashed, leaving an ugly collage that resembled the paintings of a child in preschool.

He imagined that at night very few people had a reason to be there. It was a cold and soulless location. There were no local eateries, cinemas or shops other than a local Morrisons supermarket off to his left and over the flyover. The fact that the location was not overlooked or busy at night offered the ideal spot for drug takers, vandalism and no doubt a few courting couples who could pull up for a quick bunk-up without being spotted or disturbed.

He could see Cara and Abby approaching the tent.

"Who found him?" Scott asked as he turned and leant back against the railings, exhaling deeply in the process.

"It was a council worker who was coming to do a sweep of the car park. Fucking frightened the living daylights out of him, poor old sod. He's been with the council nearly forty years and due to retire next year. Said he's never seen anything like it in his life."

"Did you get a statement off him?"

"Yes, Guv. Uniform has done that already."

"Mike, I want you to check for CCTV."

"Do we need to? He's only a jumper?"

"Ordinarily, probably not. They found evidence on the body, a white feather and the Latin inscription...the two events are connected."

Mike raised his eyebrows in surprise. "Oh, shit. I'll have a scan around and check with uniform to see if anyone in the crowd spotted anything."

"Okay, you do that. There's not much else for me to do around here. Think it's time I paid the principal another visit."

Abby was lurking around outside the tent by the time Scott

returned. Cara had also completed her brief examination and was jotting a few notes whilst sitting on her silver medical examination case.

"Great way to start the morning off," Abby said.

"The body in there looks to be of a teacher at Edmunston-Hunt."

Abby crossed her arms and pursed her lips. "Coincidence?" she suggested.

Scott shook his head. "No, I don't believe in coincidences. We need to go and have a word with Collier. There's more going on at that school than he is letting on and he's trying my patience now. Is there anything you saw that looks suspicious, Cara?"

"Can't be a hundred per cent certain, because it's a bit of a mess. I could definitely make out some type of red banding around the deceased's neck."

Scott nodded, that extra bit of evidence, if true, would lend even more weight to his theory that the two incidents were connected. The question was how.

I n just over forty-eight hours, Scott found himself
back at Edmunston-Hunt boarding school. On any
other day driving up to the school, the smell of
freshly cut grass wafting in through his car window, and the
sound of birdsong reverberating around the grounds, would
offer a peaceful and tranquil escape from the hustle and
bustle of Brighton life. However, the death of a second
teacher meant his visit took on a more sombre emphasis.

As Abby got out of the car, she put on her scary face. "You
ready for Cruella de Vil again?"

Scott smiled as they walked through the main doorway.
He'd forgotten about the charm of Mrs Hilary.

Their favourite glorified secretary was busily tapping away
on a keyboard whilst wearing headphones. They were the
old style of headphones that sat over the ears and drowned
out most of the surrounding noise. He doubted she was
listening to anything vaguely resembling music and was
probably typing from dictation. She cast a brief look in

their direction and carried on typing. Scott leant forward on the reception desk.

"Mrs Hilary, we need to see Mr Collier," he asked putting on his politest voice.

His enquiry was met by a wall of silence as she continued typing. Anyone would think that Scott and Abby were both invisible. Scott clenched his jaws and shot Abby a glance. Abby rolled her eyes in disbelief.

Scott cleared his throat loudly, and knocked firmly on the countertop. Mrs Hilary stopped typing and paused for a moment, briefly staring at her screen, before slowly raising her eyes disapprovingly in Scott's direction. She clearly wasn't pleased at the interruption.

"Mrs Hilary," he repeated, his voice heavy with sarcasm, "we are here to see Mr Collier immediately."

"Mr Collier is busy. One moment, please. I'll just finish this and get you booked in for an appointment," she replied with a long-suffering sigh.

With Scott's patience both tested and exhausted, he placed his hands on the desk and leant forward. "I'm not asking you; I'm telling you. We'd like to see Mr Collier *now*."

The woman's attitude remained steadfast. This was turning into a battle of wills and Scott was in no mood to come off second best. "What is it regarding?" she asked.

Scott lifted an eyebrow and glared at the woman to suggest *really?* They were hardly popping in for a cuppa. "It's regarding the ongoing investigation and a new development. Would you like me to draw you a diagram?" he snapped.

Scott's sarcasm was lost on Mrs Hilary who continued to throw a disapproving look in his direction as she picked up the phone.

"What did she think we were here for? A bloody parking fine? Swap knitting patterns?" murmured Abby as she stuffed her hands in her trouser pockets. Scott smiled, Abby didn't suffer fools gladly either.

Mrs Hilary replaced the phone receiver. "Mr Collier will be out in a moment. You can wait over there," she said nodding in the direction of a cluster of low-level leather chairs provided for visitors and prospective parents by the front door. She crossed her arms in defiance.

"Thank you, but no. We will wait here," Scott replied knowing full well that invading her space as they were would only rile the woman.

Mr Collier, impeccably dressed in a dark navy suit, crisp white shirt, and pale blue tie, arrived a few moments later. As he strode purposefully towards them, it reminded Scott of how army personnel marched, shoulders back, chest out, straight arms synchronised in a rhythmic swing. He looked concerned and frustrated, his eyes had narrowed, deep furrows lining his forehead.

"Inspector, Sergeant." His tone was strong; his words few and direct. "How can I help? Is this to do with Mr Johnson?"

"I'm afraid not. Is there somewhere we can go that's a little more private?" Scott asked, glancing briefly in the direction of Mrs Hilary.

"Of course. Yes, come to my office," he offered turning on his heel and striding off just as quickly as he had arrived without even glancing back to see if his visitors were following.

Abby walked quickly behind him. Scott trailed a little further behind. He had slowed to look at the portrait photos that lined one wall of the corridor. Each photo depicted a teacher at the school. He could see that it was a collection of teachers both past and present judging from the dates. Many of the former teachers stared into the camera lens with sombre, serious looks. Grey backgrounds blanched their photos further. The most recent colour additions portrayed teachers in relaxed, side-on poses, with slight smiles that softened each image. They'd changed locations of the photo shoot Scott noticed. They were taken outdoors, from the looks of it on the main lawn, with the school as an elegant backdrop.

Adrian Collier invited them into his room but on this occasion didn't offer them a seat, choosing to stand impatiently behind the closed door, his arms straight by his sides. "What is this all about?" His words were short, sharp and deliberate.

Scott rocked back and forth on his heels a few times. "Have you seen Giles Rochester this morning?"

"No, I'm afraid not. I was made aware of the fact that he didn't turn up for classes this morning. I sent a member of staff over to his cottage to see if he is unwell, but he doesn't appear to be in, and his car was not there either."

"What car does he drive?" Abby asked.

Collier looked in the direction of Scott, and ignored Abby. "He drives a silver VW Golf. Can I ask the nature of your enquiry?"

"Do you have the registration number?"

Adrian Collier looked perplexed as he scanned the officers. "Not to hand, and I'm not sure why you need it?"

"Mr Rochester may have come to some harm, so we are trying to establish some facts. It would be really helpful if you could provide us with his registration number."

Collier turned to his desk and dialled through to Mrs Hilary. "Could you give me the registration number for Giles Rochester's car?" He paused for a moment clearly listening to the woman's response. He lifted his head towards the ceiling in frustration. "Just get me the details… now." There was a long pause whilst he waited for the details before he replaced the handset. "It's FG15 FKL, Inspector."

Scott and Abby exchanged glances. It confirmed what Scott had suspected.

"Mr Collier, a body was found this morning in Worthing. We believe it's Giles Rochester."

Collier fell silent. He stared momentarily at the floor before levelling his eyes with the officers again. His eyes searched theirs; he looked for answers. "I'm sorry to hear that. It's tragic news. Are you sure it's Giles?"

Scott nodded. "We believe so, but we'll need to formally identify the body. His car was found close by. Did he have any issues or problems that you were aware of?"

"I'm afraid I don't know of any."

Scott didn't want to release too many details or his suspicions at this stage about how the two deaths were connected. "Mr Collier, what concerns me is that in the space of forty-eight hours, two members of your staff have been found dead. Call me a cynic, but do you not find that strange or disturbing? Are you not concerned about the welfare *and* safety of your staff and pupils?" he asked, staring intently into Collier's eyes.

Collier shrugged. "I admit, it's highly unusual. My job here is to run a school, provide an excellent teaching environment and deliver outstanding results. It's not my place to delve into the private lives of my staff. As long as they do what they're employed to, and get the results, then I'm satisfied. Of course the happiness and welfare of my pupils is important too, but we're not a kindergarten. We turn out a certain type of young man." The principal straightened his back, pulled his shoulders back and thrust his chest out in military fashion.

"And what might that be?" Abby asked directly.

Collier glowered, returning a steely stare. "We turn out fearless young men, the future captains, majors, brigadiers of the British Army, the leaders of FTSE 500 companies, the entrepreneurs that shape our world, world-class sportsmen and our future politicians. We have no room for weak-mindedness." He turned and walked towards the window that looked out over the magnificent striped lawns. "In battle, it's the cowards who are the instigators of defeat; bravery is a rampart of defence," he said firmly as he straightened up.

"So you'd agree with the quote, 'Weakness of attitude becomes weakness of character'?"

The principal turned and wryly smiled at Scott. "Ah, Inspector. Touché. Albert Einstein certainly had a point."

Scott let Collier's reply hang in the air for a moment even

though he disagreed. He was beginning to think that the man hadn't really moved on from his days in the army. "Did he have any next of kin?"

Collier thought for a moment as he rubbed his chin. "I believe he had a sister, but she's in New Zealand."

"No one else in the UK?"

"Not that I'm aware of."

Abby interrupted him. "Are you sure that he doesn't have any family in the UK?"

"Is it necessary, Inspector?" he asked.

Scott remained silent, surprised by Collier's response. The principal clearly had an issue responding to Abby's questions. Whether it was Abby herself, or the fact she was a female was hard to tell. Scott suspected the latter. Collier was no doubt used to commanding the superior high ground, and with his military background probably wasn't used to be challenged, especially by a woman.

"Mr Collier?" Abby pushed again.

Collier sighed in protest. "As I said to the inspector, not that I'm aware of, Sergeant," he replied looking down at Abby.

Abby straightened her grey suit jacket, and reached for her phone before stepping away to call the office.

"We'll need to search his cottage, so can you arrange for us to gain access now please?"

⸻

GILES ROCHESTER's cottage was much the same in size and

sparseness as Christopher Johnson's. Scott and Abby had taken the opportunity to look around and search for evidence to explain the last few hours of his life.

Whilst Abby searched upstairs, Scott looked around the ground floor. The lounge had a large flat-screen TV mounted above the fireplace, a stack of country living magazines sat beside a leather armchair. As he wandered through to the kitchen, he stopped in his tracks. There on the table sat a large length of thick boundary rope. Scott examined it in closer detail, leaning over the table without touching it. Despite it being wrapped in a series of circles, he could clearly make out that one end had been tied off to form a loop...*or noose*. Scott's mind whirled as he thought about why it was there. *Was it linked...to the first incident?*

He was distracted by Abby's shout from somewhere upstairs. He found her in what appeared to be the study. "We've got a rope similar in thickness and look to the one used in the first case," he said.

"Look at this," Abby said waving a piece of paper between her gloved fingers.

Scott looked at the note and scrunched up his eyes with suspicion, then read it out. "Giles you make my heart skip a beat, our secret meetings are what I live for...S xx"

"Sound familiar?"

"Just a bit. The handwriting looks the same. Get it bagged up. Any others?"

"There's a small pile in the top drawer of his desk. All pretty much saying the same stuff; all signed in the same way."

"Abby, the chances of him having next of kin in the UK

appears slim. Grab his toothbrush, that mug on his desk, and see if you can pull some hair fibres off his bed pillow. We can give them to forensics to do a DNA match with our victim for completeness."

Scott was perplexed. Two bodies in two days. The same evidence found on both victims, and now both having similar notes from possibly the same person. *Who was S?*

12

Scott and Abby arrived at the station not long after lunch. Buried deep in their PCs, the rest of the team hardly glanced up to see them arrive. One by one they lifted their heads when the smell of freshly brewed coffee filled the floor.

"Grab yourselves a cuppa and a cake," said Scott.

They had stopped at Costa Coffee on their way back to the station, and selected an array of cakes including millionaire's shortbread, teacakes, lemon tarts and chocolate tiffin.

Mike's large frame moved first as Scott had expected. His large beer belly hung over his trouser belt, the shirt buttons on his grey shirt fought a valiant battle to stop him from bursting out. Small hairy bits of flesh poked out between each button. A fine specimen of a man he certainly was not. Scott had seen pictures of Mike from his army days. Back then, he was a fit, large, well-built trained sniper that had seen two difficult tours of Afghanistan and spent time based in Germany and Africa. His active lifestyle had ensured he'd remained a healthy weight and size.

Since becoming a civvy, he'd let it go. His hair had started to thin and grey. His trim, muscular frame had given way to an ever-expanding waistline, the consequence of a diet that gravitated towards convenience meals, Oreo biscuits and sampling craft beers. The Hare & Hounds in London Road was his favourite watering hole. He would find a corner to settle down with the paper in one hand, and a pint of Meantime's unpasteurised, unfiltered, 'straight out of the brewery,' lager in the other. Mike would slowly sip his pint, savouring the slightly yeasty brew that offered a sharp hop edge and a twisting citric taste.

He lumbered towards the desk and helped himself with a welcoming nod that would normally be reserved for the return of an old friend. He would happily have hoovered up the lot if given the chance.

Raj and Sian piled in, too. Sian, ever careful of her figure tiptoed around the food. She wrapped her dark brown hair behind her ears as she peered over the goodies. Her tortoiseshell-framed glasses slipped down the bridge of her pixy nose causing her to tip them back up. She gleefully glanced over the selection with her hands firmly tucked in the pockets of her light grey trousers that hugged her backside and accentuated her slim figure. Sian finally opted for a solitary teacake biting off the chocolate layer first like a child, leaving the biscuit base and fluffy marshmallow.

DCI Harvey marched into the office. "Scott, a word please," she hollered from the other end of the room causing everyone to spin round in her direction, before she turned and headed back out into the corridor.

Scott swung through the double doors to find Harvey pacing up and down the landing. She looked concerned as she glanced at her feet, her arms tapping each thigh.

"Yes, Ma'am."

"What's the latest on the jumper this morning?"

"Well, initially it could have been mistaken for being a suicide. However, I'm fairly certain it's not."

"Go on."

"The victim appears to be a Giles Rochester, a teacher at Edmunston-Hunt School. DNA evidence should confirm that, but he looks like his driver's ID and school photo anyway. Secondly, a Latin inscription and a white feather were found in one of his pockets. Exactly the same as in Johnson's case."

This wasn't the news the DCI was hoping for. If anything, it heaped more pressure on her shoulders. Her forehead furrowed as the two incidents ran through her mind.

Scott sensed that Harvey was probably mulling it over. "What's on your mind, Ma'am? I think I know you well enough to know that something's bothering you."

Harvey hesitated for a moment. "You need to get a result on this one, Scott, and you need to get it fast," she said firmly.

"With all due respect, Ma'am, we are still very early into our investigation. I can't pull a rabbit out of a hat at the click of a finger."

"Scott, you have to appreciate that *sometimes* our job becomes a little political, and more importantly people up there," she said pointing with a finger at the ceiling above, "have a vested interest, and significant clout."

"What are you getting at, Ma'am?"

"Superintendent Meadows is on my ass. He's just had a call from Chief Constable Lennon. CC Lennon moves in the same circles as several of the governors on the board of Edmunston-Hunt. I'll go as far as to say that they are members of the same Masonic lodge. The governors were *a little concerned* about the negative publicity that Johnson's death would have on the reputation of the school. That's something they want to guard fiercely. The last thing they want are parents, and I hasten to add, very *influential* parents, pulling their kids out of Edmunston-Hunt. At forty-five thousand pounds a year per pupil, they have a lot to lose. If the second victim turns out to be Rochester, then Lennon is going to be under pressure for his force to deal with this matter quietly and swiftly, with the least amount of fuss."

"I'm not going to brush it under the carpet, Ma'am, or hope that the file disappears under the other dozens of cases that we're dealing with."

If there was one thing Scott hated, it was his team being used as a political football, a point he stressed. It annoyed the hell out of him how those who talked in hushed tones could influence how he did his job on a day-to-day basis.

"I'm not asking you to do anything of the sort," Harvey replied firmly and quickly, a hint of anger in her voice at the thought of being challenged. "Just be wary, and more importantly bear in mind who you and I report to." She shook her head furiously and gritted her teeth. "Sometimes you can't ignore *that football. We* are part of a team whether we like it or not." Harvey looked at Scott silently, her eyes conveying the delicate nature of this matter as well the ramifications if he didn't toe the line.

The corridor fell silent once again as Harvey turned and headed back to her office through the double doors at the other end of the landing. Scott's mind turned over Harvey's parting words as he leant on the stair rail. If he did his job, he'd be making a bed of nails for himself, but his conscience would be clean. If he toed the line, his career would be safe, but he'd be going against everything he'd joined up for.

His attention snapped back to the present as Sian pushed through the doors. "Guv, there's a call for you. It's Simon Barrett. He's a lecturer in modern languages at Sussex University."

"Simon, this is Detective Inspector Baker from Brighton CID. Thank you for coming back to us regarding our enquiry," he said sitting down at his desk.

"My pleasure, Inspector. How can I help?"

"I hope you've had enough time to review the information we sent over to you. We're hoping you can interpret the Latin inscription?"

"Most certainly. I have to admit, it's not the usual type of request I receive," he replied with a deep belly laugh. "Usually it's feedback on Latin inscriptions in books or photos, and even the odd artefact."

"I guess so. Can you tell me what it means?"

"*Ignavus iners timidius tu mori debes*...essentially means 'You, a coward, deserve to die.' It's pretty much self-explanatory."

Scott thanked the lecturer and hung up. He tapped his pen slowly as he leant back in his chair, the sound sharp and loud in the quiet of his office. *Coward, deserve to die* ran on repeat in his mind. *How did the phrase relate to Johnson and Rochester?* That's what he needed to find out and fast as the conversation with DCI Harvey sprang back into his thoughts.

He glanced at his watch. The PM on the jumper would be taking place now; he'd call Cara later for her results. Firstly, he needed a team update.

13

Abby made her way to the drinks machine to grab a bottle of water before the briefing. Mike blocked her access to it as he chatted with the same female officer he'd been talking to in the canteen. He was so engrossed in conversation that he didn't see Abby approaching.

"Erm hum," Abby said, clearing her throat loudly to catch Mike's attention.

He turned and gave Abby the cheesiest of grins. "Hiya, Sarge, how's it hanging?"

Abby looked at him with an open mouth, her eyes wide with incredulity. "If you know what's good for you, you'd get up to the briefing room now. The boss is about to start," she added shaking her head, as she grabbed the bottle before heading off. Behind her, she could hear Mike throwing out more one-liners to the poor girl. "Catch you later, babes," he called as he left her standing by the machine.

"Hey wait!" he shouted. His bulky frame shook the floor as he trotted up alongside Abby, a satisfying grin smeared across his face. "See that smile? I reckon I'm well in there," he said smugly.

"She's either got a screw loose, or she's taking pity on you," Abby said with a shake of her head. "I mean, do yourself a favour and find yourself some new chat-up lines. Anyone would think you're still at university and about half your age," she said punching him playfully in the arm. "'Catch you later, babes'? Really? This isn't *High School Musical*, and you're certainly not Troy Bolton. She might be ten years younger than you, and that's being generous, but lines like that aren't you."

Mike shot her a quizzical look, without kids, the reference about *High School Musical* and Troy Bolton was clearly lost on him. "Well, she seems to like me. I make her laugh, which is more than I do with you," he said in retaliation.

"You sure she's not laughing *at* you?" she teased. "Maybe she's taking pity on the less fortunate in our society, namely you."

The suggestion seemed to hit Mike right in the solar plexus, knocking the wind out of him. Even though Abby was jesting, it nevertheless caused him to reflect, the slightest of doubts slowly invading his mind. No sooner had he entertained them, had he shrugged them off. "Yeah, whatever."

Abby paused for a moment by the door to the briefing room. "Oh, and one last thing. If you ever say 'how's it hanging?' again, I'll cut your nuts off. Then you definitely won't have anything hanging. Get my drift?" she said with a mock menacing glare in her eyes as she used two fingers to mimic the blades on a pair of scissors.

Raj and Sian were already seated as Mike and Abby entered. Scott busily scribbled a few notes on to the whiteboard when he glanced over his shoulder to see them enter.

"Okay team, we've got another case that I now believe is linked to our first victim, Johnson. Initially, it was thought that the jumper from Teville Gate car park was unconnected and nothing more than a suicide. Evidence has now come to light that suggests both cases are connected. In particular, both victims were found with a Latin inscription and white feather in their pockets. According to our Latin scholar, the inscription says, 'You, a coward, deserve to die.' So in my opinion these deaths were murders and the victims were killed for a particular reason.

"Hopefully, DNA evidence will confirm for completeness that the second victim is Giles Rochester, a teacher at Edmunston-Hunt. But it's safe to assume it will. There are similarities between these two cases, one which I've already highlighted, the second being they both seem to have in their possession love notes from the same person. The handwriting is similar, and they're both signed off with the letter S followed by a few kisses. And lastly they were both teachers at the same school. I don't believe in coincidences, so we need to look for motive and the Latin inscription is key to that."

Scott glanced around, he could see that the others around the table were rolling the connections through their minds, and his thoughts were met with suitable nods of understanding.

"Mike had a quick look whilst we were there and saw nothing, but Sian I want you to widen the search and look for anything on CCTV. Check all the roads leading into the area and to the car park. It's not the busiest of areas, but there are office buildings in the vicinity, and Worthing station. So there is a chance something may have been picked up. Secondly, get on the case with the high-tech unit. I want the phone records downloaded from his phone as fast as possible. If they haven't got time to do it, let's find a designated officer who can."

Sian whistled softly as she wrote down her instructions.

"The thick boundary rope that Abby and I recovered from the second property resembles the same type of rope used in our first case where the victim hanged himself. Hopefully, forensics can confirm that through fibre type analysis. What I can confirm, however, is the rest of forensics feedback so far.

"Johnson had a significant amount of alcohol in his bloodstream that had been consumed over several hours. They estimated something in the region of half a bottle to a full bottle of red wine. The prints on the glass belong to Johnson. They were able to lift some clear impressions off the love notes from S. There's nothing showing on the database against those prints. So that person is still unknown to us. Forensics found two sets of prints in his room, one belonging to him, the other matching mystery person S. This person certainly visited Johnson in the past."

"I'll do all the usual, and start looking into the background of the second victim. The usual stuff, Guv?" Mike asked.

"Yep, friends, relatives, relationships and social media profiles. Get down to the school and speak to the teachers. Let's see if he had fallen out with anyone, find out his movements over the last twenty-four hours, and see if anyone spotted anything unusual either in his behaviour, or around the grounds of the school."

"How have we got on with Johnson?" asked Abby, addressing the others around the table.

"He seemed a likeable character," added Sian. "He was the housemaster for Ditchling House; I spoke to the pupils there. The consensus was he was fair but firm. He wasn't the type of guy to take any crap, and said it as it was."

"I've got the phone records back on Johnson. He didn't make a lot of phone calls to be honest. I guess he didn't need to. There's quite a lot of phone traffic between him and another number, though. I checked the number but it's a pay-as-you-go number, and the number's not registered."

Scott thanked her. "I've spoken to DCI Harvey, and because of the continued threat at the school, we're assigning some uniformed resources as a visible deterrent and for reassurance. Although I'm not sure how effective a panda car with a PCSO parked by the main entrance is going to be, but that's all we can allocate at the moment. The school is not in lockdown, but we need to remain vigilant there. We recommended that the school needs to consider closing for the time being. However, the school and board of governors felt it would send out the wrong message to the pupils and parents, many of which are either not in the UK or wouldn't be too pleased with the decision."

Raj shifted around in his seat. Remarkably, he hadn't come bearing gifts today. Normally, there'd be some biscuits or cakes flying around, and without them, the briefing didn't feel the same. The heat of the day bothered Raj. He'd chosen a grey shirt to wear with his black trousers. In this heat and without the air conditioning, it had proven a poor choice. A thin, dark grey patch started to appear under each armpit. His hair looked decidedly more ruffled, and his clean-shaven looks had been replaced by short, designer stubble that reminded Scott of the unshaven villains in the old spaghetti westerns.

"Guv, what I find strange, is the lack of reaction within the school. Their assistant principal is dead, and now it looks like a second teacher has died under suspicious circumstances. In any normal school, you'd have the mix of human emotions, panic, fear, outrage, sadness. But there doesn't seem to be anything like that even after the first victim. And now with a second teacher, you'd think the school would be in overdrive. I'd expect to see parents pulling their kids out and teachers panicking. There's none of that," Raj added, shaking his head in disbelief.

"I'm with you there, Raj. It's a very surreal atmosphere. On both occasions that Abby and I have been up there. The principal had an almost nonchalant, cavalier attitude. There's definitely more going on at that school than we have been led to believe. We need to find out what. I want you and Mike to look into the backgrounds of all the pupils. Look for any disgruntled parents who perhaps have a grudge against the school. And, Sian, I want you to pull the records of all teachers past and present and review them. Does anything stand out? Were there any past convictions? Any disciplinary issues? Was there anything going on in their personal lives that could have some bearing on this case?"

AFTER WRAPPING UP THE MEETING, Scott briefed the DCI. Her mood hadn't really changed much since the last time he'd spoken to her. A knot of deep tension built inside the pit of his stomach as he tried to explain to Harvey all the different avenues that they were exploring in the hope that she'd be satisfied. He'd left the meeting decidedly uncomfortable, sensing that everything he had said had fallen on deaf ears.

Whilst the team busied themselves, he'd retreated to the sanctuary of his office. The emails had been piling up in his inbox. With the case taking up most of his time, he'd not had the opportunity to sift through them. He groaned at the prospect of going through one hundred and twenty-four emails, most of which he knew would be internal memos and circulars.

He glanced up from his PC monitor to look at his in-tray. He had another eleven case files to review. With the current case taking up much of the team's resources and time, it was easy to have the case files slip to the back of the queue. Rape, burglary, aggravated burglary, an armed robbery in a small off-licence in Hove, and a team of professional shoplifters working their way through stores in The Lanes, all overflowing his review list.

It would have been easy for Scott to type up brief review comments before handing the files back to his officers. He'd come across other DIs who very rarely examined case files in detail. Typing the proverbial 'I agree with the current approach and suggestions offered' seemed to be their preferred option. Anything for an easy life.

Scott didn't want to be like that. He trusted his officers, and in return they trusted him. A good team surrounded him. At the end of the day, the buck stopped with him. He was good at his job. If it meant that he would have to review every single case line by line, then that's what he would do. He was very much in the camp of 'leaving no stone unturned'.

His body ached; his shoulders were tight. The muscles radiated bursts of throbbing pain down his back and his eyes felt heavy. He'd leave the case files until tomorrow when maybe he'd have the opportunity to look at them with a fresh set of eyes. He had somewhere else he needed to be now.

14

The heat of the late afternoon sun beamed down on Scott's shoulders. The much-needed warmth penetrated deep, relieving the tension that had built up during the day. He stretched his arms out to the side, pulling his shoulders back in the hope of relieving the nagging pain that gnawed between his shoulder blades. He loosened his top button and pulled the knot on his tie, releasing its grip from his neck before rolling it into a neat ball starting with the thin narrow end. He removed his jacket as he walked through the grounds, casually throwing it over one shoulder and hooking the hanging loop through his finger.

As the sun began its journey downwards on the horizon, the shadows of the trees and headstones began to lengthen. Scott never understood why for some people a cemetery spooked them out. To him it was a place of solitude and reflection. It offered a lasting connection with loved ones.

In the distance to his right, he could see a couple huddled around a grave. The woman gently wiped her eyes with a tissue; the man provided a supporting arm around her shoulder as he pulled her tight. Further past them, he could see a man, probably in his late sixties judging by his grey hair. He stood solemnly in front of a grave with his hands deep in the pockets of his trousers. He stood there rocking back and forth very gently as he stared down at the newly laid flowers.

Stillness hung in the air. The sound of birdsong echoed through the trees. The odd bumblebee buzzed as it hopped amongst the various plots feeding on nectar from the buttercups.

He'd finally arrived at Becky's grave. He stood for a solitary moment staring at her beautiful picture set in a heart-shaped black marble headstone. His shoulders slumped, a crippling, dark heavy sadness pulled them down along with his broken heart. His eyes misted over. He missed his family so much. His jaw clenched tight as he fought desperately to stem the flow of tears that threatened to break free. Scott blinked hard as moisture wet his lashes. That beautiful smile that greeted him every morning was nothing more than a precious memory. The very same smile that looked up at him now.

"I've brought you a present, little one. I promised to bring you your favourite toy." His bottom lip trembled. "Remember when we used to watch it together, and I'd make the piggy oink, oink noises, and you'd laugh. You would always say 'again, Daddy, again'…I loved being silly with you." He knelt down and placed a small, pink, Peppa Pig cuddly toy by her headstone. Minutes elapsed as he stared at Becky's picture, sobs ripping through his body, a release of the pain and sadness that festered and built up within him every day. Moments like this gave him the opportunity to let go, like a pressure cooker releasing steam.

"I hope you're resting in peace. I'd do anything to see your little chubba smile now."

The sounds of daily life seemed to fade into the background. Quietness surrounded him. This sanctuary cocooned him from the tribulations of daily life. If he could, he'd spend every day here. His mind needed it. His body craved it and his sanity depended on it.

Scott finally stood and straightened up. "Love you lots my little lady," he whispered as he placed two fingers on his lips, placed a kiss and touched Becky's picture. "I'll stop by real soon."

He left Angel's Corner and walked through the small meadow towards Tina's plot. A lot of care had been taken to create a place of rest that was both aesthetically pleasing and respectful. The meadow was a nice touch, a space for local flora and fauna to flourish, and a place for visitors to wander and be with their thoughts.

Tina's grave filled him with mixed emotions. Part of him ached, his mind a blur full of memories and pictures. Every time he thought of his wonderful wife, those precious moments were invaded by the lasting image of Tina on the floor, her body twisted, a narrow blood trail winding down from a head trauma. It was an image that always sent waves of repulsion through his body. His stomach seemed to repeatedly flip over, forcing him to lose his breath.

A shake of his head pushed that image back to the darkest recesses of his mind for the time being until they returned to haunt him again. Though the nightmares were few and far between as time passed, a dark cloud of anguish followed him every waking minute.

Another part of him carried a burden of guilt…for not being able to protect his family. That sense of failure clung like an acrid smell. This time around, the guilt seemed worse. Cara. This wonderful woman he'd met was helping him to heal the wounds of the past. She'd brought happiness back into his life. Or so he thought.

Was she really healing him, or was he conveniently relying on the relationship as a distraction. He was sure it was the former, but a doubt still niggled him. It bugged him, like a small stone caught inside his shoe. It made his relationship with her an uncomfortable journey at times.

Looking at Tina's picture didn't help. He hoped that through some divine or cosmic intervention, he'd know what to say or how to feel, but the right words failed him.

"I'm sorry I let you down, babes. You're always in my thoughts. I'll always be with you. There are days I question if I can live without you and Becky, but I have to move on. I know you would have wanted me to. I have to let you go at some point. I have to keep going. The only way I think I can cope is to keep working, keep busy and keep living my life. I have to remind myself what I'm here for…to make a difference to the world.

"I've met someone new. Her name's Cara. I think you'd like her; you'd approve. I can imagine you right now telling me to stop being a silly sod, to get on with my life and not to dwell on the past. But that's easier said than done." He sighed as he picked at the weeds around her headstone.

He felt a strange sense of remorse tinged with relief as he

walked away. It wasn't a feeling that he'd experienced before in all his visits. Perhaps the tide was changing. Perhaps he was easing into the present rather than reversing into the past.

———

THE DOUBLE RING on the doorbell signalled Cara's arrival as Scott sat watching the news about the latest crisis in Syria. Only Cara rang the doorbell twice in succession, more to annoy Scott than anything else.

Cara had come straight from work, her hair tidied away in a ponytail, a simple pair of black trousers, white sleeveless vest and dainty black patent ballerina pumps provided simple yet stylish attire.

"Hey, handsome," she said greeting him with a lingering kiss on the doorstep that wasn't reciprocated. She held up a white paper bag with a picture of a fishing trawler on it. "Dinner," she said excitedly as the familiar smell of fish and chips filed the air, firing off a rumble in his stomach.

Cara sensed Scott's melancholy as they made their way through to the kitchen. As Scott grabbed some plates, Cara placed a hand on his arms.

"Scottie, you okay? You seem a little distant. Something happen? Have I done something to upset or hurt you?"

Scott shook his head as he turned to face her. Her deep brown eyes were soft, alluring and inviting. How could she possibly hurt him? Her loving nature was one of the qualities he loved the most. He needed to tell her.

"I went to their graves this afternoon."

Cara gave his arm a gentle and reassuring squeeze. "I'm sorry."

"I know you'll think this sounds silly, me talking to them and all that, but I told Tina about us, well you in particular. I know she's gone, but I still think she's around. Daft—I know." He paused. "I needed to tell her. I felt like I was betraying her...betraying her memory. I...I can't really explain it, but I needed to tell her so I could move on and not feel guilty all the bloody time."

"Guilty about us?" Cara asked.

"I guess..." He shrugged.

Cara pulled her hand away in the awkward silence that followed. "Would it be easier for you if we didn't see each other?" She frowned. Her words hung in the air and filled the uncomfortable void.

Scott studied Cara. Her milky, flawless complexion, her high cheekbones and firm full lips. She was mesmerising. He was afraid to admit just how much she meant to him.

She tilted her head to one side unsure as to what Scott was thinking. "Speak to me, Scott." Her words were conveyed with sincerity and meaning. Her chest heaved. On the outside she was trying to act cool and collected. But on the inside she was a mess, hoping against hope that this wasn't Scott's way of letting her down gently with the old "we can still be friends," line to wrap it up.

He held her by her arms. "Cara, I need to move on with my life. I've been through hell and back. Sometimes I've felt like I'm in quicksand and I'm paralysed, and the harder I try and fight it, the stronger the pull is to a place I don't want to go."

Cara offered the smallest of smiles, a sense of vulnerability apparent as she wrapped her arms around herself.

"I've no intention of letting you go, Cara."

She was pleased to hear that, but a part of her trembled as she fought to breathe normally. Now wasn't the time to tell him.

15

Scott left Cara putting on her make-up as he threw his jacket on to leave. He felt good this morning and put that down to an evening of closeness and affection with Cara. She had a unique knack of effortlessly blending love with the odd sprinkling of laughter to lighten the mood. He opened the door whilst simultaneously pressing the unlock button on his car fob. Brilliant sunshine and the warmth of the morning bathed his face.

Horror fast replaced his enjoyment as he paused mid-step, and looked down. He tried to fathom whether his mind was playing cruel tricks on him or if it was real. Staring back at him with black, lifeless eyes was a pig's head...a fresh pig's head. Alarm bells rang in his mind, his pulse quickened as he stepped over the head and walked a few steps down his path to the front gate. He looked up and down the road to see if anyone was lurking about.

In his job as a police officer he'd been called many names, but the undesirable element of society that officers had to deal with often referred to them as pigs. And indeed he had been referred to as a pig on more than one occasion that he could care to remember.

Part of him thought that the severed head was perhaps a prank of some sorts. But there was another part of him that had to take it seriously. He paused for a moment and scanned every single car as far as the eye could see. If they were around, they could be parked up and watching. From where he stood, there was neither anyone hanging around in the street nor anyone sitting in a car observing him.

"Cara, you better get down here!" he shouted.

"I'm nearly finished, hon."

"No, I mean get down here now," he repeated.

The severity in his tone forced Cara to curtail the finishing touches in applying her make-up as she rushed downstairs. "What's the matter?"

Scott stood to one side so that Cara could see behind him and to the porch.

Her eyes widened in surprise and disbelief, a hand covered her open mouth. "Shit almighty...what?...Oh my God." She was struggling, her eyes darting back and forth between the pig's head and Scott, searching for answers. "That's just disgusting. What's it doing here?"

"I don't know." Scott shook his head. "It could just be a prank, but in my line of work it could equally be something more sinister."

Cara came to stand beside him, looping her arm under his, her gaze firmly fixed on the head. "What are you going to do?"

"I'm going to bag it up, take it to the station and report it.

I'll have to inform the DCI, and get a uniform to phone around all the butchers just to see if any have sold a pig's head to anyone. You get yourself off to work and I'll sort this out."

Scott's mind whirled. Maybe it was just a coincidence, even though he didn't believe in them. He played it calm, appearing to brush it off in front of Cara. The last thing he wanted to do was alarm her. In his line of work, he couldn't be too careful. He'd heard of officers' cars being vandalised in revenge by suspects that had been arrested or charged. But two random events in the space of just a few days seemed odd to him. *First Cara's car was vandalised at work, and then I get a pig's head on my doorstep.*

As he drove off, his eyes scanned the area in the hope that he'd see a couple of teenagers on bikes giggling to themselves as he drove away. He passed a black BMW, its windows blacked out. Scott didn't see the man in dark clothing hunkered down low in the driver's seat.

ABBY STRUMMED AWAY RHYTHMICALLY on her steering wheel to the sound of Coldplay as Scott pulled up.

"Where have you been?" Abby asked, tapping the clock face on her watch.

"You wouldn't even believe me if I told you."

"Seen him?" Abby said, nodding in the direction of the man they'd seen on their earlier visit.

This time he wore grey overalls as he slowly swept the flagstones that skirted the building. The slow sweeps of the broom equalled by a long, fixed stare in their direction through narrowed eyes. His mouth slanted down, his chin jutted forward and his forehead creased as he stared intently at them.

"Must be a groundsman or caretaker of some sorts," Scott suggested.

"More like old man Smithers the creepy janitor from *Scooby-Doo*, but with hair."

Scott didn't reply. He didn't have a clue what Abby was on about.

"Let me guess, another late night with Cara and she's worn you out?" she asked, elbowing him in the ribs as they walked to the front door of Edmunston-Hunt School.

"Well, that's partly right, but as I was leaving this morning I found a bloody pig's head on my doorstep...a *proper* pig's head," he said with wide eyes.

Abby looked at him suspiciously, her eyes narrowing, unsure if he was winding her up. "You're joshing me...right?"

Scott shook his head. "Nope. I'll show you if you want. It's in the boot," he said nodding over his shoulder towards his car.

"Kids playing a prank?"

Scott shrugged. "I'd love to say yes; I can't be certain. How many times have you been called pig in your career?"

"Um...I couldn't even put a figure on it, but a fair few times."

"Exactly, and I bet at least half of those slurs involved

someone that we had apprehended or charged. How many scrotes have said they'd get us back?"

"What are you going to do?"

"Report it, make a few enquiries and just remain vigilant." He sighed.

Scott's mood didn't lighten as he stood in front of his favourite receptionist, Mrs Hilary, waiting for her to finish her current phone call. She neither looked up nor acknowledged them.

Scott rapped his knuckles once on the desk before walking off in the direction of the principal's office, much to Abby's surprise. She first looked towards Mrs Hilary and then back towards Scott before deciding to chase after her boss. Behind them, they left Mrs Hilary abruptly telling the caller "one moment please, one moment," before she began to shout after them, the sound of rapid footsteps emanating from the reception area as she quickly tried to intercept them.

"Welcome, Inspector," greeted Collier, his back to Scott and Abby as they strode into his office. Collier had clearly been expecting them as he stood by one of his windows. He looked out over the front lawns of the school, the brilliant sun offering warmth on his face as he admired the rich, dark vibrancy of the immaculate frontage. He turned with a tight-lipped smile; his shoulders pulled back, the thumb of each hand hooked into the pockets of his waistcoat. "How can I help?"

Collier was either as cool as a cucumber, calculated and cunning, or plain ignorant and unaware of the severity of the situation that the school faced. Scott's guess was that he was a bit of both.

"Mr Collier, I believe that you're not being entirely forth-coming with the goings-on at the school. You have two members of staff confirmed dead, and you really don't seem to be alarmed or concerned in any way."

Collier cleared his throat, and levelled his eyes with Scott's. "I'm not entirely sure what you're insinuating, *Inspector,* but I'd be careful if I were you about throwing around assumptions," he replied in a firm, plum tone.

"Oh, I think you do, Mr Collier. I think you know exactly what I'm talking about. And I don't take too kindly to being threatened."

Abby watched her boss play out this gladiatorial battle with Collier, and started to feel sorry for the principal as the heated discussion continued. The memory of how he'd dismissed the deputy governor at Pentonville prison sprang into her thoughts.

Collier shrugged and turned to face the window again. He chose to remain silent.

"Both of the deceased had identical evidence placed on them which is why we believe the two events are connected. What does the phrase 'You, a coward, deserve to die' mean to you, or a white feather?"

Collier bowed his head. With Scott's knowledge about patterns of human behaviour, the silence and turning away were classic ploys that people employed when they wanted to avoid giving anything away, especially in their eyes. He knew, from experience that 'The eyes are the window to the soul. The mouth the door.'

Collier shook his head as he turned and walked towards Abby, casting her a derogatory glance. "I'm afraid I haven't got a clue. All sounds rather sinister if you ask me, straight out of a *Poirot* episode."

"Mind if we have a look around the school?"

"Of course, be my guest. I'm here if you need me."

Scott nodded. "By the way, who's the chap in the overalls sweeping up outside?"

"That's Alan Bennett, our caretaker."

"Been with you long?"

"As a matter of fact, yes. Seven years. Keeps himself to himself. A bit of a loner but gets the job done and I don't hear a squeak out of him."

"And before that?"

Collier paused for a moment, unsure whether to divulge Bennett's prior history. "He's an ex-prisoner. Came to us via a charity and Jobcentre Plus."

"Do you know the nature of his offences?" Scott enquired, knowing full well that he could check once back at the station.

"Some type of violent assault or fracas outside a pub in Soho, London…but I can assure you that he's a reformed character now. He's given me no cause for concern, and is of no threat to our pupils…or staff."

"Where does he live? I assume he has accommodation on-site like most school caretakers?"

Collier stiffened, jutting out his jaw and pulling his lips down at the corners. "Yes, he does. He has small lodgings around the back, set back behind the row of cottages designated for teachers."

Alan Bennett lurked in the corridor listening to this exchange. He didn't like people knowing about his life, or his previous misdemeanours. He slowly retraced his steps back around the corner of the corridor, one foot quietly placed behind the other, resting the balls of his feet first, ensuring that his leather workwear boots didn't creak.

16

Matthew Edrington was trapped. They'd caught up with him whilst he was on his way to the music room during his free period. The first shove against the dark oak panelled walls of the corridor had startled him, the unevenness of the surface rubbed against his thin shoulder blades. The back of his head ached from where they'd slapped him hard. *If only I'd run*, he thought, feeling angry with himself.

It would have been easy to say that he was getting used to being singled out, but the truth of the matter wouldn't bear the lie. The attacks, the verbal abuse and the intimidation had broken him further.

"You never learn your lesson, do you, Edrington?"

"Please, please leave me alone. I don't understand what I've done for you to keep hurting me like this."

"You…you just being you is what you've done to deserve this. You're a liability, the weak link. *Everyone* is expected to give a hundred per cent to the house; we're lucky if we

get fifty per cent from you!" Hunter screamed as he delivered another slap to the side of Edrington's head. The sting
spread through Matthew's scalp.

James Rollings pushed the other two boys aside, parting
them as he stepped in between. He grabbed Matthew by the
throat, pushing him hard into the wall. "You don't belong
here. I think you'd be better suited at Roedean," he sniggered before releasing the boy with a step backwards.

Ford and Hunter stepped forward again. They crowded
Matthew, their faces just a few inches away from his. He
could smell their stale, hot breath on his face. Matthew
gritted his teeth, his jaws clenched tight. He needed to be
strong even though all he wanted to do was cry. He
couldn't handle this anymore. He hated being here, hated
the way they treated him.

"Enough!" boomed a voice from behind them, startling the
boys as all three spun round to see Timothy Saunders, the
catering manager, stride towards them. "What do you think
you are doing?" he demanded as he shot each of them a
glance.

A wall of silence met Timothy's question as Rollings stood
there, his hands buried deep in his pockets, his long fringe
swept down partially covering his eyes as it fell across his
face. The corner of his mouth turned up, the slightest of
smiles broke out on his face. Ford's face remained impas-
sive. His light brown eyes appeared to be glazed over as if
affected by illegal substances, which knowing Ford may
have been true. His eyebrows seem to be permanently raised
as if a brow lift had gone horribly wrong, and together with
his pale complexion, he took on a macabre ghostly appearance. It was Hunter who appeared to be the aggressor in the

pack. He had tight, cropped hair and a thin face. Hunter had a penetrative, menacing stare that seemed at odds with his boyish looks. His head slightly bowed, he stood his ground, goading Saunders, his fists clenched tight by his sides.

"I've seen enough of this to last me a lifetime. Leave the boy alone. If I see you do this again, I'll frogmarch the three of you to the principal's office. Do I make myself clear?" he said in a firm and deliberate voice.

His threat was met with a continuing wall of silence. The only response was a defiant smile from Rollings as he turned towards Matthew and said in a hushed tone, "We'll see you later."

Saunders and the boys heard a series of footsteps behind them. Abby and Scott had overheard the altercation whilst they wandered through the school and grounds.

"Everything all right here?" Scott asked, sensing the tense, icy stand-off.

He could see the terror in Matthew Edrington's eyes as they flicked nervously between Scott, Saunders and the boys. His hands were clenched tight in a ball under his chin, his arms protectively shielding his chest.

"Nothing I can't handle," Saunders said in frustration.

"You okay, Matthew?" Scott asked.

"I *said* nothing I can't handle," Saunders insisted.

Matthew opened his mouth to speak, but immediately decided against it when Rollings turned his head shooting him with a threatening glare. The boy's eyes were wide, his lips pursed tight and his jaw muscles flexed as his stare pierced Matthew's fragility. Matthew shot Scott a quick look and gave a tremulous nod.

"Get on your way now, the lot of you…go!" Saunders shouted, before he too turned and hurried away.

Rollings shoulder barged Matthew as the three boys walked off. "We'll see you *later*…" he snarled.

Scott watched as they sauntered off nudging one another and laughing. "Matthew, wait…"

Matthew paused in mid-step, slowly turning on his heel to face Scott, with one eye firmly fixed on his aggressors. He hung on tight with one hand to the rucksack over his shoulder, his other hand buried deep in his trouser pocket.

Scott walked over to him and placed one hand on his shoulder in support. "Are they always picking on you?" A wall of silence met his question. Matthew stared at the ground as if it might open up and swallow him whole. Scott decided to change tact. "Do those boys pick on other kids?" Matthew shrugged his shoulders, not answering. Scott could feel the bony shoulders of the boy through his blazer. Scott gave him a reassuring pat on the back. "Listen, if there's anything you want to talk about, here's my card. Give me a call," Scott offered pulling out his card from the inside of the suit jacket.

Matthew scurried off in the opposite direction, keen to put some distance between him and the others.

"The poor boy looks terrified," Abby tutted. "Kids can be so cruel."

Scott paused for a moment. Bullying was something he knew happened in every school. Whether it was a state comprehensive, or an elite boarding school, boys or girls, it happened. Schools would try their hardest to stamp it out, but in his experience, as soon as a victim sought help from the teaching staff it inevitably led to further victimisation from the aggressor.

For that very reason so many victims chose to remain silent. They would endure years of torment looking forward to the day they could finally leave school. Their lasting impression of school wasn't one of carefree fun and learning. It was one of fear and sadness.

"What makes you think that Matthew's been singled out?" asked Abby.

"When we first turned up here, do you remember how he was talking about how he had let his house down and they were going to be angry with him?"

Scott stared down the corridor, his eyes drifting in space. There were just too many things that weren't adding up for him.

17

L aurence Goddard attempted to put his key in the lock for the third time as he leant against the frame for support. Each time he'd tried, the key had slipped or refused to slide into the keyhole. He'd cursed, "Useless piece of shit." To him, the task seemed as impossible as threading a needle with the naked eye. He finally drove the key home with a satisfying grunt, and pushed the door wide open and stumbled in. Another day of dealing with illiterate adults and snotty-nosed kids had left him with little patience. He had decided to seek solace at a pub around the corner. The last thing he wanted to do was come home.

Earlier this evening, he'd felt safe with his favourite friend, Jack. Several rounds later, the tension had eased from his shoulders, so much so that his eyes felt heavy as the world around him spun. He'd not eaten anything since breakfast. Glancing at his watch, he'd gone more than twelve hours without food. Goddard's mouth was tinderbox dry and his throat still parched. He looked down at his bruised hands. His knuckles were red and purple.

As he rubbed them, the anger once again bubbled up inside. His stomach tightened causing his body to shiver. *She did this to me. She forced me to hit her. She never listens, that filthy, fucking slut of a wife of mine.*

His eyes had fought hard to focus on the other punters in the pub, a mixture of old, sad and lonely men like him offset by young city types and their floozies. "Women, bloody women," he snarled through clenched teeth. He hated the way they had this Amazonian quality to twist any man around their little finger. The short skirts, high heels and big breasts were all that any hot-blooded man needed to fall under their hypnotic charm. *How could men be so weak?*

But he was just as weak. A saying rolled around inside his head, *Women, can't live with them. Can't live without them.* He was guilty of thinking it. Believing it. Living it. He'd been staring at the silky, cream flesh of those floozies all night, dulling his raging senses with booze. But it hadn't worked. Their slender thighs and tight calves, oh, how he'd wanted to touch them. And their feet...how could a man forget their heel arches peeking out from the sides of their high-heeled shoes. God, they turned him on. His cock twitched in his boxer shorts. His heart pounded. His head spun...He needed sex. Now.

Back home, floozies became a distant memory as Goddard took one step at a time to haul himself slowly up the stairs as he gazed into the darkness of the landing. The stillness of the night was broken by the sound of his laboured breathing. The drink hadn't dulled the cacophony of voices inside his head. They were banging off the walls of his skull like a pinball machine. A heavy throbbing in his neck seemed to keep him company more and more these days.

A thin crack of orange light that seeped underneath the bedroom door pierced the darkness of the landing. He paused for a moment as his mind took a few seconds to catch up with what he'd seen. She was never one to go to sleep with the bedside lamp on and this confused him as he swayed back and forth on his heels.

Goddard pushed open the bedroom door, expecting his wife to be fast asleep. *Wife...That was a joke*, only to find her sitting on the end of the bed fully dressed. He glared at her, bewildered. Samantha Goddard sat there fiddling with her wedding band and engagement ring that rested in the palm of one hand. He steadied himself in the doorway with one hand as his eyes trailed down to the floor where a small suitcase rested by her feet. She looked up at him nervously, neither of them breaking the silence.

"What...What theeee fuck do you think you'rrree doing?" he slurred.

She fiddled even faster with the rings in her clammy hands, as she took short, sharp breaths. She'd had this planned for a long time, knowing exactly what she was going to say. The events of the last few weeks had pushed her to the edge. Any hope of happiness had been cruelly dashed in the past few days. Samantha thought she could put up with the beatings if she was happy in other parts of her life, but soon realised she'd been kidding herself all along. The people she loved were never there when she needed them, leaving her full of resentment, anger and deep sadness. Was she that unattractive?

The speech had been rehearsed over and over in her mind,

but her words fell at the first hurdle. "I'm...I'm...leaving you, Laurence. I can't...stay here anymore. I need to leave now."

Goddard glanced around the room, his head bobbing slowly like a nodding dog toy on the parcel shelf of a car. His jaw dropped as his expressionless face started to contort. His eyes narrowed as thick crease lines ploughed his forehead. "You're not going anywhere..." he seethed.

"You can't stop me, Laurence. The only person you're interested in is yourself. You never confide in me, and yet keep telling me that you can't cope any more. You drink too much and then come home and beat the shit out of me...I'm not going to be your punchbag anymore."

"Do you not think I know what you been up to?" he slurred, as he jabbed a finger in her direction. "The way you dress up, you're inviting it. How many has it been... one...two...ten? You're a disgrace, you filthy whore."

"No, Laurence," she said, finding her voice and fighting back. "You're the bloody disgrace. Look at you. I don't even know who you are these days. You're drunk all the time. You're fat, losing your hair and obsessive and secretive. You're not the same person I married."

Goddard hated being challenged. The kids challenged him. Their parents argued with him, and now his wife dared to challenge him. He was fed up of been taken for granted.

Without a moment's hesitation, he clumsily launched himself in the direction of the bed, his forward momentum carrying him as he part walked and part stumbled. He rushed towards her and gripped her by the throat, pinning her to the bed. Samantha was taken by surprise at the power of his grip as he pressed down hard on her windpipe. She fought to rip his fingers away, but he sat his ample body on top of her, his weight crushing the air from her chest.

Her legs flailed as she thrashed around on the bed but she couldn't breathe, couldn't do anything. Drool escaped from her open mouth, as it ran down either cheek. Her face felt tight and hot as the blood gathered. Her eyes felt like they were bulging in their sockets. All the while, his hand kept squeezing, squeezing so hard that she felt her head might explode at any moment.

Goddard leant into her, his face just inches away. She could smell his warm, vile whiskey breath, which made her head spin with nausea. He tried to kiss her but with each attempt to lay his lips on hers she'd thrash her head from left to right. Her resistance was met with a heavy slap that whipped across her face. The crack of skin contacting skin echoed off the walls, vibrations of pain in his palm numbed by the drink. The redness in his hand matched only by the redness on her cheek. Her skin stung, her eyes wide in fear as he hit her again.

He hadn't loosened his grip on her. Unbearable pain rocketed through her body as his thumb pushed down hard on her windpipe and black spots took over her vision, spreading like a contagious disease. Samantha's mind raced with images of imminent death reaching out its icy cold hand to clutch her. Her vision flooded with blackness. Moments away from passing out, he loosened his grip on her neck. Samantha lay there gagging, desperate to draw huge lungfuls of air into her constricted throat. She gasped once, twice and heaved as some oxygen started to reach the rest of her body.

As she lay therefighting for breath, her whole body ached, her vision just a daze as the room spun around her. Any hope that the attack was over became short-lived as his next atrocity loomed into her awareness. Goddard had unzipped his trousers and dropped them to his ankles. He scratched and clawed at her skirt pushing it up to her waist. She kicked out furiously in a desperate attempt to push him away. Her attempt to defend herself was soon crushed as he punched her hard in the stomach, forcing all the air out of her still struggling lungs. She gripped her stomach as the pain spread through her abdomen in waves like ripples on a pond.

"Stop fighting, you silly bitch," he hissed. "You're mine... do you hear me? You're mine!" he shouted, as he violently pulled at her underwear, snapping the elastic and tearing fabric before discarding the fragments like empty sweet wrappers. He fell on top, thrusting himself into her with an aggressive grunt as he grabbed her hair and pulled violently with each thrust.

Samantha's weakened body had lost the will to fight. She lay limp on the bed, eyes clamped shut. Her body ached in so many places. Her scalp prickled with pain as he tugged harder. She scrunched up her eyes, tears broke free from the closed edges. She escaped deep inside her mind, trying to block out the violation to her body. *You'll never do this again to me.*

18

Matthew had spent the best part of an hour cowering under his duvet. He gripped the top of his bedding and pulled it tight under his chin. His eyes darted left and right in the darkness. His body craved sleep, but his mind raced in fear. He couldn't win either way. If he fell asleep, he knew the nightmares would wake him as they had done so often. If he stayed awake, the waves of anxiety that racked his body would only intensify.

He finally succumbed to physical and mental fatigue as he drifted off into a deep sleep. His subconscious mind replayed the events of the day as his head jerked from left to right, beads of sweat bubbling on his forehead. His body jerked as tiny micro-muscular movements systematically repeated the assault from earlier today.

The door to the dormitory opened quietly and the three figures silently made their way to his bed in slow motion. They glanced around at the other boys, deep in sleep and blissfully unaware of the fate that awaited one of their

room-mates. The odd groan and snort punctured the silence
of the night. They gathered around his bed, their eyes fixed
on him. Rollings gave the other two the nod to proceed.
Hunter leant forward and forcibly pushed a length of duct
tape over Matthew's mouth whilst Ford held the boy down
by his shoulders.

Hunter's eyes drilled into Matthew, menace pouring from
them as his eyelids twitched. One corner of his mouth was
fixed with a sadistic smile. He wanted to hurt Matthew; he
wanted to hurt him real bad. Many students had privately
thought that Stephen Hunter was unhinged and a complete
nutter. He had a reputation around school, a reputation that
was fully justified. Several months earlier students had
witnessed Hunter capture a bird and break its neck as it
thrashed around in his hands. He'd laughed as the bones in
its fragile neck cracked. He seemed to relish seeing those
around him wince in disgust and horror as he threw the lifeless bird in nearby bushes.

The year before, another pupil had burnt his arm in a chem-
istry class after bleach had been splashed on it. Despite an
internal school investigation, the perpetrator of the crime
had never been officially identified. It was widely accepted
by his peers that Hunter had been the instigator, but a wall
of silence fuelled by fear meant that no one would come
forward.

Rollings stepped forward as the two boys dragged Matthew
out of bed. The poor boy's eyes widened with terror as his
arms were forcibly held behind his back, a tight vice-like
grip caused his hands to throb. When a black hood was
placed over Matthew's head, the overwhelming feeling of
fear intensified and engulfed his tiny mind and body.
Matthew let out a faint squeal as he tried to cry, his silence

instantly assured as Hunter punched him hard in the kidneys with gritted teeth and fiery aggression in his eyes.

They forcibly pushed him towards the door. Rollings peered into the dark, cold corridor to check the coast was clear before he nodded at them to follow. Hunter and Ford held Matthew tight as he stumbled blindly. His bare feet shuffled along the hard, cold parquet floor.

They led him from Stanmer House, through the winding historic corridors that over the years had been graced by future politicians, CEOs, army generals and doctors. At night, they took on a different meaning to Matthew. They were his hell. He'd rather face a night on his own in the middle of the forest with nocturnal creatures, than endure the fear, humiliation and degradation that he faced every day. School was supposed to be the happiest, most carefree days of your life. Matthew saw them as something entirely different.

They walked through a much older part of the school, long consigned for redevelopment many years ago and not fit for purpose. Through a lack of maintenance and upkeep, it fell victim to ongoing disputes between the school and the planning department at Brighton and Hove Council over proposed plans for expansion. It was out of bounds to all students.

Plaster crumbled from the walls as damp crept up from the floor like an evil, cancerous disease destroying everything in its path. The parquet floor had been long removed and replaced by dusty, uneven concrete that felt as rough as sandpaper on Matthew's bare feet. A lack of ventilation caught him off guard, a claustrophobic stench like overturned earth or a damp cellar. Matthew heard a door creak open, the swollen timber dragging on the uneven floor. He was thrust into the room before coming to a stop.

After the hood was yanked from his head, Matthew blinked furiously as he tried to adjust to the semi-darkness. It was a soulless place. The dirt and dust from years of neglect gathered on the boarded windowsills. Cobwebs draped from the ceiling and dust particles drifted in the still air. Small candles placed around the room flickered, their ghostly shadows dancing on the walls. Matthew felt the faint trace of heat from the fireplace warm his face, the orange and yellow glow illuminated the features of those gathered.

"I told you we'd see you later. The weakest amongst us need to be weeded out," Rollings said as he circled Matthew. "You faggot. Now for your punishment...you'll take this like a man."

Without another word, Ford and Hunter secured ropes to Matthew's ankles and wrists before pulling them tight through iron wall fixtures. Strung up like a starfish, his shoulder blades and hips ached from the stress position. Confusion clouded Matthew's senses. He pulled and thrashed in the vain attempt to free himself, but the harder he toiled, the more the rope cut into his skin. The stinging sensation burnt as red welts formed.

His eyes widened in shock as he watched Rollings bend down by the fire and retrieve a small tin of black shoe polish bubbling away in the red embers. Matthew struggled, his breathing fast and heavy as panic consumed him. Ford grabbed Matthew's face, firmly gripping his chin and forcing him to look forward. Tears streamed from Matthew's eyes as he shook his head violently trying to free himself. Only high-pitched, muffled cries indicated the terror that engulfed Matthew.

He became increasingly frantic, his head tossing and turning left and right as he tugged on the ropes that secured his arms. His body twisted and contorted as if possessed, beads of sweat racing down his face with the increasing effort.

Rollings walked slowly towards Matthew with a glint in his eyes. One gloved hand carried the bubbling tin, the other held a thick paintbrush. He nodded at Hunter who pulled down Matthew's pyjamas bottoms and underwear. He sniggered as he relished the opportunity to break the boy's fragile confidence and self-esteem even further. Matthew stood trembling, naked from the waist down. Cold, sweaty and humiliated, his fate was in their hands. He had nowhere to go and no way of releasing himself. Tired, exhausted and dazed, the last shred of fight drained from his small body.

Rollings stood before Matthew, his face expressionless, a cold stare fixed on the boy. He knelt down and smothered Matthew's testicles with hot, black liquid shoe polish. Blackballing was the ultimate punishment and a long-standing ritual in boarding schools up and down the country. Once cooled and dried, the polish would be hard to remove.

Matthew's high-pitched screams intensified as they echoed around the room, each piercing cry bounced off the walls. He writhed in pain as his body bucked back and forth in an attempt to escape the searing heat that torched him. Tears streamed from his sore, wide, scared eyes. His cheeks reddened as the pressure built in his face. Each stroke of the polish-laden brush left him clenching his fists and curling up his toes.

Rollings ripped the duct tape from Matthew's mouth. His skin pulled and burnt as the firmly fixed tape tugged at his wet, stinging skin. He screamed in agony through bleeding lips.

Another stroke of the brush prompted a haunting, shrill of a scream that raced through the room. His raw and hoarse throat burnt as if a hot poker had been shoved inside it. The blood-curdling screams were in vain because no one would hear him. The old room had been the former music room. Despite its state of disrepair, the walls still reflected sound from soundproofing that remained intact.

He prayed the torture would stop. He pleaded in his mind with silent words unable to escape from his mouth. His ginger hair now heavily matted in sweat clung to his face shielding his eyes. He couldn't take any more. His body was spent. His pain threshold had been breached.

19

S cott's thoughts still troubled him as he made his way into work. The intimidation he'd witnessed yesterday had not only distressed but concerned him as well. Three against one meant the odds were heavily stacked in favour of the bullies who'd been harassing Matthew. An early morning run along the seafront hadn't helped to shake off the nagging feelings that clung to him like glue.

On this occasion, Abby had joined him. She was a far more competent runner than Scott. He saw it as a way to stay relatively fit and get a bit of a cardio. Abby, on the other hand, always saw it as a competition. Rivalry was some-thing he had noticed in Abby. She would strive to be the best in everything she applied herself to. She was a good mum to her kids, and a top-class copper. She hated failure, and that was the catalyst that spurred her on. It was a quality he admired in her.

His gentle jog along the seafront had become yet another challenge for Abby. She'd left him for dust at the 3K mark when he'd chosen to turn around, leaving Abby to run an extra 5K, which was closer to her preferred distance of between eight and eleven kilometres. She had wanted to shake off a mild hangover after her date the night before with Jonathon, an optician.

Scott had teased her as they ran together, questioning whether Jonathon had forgotten his glasses at the office. She replied by saying that she'd quite enjoyed this whole dating lark but found it stressful with the whole dressing up thing and sorting out childminding. It was typical Abby, the pessimist.

The duty sergeant had buzzed Scott in acknowledging him with a nod. Scott could hear Mike's voice echo from the floor above as he made his way up the stairwell. He found Mike outside the CID office in deep conversation with the same female police officer that he'd seen on previous occasions. They were talking in hushed tones which came to an abrupt halt when Scott loomed nearer. Mike had a pathetic grin on his face that suggested things were going well. The female officer looked rather more sheepish as she made her excuses and scuttled off down the stairs, casting a brief, embarrassed sideward glance at Scott as she brushed past him.

"Don't tell me you…" Scott added, pointing over his shoulder and shaking his head.

"Oh, yeah…well worth a round of drinks and curry that I paid out last night."

"One of these days, all these women are going to gang up on you, strip you naked and tie you to a lamp post…as revenge."

Mike didn't have an answer as he followed his boss through the double swing doors on to the main floor.

Scott headed over towards the incident board to see if anything new had been added. The before and after photos of the two deceased men stared back at him. The images of victim two were less encouraging to look at, his face half the size of what it would have been prior to the fall.

"Okay team, let's get an update. What've we got?" he asked as he perched on the edge of a desk.

Raj threw his pen on the table. "I've been talking to the other teachers and Mary Harrison the deputy principal. Johnson was a well-liked man, firm but fair. I got the impression from talking to some of the staff members that he kept his private life to himself. They weren't able to shed any new light on the situation. Some seemed devastated at recent events, and others appeared unaffected which to me seemed so weird."

"Mary Harrison has been signed off work with stress, so I went to see her at her home. Apparently, the whole situation is getting too much for her. She seemed at odds with the principal. I got the impression they didn't see eye to eye."

"In what way?"

"Not sure to be exact, Guv. I pushed her a bit, and came to the conclusion that Collier wants things done in a strict, traditional way, and Mary Harrison wants to inject more variety into the school and make it more appealing and modern."

Despite Abby having run further than Scott, he couldn't believe that she'd still managed to complete her run, get to the station and shower, and be at her desk before he'd arrived.

"The pathologist's report on Giles Rochester is on the system now, Guv," Abby said, chipping in. "We know he died as a result of the fall. He had multiple fractures to both arms, his hips, several broken ribs and severe trauma to the head. However, Dr Hall also identified a red band of bruising around the victim's neck. It's about an inch wide."

"Strangled?" Mike interrupted, looking bemused. "I thought he just jumped or was pushed."

Abby continued flicking through the notes online. "Yes, he did die as a result of the fall, but Cara, I mean Dr Hall, identified a red banding, but only around the front of the victim's neck. There's some localised bleeding where whatever was used cut into the skin. The tiny lacerations, she believes, are from applied force."

"Could he have been strangled and then thrown over?" asked Raj.

"I doubt it. You'd have to be pretty strong to lift a dead weight and throw it over some barriers," Scott replied.

Scott turned to the incident board, and put a question mark by the word suicide. This potentially looked like a second murder investigation. He made a mental note to talk to forensics about it. The victim's car needed to be examined in closer detail.

"Sian, what have you got for us?"

"I'm still working through the phone numbers and contacts, Guv," she said, resting her elbows on the desk and leaning forward, her hands clasped together. "But what I did notice was that the same number we repeatedly found on Johnson's phone was also on victim two's phone. There are lots of lovey-dovey messages between the two numbers, and lots of calls placed between them. As we know, it's a pay-as-you-go number that hasn't been registered, so I've drawn a blank there so far. I've sent the phone back to the high-tech unit to see what they could retrieve."

"How about CCTV?" Scott enquired.

"There isn't a lot of CCTV coverage by the car park, or in the surrounding streets. However, we picked up the silver VW Golf driving past Worthing rail station in the direction of the car park. It's a bit of a grainy image because it was dark, but from the stills I pulled off, there only appears to be one person in the car, the driver," Sian said, passing round a few copies.

Scott tapped his whiteboard marker by the images of victim two, before pinning one of the still images beside Giles's case details. "So he went alone. Who did he meet there?" he asked quietly as he stared at the grainy image depicting the single outline of a figure in the driving seat of the VW Golf.

"Quite possibly, Guv, but there's nothing on CCTV. There's no one walking towards the car park, and no one walking away either," Sian said, scratching her forehead.

Scott stepped up to the board and stared at the grainy image for a few moments. "Sian, if you look at the image closely, something looks odd. I can't tell if it's a street light reflection distorting the image or something else. I'll get it checked out anyway."

Scott's observation caused the others to examine their copies in closer detail. Mike squinted as he strained to see the finer detail and Sian rested her glasses on her head to get a closer look.

"Well, even though he hasn't been formally identified yet, we're working with the assumption that the victim from the car park is Giles Rochester. Forensics will no doubt confirm that with DNA sampling taken from his tooth-brush. He's too messed up to have a visual ID and Collier would have been best suited to do that."

"In the meantime, Sian, what happened with the search of staff members?"

"One name has come up, Guv. John Morecombe. He was sacked about a year ago after confronting Collier about bullying of both staff members and pupils. He wasn't there long, one academic year. Last known whereabouts according to the electoral register has him down in Crediton in Devon."

"Did you follow up?"

"Yes, Guv. I spoke to our colleagues down there. Crediton is a bit of a backwater to be honest. They had less than fifty crimes reported in the previous twelve months, and the local station is just a neighbourhood unit mainly manned with PCSOs. They checked his last known address and he's since moved on. He's not known to them. I checked with DVLA and the Motor Insurers' Bureau, and there isn't a car registered in his name. He's disappeared off the radar. I'll check with DWP in case he's been drawing benefits some-where. There's also the local authority and local education authority in case he's been working in schools, and I've still to do financial checks with Equifax."

Scott shifted as he settled on the edge of her desk. "Good job, Sian. Circulate his details locally and with the Devon lot. Check neighbouring counties too. We need to find him if nothing more than to just eliminate him from our enquiries. He may have an axe to grind…"

"Enough to kill?" Sian asked.

Scott shrugged in reply.

The team headed back to their desks in a flurry of activity.

———————

SCOTT PUSHED through the door and was greeted by the constant tapping of keyboard keys that bounced off the walls around him. To him, this office was where the magic happened. Highly trained specialists partnered with forensics and outsourced specialists to scrutinise evidence that in his experience made the difference between a conviction and a crime going unsolved. He thought of them as techies and geeks, but in reality, they were talented, calculated individuals with naturally curious minds.

Digital forensics was the more formal title for the unit. A team trained in forensic video and image analysis. Technically Scott wasn't well versed in the finer points of their role; he just needed them to deliver results. They'd be called upon to assist with tasks like transcoding, image enhancing, slowing and enlarging video footage, right through to more complex tasks that officers needed such as reverse projection and reconstructions, height calculation and comparative analysis. Whatever they did always left Scott in awe.

Martin Jones was a thin, middle-aged man with bony fingers that hovered over his keyboard like the spindly legs of a daddy-long-legs spider. They moved with grace and speed as his fingers splayed out, reaching all corners of his curved keyboard with ease.

"Hi, Martin. Good to see you. Everything okay?"

"Yep, all good on the Western Front. Hear you've got a tricky case running. What do you need?"

"I need the image on this video still enhanced if you can," Scott said, handing Martin a memory stick.

Martin plugged the stick in and opened its directory. The still image of Giles Rochester behind the wheel of his car filled the screen. "Any part in particular?"

"Yes, the driver in particular."

Martin opened up another application on his screen and then dragged the image into it. A few clicks isolated the area in question and then he scrolled on the wheel of his mouse. Each click sharpened the image a fraction until it was clearer.

"That's the best I can get it," Martin said.

They both peered closely at the highlighted section. Rochester had a distressed expression on his face. His head was firmly pulled back into his headrest and his teeth were clenched with his lips pulled back in a snarl.

"Looks like he's got some sort of restraint around his neck. See that white line?" Martin pointed out with a flourish of tapered finger.

"Looks like he's being held in place?" Scott offered.

"Looks like that to me, too. You've got someone else in the car with him."

20

The figure smiled. He'd gained access to the ground-floor apartment with remarkable ease. Posing as a delivery driver, he'd pressed the buzzers of the other apartments in the block. No one had come to meet him, or even questioned him, such was the frequency of this type of request; other residents had become blasé about security.

Using a crowbar, the door had offered little resistance as it cracked open, splinters of wood littering the floor. He gently closed the door behind him. He stood there in the hallway with his eyes closed. His heart thumped violently in his chest; his shoulders rising and falling quickly. He inhaled deeply, taking in the heady concoction of lavender scented air fresheners and her perfume. *Yes, her perfume. She still liked her Armani Code.* His stomach flipped and his cock twitched as he licked his lips. He slowly opened his eyes, revelling in the sensual feelings that rippled through his body.

He walked through the apartment going from room to room

admiring the decor. She still had taste; he could see that. Everything was perfectly matched and laid out. *She had expensive taste now.* The main bedroom was to the left, the bathroom to the right. A large reception room opened up further on the left with a secondary small bedroom directly opposite which had been converted into a study. Beyond them lay the kitchen, with white double French doors that led out onto a small courtyard garden. He glanced through the doors. "How cute," he said, looking at the small wrought-iron circular table with two chairs, a small potted red plant adding the contrasting feature.

Walking back into the large reception room, he stroked the back of the L-shaped chocolate brown, crushed fabric sofas that added grandeur in proportion to the room. Two empty Veuve Clicquot champagne bottles sat at opposite ends of the mantelpiece above the wrought-iron fireplace. A vase with daffodils took prominent position on the hearth. Magazines had been splayed in a fan shape across the white chunky IKEA coffee table. *Far too neat.*

He wasn't here to sightsee as vivid thoughts about her shocked him back to reality. He spun on his heel and headed back towards her bedroom with a sense of urgency in his step. He smiled to himself as the smell of perfume enveloped him as he stepped over the threshold, stirring his senses once again.

He loved her bedroom; it was exactly how he'd imagined it. The bedroom was minimalistic white, even down to the duvet cover. He gently stroked the soft cotton before moving to the pillow, picking it up and burying his face in it. The bristles from his stubble scratched the surface. He inhaled deeply; the smell aroused him. It was a familiar smell, something he found hard to pull away from. The way her smell lingered on the pillow, even in the air, that deep, intensely sexy scent she continued to wear.

He headed towards a four-drawer chest that was nestled in one of the alcoves. Pictures of her posing with friends in a bar sat on top, along with a silver ornament that said 'Love'. He pulled each drawer out, fondly stroking all the items of clothing before pushing each one back in. He reached out for one of the two small drawers at the top, his pulse quickening. He was excited at the prospect of what he'd find; he could now reacquaint himself with her intimately.

He loved this drawer and what it said about her. How tidy, how ordered, how sexual, how teasing she was. He pulled out several pairs of knickers, the soft, delicate fabric brushing against his coarse skin. Thin, tantalising, frilly knickers, lots of creams and whites. *She'd always loved those colours.* He was excited at discovering that she had a few pairs of G-strings hidden towards the back, neatly out of view behind her day-to-day practical M&S knickers.

Every woman had some; he was sure of that, whether bought by themselves or by their lovers as a special treat or on impulse. *Maybe she'd bought them for herself to feel sexy, or bought them for him.* They were nothing more than little threads of fabric that masqueraded as underwear. Lacy strips, delicate red bows, see-through lace. Scrunching them up in his hand, he smelt their fresh, clean femininity. He smelt her. They were soft, so sensual, so sexy. He could almost imagine his lips pressed against her flesh, tasting her, her scent deep within his nostrils.

He couldn't leave without taking his souvenir pair, stuffed into his back pocket now and even the illicit thought excited him.

There was an even better treat in store for him today as he opened the laundry basket that was tucked into the corner. He sifted through her dirty linen. *She must have some.* There were blouses, *no*, a pair of jeans, *no*, jogging bottoms, *no, no, no*, several towels, *you better have some for me.* "Yes!" he shouted as the thin fabric of a pair of her knickers wrapped around his fingers. He stared at them for a few moments like a child too excited to even open their Christmas present, before drawing them to his face. He buried his nose into her most intimate clothing and inhaled deeply. *Oh yes...yes...yes.*

His head spun wildly as his eyes rocked back in their sockets. His mind became a melting pot of emotions. Anger surged through his veins, swiftly replaced with a longing desire for her body. His own body responded immediately. He tucked one hand into the waistband of his jeans, thrusting deep inside his boxer shorts and began to masturbate. *This is such a turn on...I want you, I want you now.* He pressed on, moaning in desire and ecstasy as he climaxed. He clenched his teeth as veins pulsated in his neck, his eyes rolling up once again disappearing under his lids. His body jerked in satisfaction.

He held her underwear in his hands one last time, inhaling deeply, the fragrance caressing every cell in his body.

He needed her. He'd have her.

21

Matthew Edrington paused for a moment, his hand hovering just an inch or two away from the door. With dry sticky lips, his jangled nerves stopped him from catching his breath. He stared at the oak panelled door, in two minds as to whether to knock at all. He knew that once he walked through the door, there would be no turning back. He just wasn't sure if he had the courage to follow through.

He'd already attempted to knock once, pulling away as his hand twitched. With a deep breath, he finally knocked twice. He waited for what seemed an eternity, and when no response was forthcoming he knocked again, his knuckles smarting from the extra force. The noise echoed up and down the corridor. It was sharp and short like a cricket ball striking willow.

"Enter," came a firm, booming voice from behind the door that made Matthew jump.

Matthew tentatively turned the handle and took half a step in, peering around the door.

"Come in, Edrington…don't just stand there," continued Edward Chapman the housemaster for Stanmer House. "Take a seat."

He motioned to a metal-framed leather seat that sat by the side of his bureau desk. He swivelled around in his chair, smoothing out the creases in his grey corduroy trousers. He was a rotund man with a rosy face and double chin. He had an unusual-looking face, small eyes closely set together with a pointed, thin, Roman nose.

Matthew took a seat and nervously wrung his hands in his lap, his jaws on the verge of chattering with nerves.

Chapman placed his hands on his thighs as he leant back in his chair. "How can I help Edrington?"

Matthew looked around the room. His nerves were paralysing him, threatening to engulf him in a dark whirl-wind of fear and panic. He still had an opportunity to make his excuses and leave, his mind a mix of confusion and fear. *Should I? Shouldn't I?* His stomach flipped, and he couldn't tell if he was going to throw up or shit himself, he felt that bad. And all this time Chapman stared at him with a raised eyebrow.

"Well?" A sense of annoyance in Chapman's tone suggested frustration with Matthew's silence.

"Sir sir," he stammered, his mouth as parched as the Atacama Desert, making it difficult to say anything. "Sir… I'm…being bullied…" There, he'd said it. There was no turning back now. He thought he'd feel a sense of relief for sharing his burdens, but it didn't feel that way at all. He felt as if he'd just opened up a huge chasm in the side of Vesuvius and now all hell would break loose. The secret that he'd carried for such a long time was now exposed. He started to doubt whether this had been a good idea.

Chapman raised a brow again and cocked his head to one side as he studied the boy for a few moments unsure as to how genuine the claim was.

"Can you tell me *exactly* what you mean by being bullied?" he asked slowly, resting his hands on his thighs as he leant in towards Matthew.

Matthew clenched his hands tighter as they glistened with sweat. He shifted nervously in the chair, every ounce of courage being drawn upon to reveal more of his treatment.

"Some boys have been hitting me. They corner me in the corridors and push me around. Sometimes they punch me. They've attacked me in the dorm at night and done other things to me…" His gaze dropped to the floor, his voice nothing more than a whisper.

"You do realise that allegations of this nature are not to be taken lightly?"

Matthew nodded slowly but didn't look up, a mixture of embarrassment and fear paralysing his thin, pale body.

"Listen young Edrington, are you sure about this? There's plenty of argy-bargy in every school up and down the country. A bit of tomfoolery comes with the territory I'm afraid. It's part of the toughening up process. You know sometimes it can get a bit out of hand, but there's no malice ever intended."

"But…sir…" Matthew fell silent, unable to find the right words to explain his plight.

Chapman raised his palm to stop Matthew. "Here's what I suggest. Why don't you start by having a chat with the house prefects. They lead by example, and it's their job to support boys like you in tough times. They have been chosen for their exemplary record, their leadership, confidence and initiative. And I hasten to add, their job is to create an atmosphere of friendly cooperation, peace, discipline and unity in the school. Prefects should serve as counsellors to junior students like yourself," he said proudly as he took in a deep breath and puffed out his chest.

"But, sir…"

"Yes, I know lad," he interrupted. "It can be a daunting thing to talk about, but you've done the right thing. The prefects are there to maintain the front line of discipline; we want the pupils to sort out their differences. If they can't, then we step in as housemasters," he said with an exaggerated shrug holding his hands out in front.

"Yes…sir," Matthew replied. His shoulders drooped as the dejection played heavily on his mind. Resignation washed over him.

"Good man, now why don't you go and find them. Have a little chat and see how you get on…hhm?"

Matthew swallowed hard as he stood and made his way out. The fear rose in him, bile burning the back of his throat. How could he? He couldn't turn to them. His prefects were Rollings, Ford and Hunter. Would even believe him? Maybe the police would. Mr Saunders would.

AT FIRST, he'd stood alone looking around. It was a room that brought back a multitude of memories. Back then, he'd visited it once a week for his guitar lessons as he was growing up. A wry smile broke across his face as he recalled his attempts at learning his chords, scales and progressions, much to the dissatisfaction of his teacher. Back then, opting in for music lessons meant an easy way out from attending other timetabled lessons.

The room had seen better days, now just a former shell in comparison. Crumbling plaster lay scattered amongst the dusty, uneven concrete. Dampness hung in the air and dust gathered on the boarded windowsills. *Old traditions die hard*, he thought as he noticed the small candles dotted around the room, a sombre cloak of melancholy replacing the smile that filled his face.

His moment of reflection was disturbed by the arrival of the two other figures. One stood holding the door frame for support, his face pale and hollow with prominent cheekbones. The effort to climb a few flights of steps and navigate empty, dark hallways clearly evident as his tightly cropped hair now beaded with tiny droplets of sweat. A walking stick helped with balance as one hand gripped the door frame architrave. Sharp, heavy intakes of breath were equally matched by long whistling exhales that seemed to bounce off the walls.

The other figure fidgeted, shifting on the spot, undecided whether to leave his hands in the pockets of his bomber jacket or jeans. He clearly felt uncomfortable meeting with the others. Their numbers were fast shrinking which increased the apprehensive churning he felt. His dry mouth screamed for a drink from the nearest pub.

"We…we can't go on like this," said the first figure, as his breath slowed.

A slight whistle and crackle in his breath indicated asthma and COPD. Years of a twenty-a-day smoking habit had left him with chronic obstructive pulmonary disease. He'd been warned about it on many occasions, but he'd never managed to give up his Marlboros. The deadly weed had finally claimed his health and his job, forcing him to retire early.

The second figure nodded in agreement but was too wary to speak up. He was scared of himself and what rubbish might tumble out of his mouth. His head felt like it had been hit with a sledgehammer, a thumping headache eating away inside of him. The culprits being a lack of sleep and dehydration. He couldn't think straight, a dull fog clouding his thinking on a daily basis.

"The other two brought it amongst themselves. They weren't careful enough. For all we know, they may have blabbed to some fool and…well, who knows? I want you both to keep your mouths firmly closed and remain vigilant at all times…understood?"

The two visitors nodded quickly in unison, both lacking backbone to challenge the man as they exchanged nervous glances between each other.

"If anyone asks, you stick to the story. You didn't know the others particularly well and you can't explain why anyone would wish to harm them. Now return home and wait for further instructions and updates from me. Carry on as normal. Don't do *anything* that might attract attention," he ordered before falling silent and turning to face the fireplace, placing his thumbs in the pockets of his waistcoat.

The figures stood there for a few moments exchanging awkward glances, unsure what to do in the darkness. The room had turned decidedly chilly following their brief encounter. They turned and left, one scurrying away, his rapid footsteps echoing in the corridor, the other, a slow steady tapping from the walking stick as it signalled his slow departure.

22

H is drive home had been one filled with a swirling mass of confusion. His chest burnt, his lungs felt tight and saliva kept pooling in his mouth. In recent years, he'd noticed the COPD worsening. The reality dawned on him that in the near future he'd become reliant on an oxygen bottle in order to survive. The thought of dragging a bottle around on a trolley grated his nerves. He looked like a man twenty years his senior, already consigned to the pipe and slippers brigade. He walked with a slight hunch, deeply set lines prematurely aged his face and rarely smiled through his tobacco-stained teeth.

Under his breath, he cursed his misfortune. *It's just my fucking luck; bad luck seems to follow me around like a bad smell.*

How could they be so blasé about this? People are dying, he argued to himself, thumping the steering wheel every few minutes. "What's the point in keeping my mouth firmly closed and remaining vigilant at all times…are you having a laugh?" he shouted. "When will this end?" he mumbled through a raspy cough that rattled his chest.

Slow, deep breaths helped. He needed to be careful of his hypertension. The last thing he needed was more health complications. On numerous occasions, the doctor's advice had been to take it easy. It was advice he'd heeded by tending to his potted plants in his small greenhouse and chatting to the neighbours as he passed the hours. Many of them were retired and seemed to relish the opportunity to fill the massive voids of loneliness that now filled their lives.

Turning into his road, he reflected on how much he enjoyed where he lived. For as far as the eye could see bungalows surrounded him. It was a safe neighbourhood, a place where he looked forward to seeing out the rest of his retirement. He'd deliberately chosen this property, a corner plot which naturally added generous dimensions to this property with an L-shaped front lawn that wrapped around two sides of his house. To the right was a small cul-de-sac, something he was grateful for. It meant less traffic noise to spoil the serene moments he enjoyed in his garden.

He carefully turned into his driveway leaning over the steering wheel to get a better view as he navigated the narrow lane. The darkness of the night played tricks on his eyes. He crept slowly up the drive careful not to damage the assortment of plants and shrubs that provided a natural border.

He remained in the car for a few moments, tiredness consuming him. Devoid of all energy, the prospect of walking just a few yards to his front door seemed like a Herculean task.

A dark-clothed figure leaning up against a wall on the other side of the road observed his every movement. His patience had worn thin whilst waiting for the resident to come home. Incensed and enraged by the news he'd received today, he was reminded of history repeating itself once again. He'd promised to take care of it, and was now more determined than ever. *The silly old fool is taking his time.* He had other pressing things that required his attention. Waiting around in the dark would only attract attention if he stayed longer.

His tenuous patience had been rewarded, when the car door opened and flooded the inside cabin with light, outlining his target. Beads of sweat chased each other down his back; his heart pounded like a drum…his next victim was in sight. He watched as the light extinguished, and a familiar thud echoed in the street as the car door slammed shut. The man shuffled slowly around to the front of his house, a methodical scraping noise punctured the silence as he dragged his feet, each step harder than the one before. His breathing laboured, a fast, shallow wheeze signalled the need for his medication.

He'd chosen to walk to his front door via the pavement rather than risk walking across his lawn in case he tripped. A stone path bordered by white plastic chain-links that looped between short wooden posts offered a natural hazard for those a little unstable on their feet. Pushing open the small wrought-iron gate, it creaked eerily from its rusty hinges. He took the final few steps up to his white front door. His heavy laboured breathing had drowned out the light footsteps that had trailed him for the last few feet.

Without a moment's hesitation, the dark figure deftly threw a length of thin white plastic tape around the man's neck cutting into his skin. The man staggered backwards, his teeth tightly clenched, his eyes wide with fear. He pulled frantically at the tape that was fast blocking off his airway. He wanted to shout, but all he could manage was a faint hiss, his body unable to either support him or fight off the attacker who was now pulling him backwards down to the ground.

He fell back hard on his elbows. The sound of bone cracking beneath him caused him to let out a muffled yell in pain…a deep throbbing pain that radiated up his arm and into his shoulder. His mind whirled. His frailness only added to his inability to fight back. His assailant had pushed him over onto his front, and knelt on his back, forcing the air out of his weak lungs. The plastic tape did its job. The veins throbbed in his neck as black spots appeared in his vision. Darkness took over and his life ebbed away. He gurgled, the mucus stuck in his throat finding no place to escape.

The figure looked around to see if they'd attracted any attention. He'd done what he needed to do, and now stood over the lifeless body, waiting for the adrenaline rush to die down. *What a pathetic, useless tosser.* There'd been no resistance, no challenge, an anticlimax even. It was almost as if he'd accepted his fate or perhaps saw this as a blessing, an opportunity to put an end to his misery and his ongoing pain and debilitating illness.

23

Hangleton Valley Drive was the last place Scott anticipated being called out to for a suspicious death. Situated on the northern-west fringe of Brighton, it was skirted by the Benfield Valley Golf Course and the A27 which was conveniently hidden behind dense woodland, but nevertheless gave its location away by the low drone of traffic that thundered along the Shoreham bypass.

A safe, quiet neighbourhood sprung to mind as he made his way along the wide road. It was the type of place that families and downsizers moved to when they wanted a better balance between the quietness and buzz of Brighton. He figured it was a place for retirees who wanted a more laid-back, community feel.

On either side of him, were clean, well-maintained, deep driveways proudly sporting well-tended lawns and shrubs. Bungalows stretched out in front of him as far as the eye could see. There was no evidence of loitering youths, litter or boy racers who annoyed residents. It was in marked contrast to some parts of the town that were plagued with this type of antisocial behaviour.

High performance cars driven recklessly were the bane of society and one of the main topics that his uniformed colleagues had to deal with at local neighbourhood meetings. With ridiculously oversized chrome exhaust pipes, lowered suspensions, blacked-out windows and paint jobs that cost more than the car itself, they belted out the latest heavy drum and bass sounds from expensive in-car systems that shook windows as they passed at all times of the day and night.

He took an instant shine to the area. It wasn't a place he'd usually have cause to visit in the line of duty...until now, and that took the edge off the pleasant thoughts that ran through his mind. The area had a close-knit feel and he could imagine living around here himself one day which made him smile. *Look at me, I'm already planning my retirement, picking my house and choosing the right lawn-mower...just need to find out where the nearest lawn bowls club is.* Scott shook his head in light-hearted disbelief.

The cordon was well established by the time he'd arrived. Having signed in with the scene guard, WPC Willits, and put on a paper forensic suit, he headed over to the white tent that was positioned by the front door of the property.

Matt Allen, the crime scene manager, packed away his notepad when he saw Scott approaching. "Morning, Scott. We've got another one for you, same MO from the looks of it," he said, holding up two clear plastic evidence bags.

Even from a few feet away, Scott could make out a white feather in one and a small piece of white paper in the other.

He grimaced and sighed as he leant in further for a closer inspection. "Strangled?"

"Yep, looks like it…how did you guess?"

Scott didn't reply, offering a shrug instead as he crossed his arms in frustration and glanced around the plot. "The pathologist here yet?"

Matt looked at Scott, a small knowing smile curling up the edges of his lips. "You should know, mate…"

Scott stared at the floor for a moment unsure of a response. "I don't get your drift?"

"Mate, you and the *path* are the worst kept secret in the station…everyone knows you two are an item." He laughed.

"Erm, really?" he asked shaking his head. "So much for keeping it quiet."

"No chance, mate…you're front-page news, and I have to say that a few of our female colleagues are a tad upset that you're off the market," he added.

"That's all I need…more gossip."

He turned towards the tent keen to change the subject as he peeked in. He knew Matt would push him for the gory details of his relationship if he'd discussed it any further. Another crime scene officer was crouching down taking close-up photos of the victim's neck. He had been turned onto his back for closer examination.

"He's got ligature marks around his neck, but no other signs of assault or bruising," Matt added over Scott's shoulder. "We did find some plastic tape still wrapped around his neck. We'll get that analysed to see if we can get anything from it."

Scott spun around. "Seriously?" He hadn't been expecting that. They'd not found evidence on the last victim, so either the killer was getting sloppy or...wasn't bothered about it being found. "Okay, Matt. Keep me informed."

Scott made his way towards the cordon tape where Abby and Raj were talking to neighbours and bystanders who'd stopped to watch the macabre scene. Cara had turned up moments earlier, and was already making her way to the tent. They'd travelled in separate cars and staggered their journeys to avoid the awkward moment of them both arriving in one car. The intention behind that master plan had clearly backfired on them.

"What do we know about the victim?"

"Guv, residents have confirmed that an Alex Winterbottom lived here. The car over there..." he said stopping in mid-sentence to wave off to the side of the house, "is registered in the same name, and the contents of the wallet found on the deceased match up too."

Scott ingested the information as he glanced around at the surrounding properties in the hope that someone had CCTV set up on the front of their house, but his optimism was short-lived. It didn't call for such measures around here he figured. Nevertheless, he saw the familiar yellow sticker of the neighbourhood watch scheme in all the windows and made a mental note to get Raj to contact the coordinator to build up a picture of the area.

His thoughts were interrupted as Abby continued with a review of her notes that stopped him dead in his tracks.

"What was that?" he asked quickly.

"He's an ex-teacher… Edmunston-Hunt boarding school… neighbours said he'd been retired a few years now due to ill health."

"Anyone see or hear anything last night?"

"Nope, a neighbour who lives a few doors down in The Meadows walked past about nine-thirty p.m. last night after walking the dog, and swears that he looked in the direction of Winterbottom's house and saw nothing out of the ordinary."

Scott's phone vibrated in his pocket. Pulling it out, he saw Mike's number flash up on the screen.

"Yes, Mike…" Scott listened intently, throwing in the odd "hhm," "yes," and "okay," before hanging up. "Abby can you take over here? Liaise with the pathologist when she's out. I need to head over to Edmunston-Hunt. Mike's just had a call from your *creepy caretaker*. He's found something and alerted the station."

24

The case played on Scott's mind as he headed out of Brighton towards Ditchling. *Three deaths in under a week.* At first his thoughts centred on a problem with the school and the current teaching staff, *a disgruntled member of staff perhaps?* But most of the staff had been interviewed, background checks had nearly been completed with a few outstanding. Nothing stood out that rang alarm bells, not even a bloody parking ticket.

He pondered the prospect of a disgruntled parent, but that was highly unlikely. The majority of parents held important positions, had wealth and status. Murder wasn't on their agenda, *would they risk losing all of that?* he thought as he tapped his thumb on the wheel in time with a random song on the radio.

As he made his way down the long access road towards the school, a lone figure stood by the main entrance. As Scott neared, the outline of a man in blue overalls came into focus.

There's your creepy caretaker, Abby.

He was a man with short, dark hair that had no particular shape or outline, but nevertheless was neat and tidy. His face was deadpan. Scott noticed how his lower jaw jutted out further than appeared normal. Bubba's jaw in the film *Forrest Gump* sprang to mind as he thought about it. A small mouth, with the edges turned down gave him a forlorn appearance. It was either his natural look or something had upset him big time. Scott thought it was probably the former as he studied the man's drooping shoulders and loose, limp arms that hung by his sides.

The man shuffled slowly towards Scott as he got out of the car, his steps small and quick as the oversized overalls hung low between his legs limiting his stride length.

"Alan Bennett?" Scott asked.

The man nodded once. His face remained fixed and stoical in a strange way, almost as if he'd had Botox and had lost all sense of facial muscular control.

"I'm Detective Inspector Baker. You've probably seen me around here a few times. I understand you called my team because you've found something?"

"Erm, yes I have."

Scott wasn't sure which part Bennett agreed with, seeing him before or finding something, but nevertheless carried on. "Do you want to lead the way?"

Bennett looked sullen as he turned without another word, his head a little bowed, and made his way around to the side of the building. Scott followed, his feet raked over the large gravel that skirted around the front of the school, the crunching sound amplified in the stillness that surrounded them. He was led through a smaller side door that took them through to an older part of the school.

From the look of it, Scott realised it formed the fabric of the original school, and judging from the dusty floors, and musty smell that hit his nostrils, hadn't been used for many years. A dull light streamed in through the old murky steel Crittall windows.

Bennett continued to lead them through the winding corridors, barely stopping to check if the detective was still keeping up with him. He stopped outside a room and pointed at a padlock and shackle that had been forcibly prised away from the door. Thin marks were etched in the wood at various angles from a blunt instrument.

Scott glanced at the door before looking back to Bennett, the lack of information or reason for being here perplexed him. He held his hands out in front of him, searching for an explanation from Bennett.

"I locked the door myself many years ago, not been in this part of the building for just as long. But I found this last night on my rounds."

"Who has access to this part of the school?" Scott enquired, as he leant in to take a closer look.

"No one, I have the only keys, someone's broken in…"

Bennett's powers of deduction were remarkable.

"Is the route we took the only means of access to this room?" Scott asked, glancing up and down the abandoned corridor.

"No," Bennett replied, scratching his temple slowly. "It can be accessed from an old storeroom in the main building; the lock to the door in the storeroom has been broken, too."

"Have you been inside?"

"Yeah, someone's been inside…"

Scott sighed and ran a hand through his hair. Having a conversation with Bennett was painful. He'd much rather pluck his own eyebrows than stand here with a man who appeared to be one stick short of a bundle.

Bennett opened the large, heavy door. It had dropped over the years and scraped across the floor as it was opened. He looked at Scott stone-faced, telepathically inviting him to take a look inside.

Scott raised a brow in consternation as he stepped in. The room was dark, however, judging from the footprints that criss-crossed in random directions, recent activity had disturbed the grey matt carpet of dust that had built up over the years.

An acrid smell hung in the air. Half-burnt tea lights lay scattered around the floor, the window ledge to his left, and on the old, dark oak mantelpiece that framed a small fireplace and hearth. Scott walked over and knelt beside the fireplace, his footsteps muffled by the bed of dust. He picked up a shard of scorched kindling that lay close to the base of the fire. He sniffed one end and immediately noticed the distinct smell of an accelerant, *perhaps lighter fuel*.

The remnants of a singed newspaper lay scattered around the hearth. He ran his fingers through several pieces before picking up a small fragment, scalded brown and black around the edges. As he scanned the words left legible, he noticed it was the header of a newspaper…dated two weeks prior.

Scott rose and turned to continue to look around the darkened room, no doubt used by persons unknown…and recently. Thoughts turned over in his mind, *was this connected in some way to his current investigation, or was it some of the pupils using it as some sort of den?*

Then it caught his attention, hanging from a silver hook screwed into the wall by the window. Not wanting to disturb the scene any further he remained fixed to the spot. Hanging loosely was a length of rope, about four feet in length. That in itself could be seen as strange if you had an inquisitive mind, however, what sparked Scott's curiosity further was the loop that had been tied in the end. As he looked to the opposite wall, there was a similar hook and rope attachment…*some sort of improvised bindings*, he thought.

"Mr Bennett, I'm going to organise for some officers to come down here to take a closer look at this room. No one is allowed in, and nothing must be touched…understand?" Scott instructed as he breezed past Bennett, not waiting for a reply.

Scott left a bewildered Bennett standing at the entrance. His deadpan expression firmly fixed and unfazed.

Scott stood outside close to the doorway that he and Bennett had gone through. As he paced around, he placed a call to the station to organise for uniformed presence and SOCO. Ordinarily he could perhaps dismiss it, but with three deaths on his watch, and rope being used in at least one of those cases, he needed to cover all bases. With DCI Harvey on his back for a speedy result, and Chief

Constable Lennon taking a personal interest in this case, Scott had little margin for error. Every lead, every piece of evidence and every hunch needed to be thoroughly investigated.

With one ear glued to his phone deep in conversation with Matt Allen, Scott's attention was distracted by what sounded like a large flock of birds off in the distance. It reminded him of the aviaries he used to visit as a boy in his local park. From his location, the only visible point of reference was a small cottage that sat close to the edge of the forest.

As far as he could recall, Bennett's small lodgings were the possible source of the avian cacophony. The dwelling was as small up close as it was from a distance, possibly just a single bedroom and what he'd call a two-up two-down compact des res. A dull white pebble-dashed exterior in need of some TLC was in marked contrast to the chocolate-box cottages offered to teaching staff.

Scott strolled around the back of the cottage only to discover the source of the noise. A purpose-built aviary with an assortment of birds fluttering from one stand to another. His arrival intensified the volume and intensity of the chirping and cooing. Scott leant on the wire mesh that formed the walls, and this only served to agitate the birds further, as their fluttering wings wafted air in his direction.

He couldn't pick out the breeds of the smaller birds, but what spiked his interest was the presence of several white pigeons. He stored that information for later, as he noticed more boundary rope stored neatly by the back door of the cottage as he walked away.

"Matt, on an entirely different matter, bit of a random question, but can DNA analysis be done on a pigeon feather?"

Matt groaned on the other end of the line. "I would imagine so but it's not really my field of expertise. Considering you can do DNA analysis, DNA screening and profiling of animals, and pretty much everything else, I can't see any reason why you couldn't. I'd imagine there are specialist companies for that. Any reason you're asking?"

"Just something I'm playing around with," Scott replied, placing a few feathers in a clear evidence bag and hanging up.

25

S cott left the room in the hands of SOCO after they'd arrived. With it being a derelict part of the school, it attracted little attention as pupils and school life carried on around them which in itself worried Scott. There was a sense of suspended reality to this place, the school had carried on as normal, teachers delivered classes, pupils appeared unfazed and the atmosphere felt controlled, clinical and sanitised. It certainly wasn't what Scott had expected, but then again, he wasn't sure that this was a *normal* school.

Collier, the principal, was seated in his red leather wingback chair facing out through a large leaded window over the front of the school. He had his back to Scott but nevertheless heard his footsteps tap across the parquet floor as he strode along the corridor. For a man leading a school engulfed in a series of murder investigations, he seemed unabashed, which should have surprised Scott, but having witnessed the man's demeanour on several occasions and the general atmosphere around the school and staff, nothing surprised him now.

"Mr Collier, you and I need a chat," Scott said firmly as he walked in.

Collier replied with nothing more than an, "Ahem."

Scott placed himself between Collier and the window, his arms crossed, staring intently at the principal. "I've just come from the old music room, and it appears that despite it being out of bounds, it's been used recently. I need answers, Mr Collier, and I need you to start talking now."

The harsh, firm tone in Scott's voice left Collier with little doubt as to the gravity of the situation the school faced. Collier sat with his elbows resting on the armrests, his fingers joined in a steeple that supported his chin. His eyes were firmly fixed in a glaze, a vacant stare that seemed to bore through Scott and out into the gardens beyond. He looked weary, the events of the past week had clearly taken their toll on him. Fatigued and stressed, the past was slowly catching up to him, and he had neither the strength nor energy to fight off the growing tide of suspicion that engulfed the school.

With a jaded sigh, his shoulders dropped and his eyes slowly rose from over the top rim of his spectacles to meet with Scott's. Pulling himself up straight and out of the chair he looked at Scott, resignation etched into the creases across his forehead and around his eyes.

"Walk with me, Inspector?" he asked as he turned and trudged towards the door.

An eerie silence followed the pair as they made their way back out through reception past Mrs Hilary, who watched open-mouthed unsure as to what was happening. She'd already locked horns with Scott earlier as he'd breezed past her, ignoring her grating voice that echoed in the air as he left her behind.

Stepping out into the sunshine, Scott squinted. The mood didn't change as they walked slowly around the grounds of the school. Their footsteps were muffled as they trod across the closely cropped lawns.

"So much has changed since I was a pupil here," Collier reflected, melancholy tinging his voice. "It was a good school, the best. It's why I came back here after my military service to begin my teaching career. It was in my blood, you see.

"It was fair, but well oiled. Discipline was key," he remarked as he cleared his throat. "We were the future leaders of industry, the future of the British Army…the future ambassadors and attachés of the British government in far-flung countries. This establishment comes with a strong, proud history. More than one hundred years, Inspector, a strong pedigree you see. Did you know that it was set up by a Brigadier General Edmunston of the Queen's Royal Artillery and The Reverend Christopher Hunt, a chaplain to the forces who held the rank of major?" he said without looking or waiting for an answer from Scott.

"Then she came along…"

"Who?"

"That Harrison woman. That wretched woman…she wanted to modernise the school, make it coed. Many objected…me included. All the traditions we valued and lived by have been replaced by modern-day thinking, the prospect of coed education, whatever's next? Eh?"

"Hmm," Scott replied, mulling over the pontification in a search for relevant clues.

"The board of governors, well, the majority, agreed with the changes," he continued through gritted teeth. "She convinced them, batted her bloody eyelids, and had them eating out of her hand. The modernisation programme included knocking down the older parts of the school, including the music room, and replacing it with dance studios, a small theatre, drama room. There was even talk of selling off some of our land to build an elite finishing school for girls, some bloody joint venture with the Roedean crowd." Collier hung his head low, worry lines creasing his forehead. Sadness and anger ate away at his core, his hands tightly locked behind his back.

"So what can you tell me about the music room?"

"Ah, the music room. I never really had a reason to go there as a teacher when I came back. I taught history and poli-tics…my forte. To be honest, I didn't even know it was being used now." He shrugged pathetically.

Scott felt a degree of remorse for the man. He was well and truly attached to the past, a past that had shaped and guided him, but nevertheless, Collier knew more than he was letting on. Scott was sure of that.

"I knew that things went on there. They happened even when I was a lad here, but it was just how the school was run. Of course there was a bit of argy-bargy, and the prover-bial initiation ceremonies to be accepted into a house by the senior pupils. The prefects got a bit heavy-handed, but it was boisterous more than anything else. If you can't take a bit of aggro, it's unlikely that you'd survive in the real world."

The pair came to an uncomfortable pause on the lawns as Collier glanced around to survey his domain.

"Obstruction or withholding information that could help my investigation is a criminal offence. I hope you realise that, Mr Collier?"

"I've nothing to withhold, Inspector. We live by the sword, we die by the sword."

Scott thought that was an odd and perhaps extreme ideology. "Mr Collier, let me remind you that two members of your current teaching staff are dead, a former member of staff is dead too. This is a multiple murder investigation, and this school, *your school*," Scott said, waving his arm in an arc in the direction of the main building, "is at the centre of it. My team is currently poring over every detail of this school, its history and its staff. We will find out who's committing these crimes. It's only a matter of time, and I hope for your sake and that of your career, that you're not tied up in this."

Collier turned back in the direction of the school, pausing for a moment as he came alongside Scott, turning his head slightly, his eyes deceptively cold and empty with a hint of resignation. "My career is already over, Inspector."

26

Any hope of Scott slipping into the station unnoticed by DCI Harvey soon evaporated as the desk sergeant pointed out that the DCI had been asking for him. She was clearly tracking him down as several other officers stopped him in his tracks to mention it on the way to the CID office.

He breathed a sigh of relief as he turned into his office only to jump at the presence of DCI Harvey sitting in his chair, her hands clasped together on the desk, fingers interlocked. She raised a brow at him. He'd seen that look many times on his boss' face. She was pissed off; that he was sure of.

"Ma'am?"

"Scott, CC Lennon is, shall we say, a little *concerned* at the lack of progress, and frankly, I don't take too kindly to getting a barrow full of elephant shit from him on the phone first thing this morning. I've got three deaths in under a week on my watch, no evidence of substance, no witnesses, sketchy CCTV and more importantly, no one sitting in a bloody cell downstairs...have I missed anything, Inspector?"

Scott hoped to correct her on some of those facts, but she wasn't far from the truth. It looked just as grim for her as it did for him and the team. They'd made little progress, and a week on, questions were being raised from management, questions he didn't have answers for.

"Ma'am, I know it doesn't look great, but we're dealing with a bit of an unusual case here and..."

"There's nothing unusual about it, Scott," she interrupted. "We've got three suspicious deaths. They appear to be connected. Statements need to be taken and reviewed again. Forensics need to be re-examined, and questions need to be asked..." She paused for a moment. "What's difficult about that? You're a *detective*. You lead a team of *detectives*. Do what you're supposed to do, or do I need to find someone else to take over the investigation?"

Scott had never seen Harvey react quite like that. She was enraged and frustrated, her words delivered in a sharp, precise tone. In all the time he'd worked for her, she'd never questioned his authority, management of his team or his capability. If he felt pressure, then she certainly was experiencing it tenfold from CC Lennon.

"It's not as clear-cut as that, Ma'am..."

"Don't mug me off, Scott," she said, thumping a fist on the desk.

Scott sighed and blew out his cheeks as he collapsed in a chair opposite Harvey. Any investigation involving a suspicious death could take weeks and sometimes months to solve. He had a stack of files somewhere on the floor filled with unsolved deaths, cases dating back months and years that without new evidence, new breakthroughs in forensic science or witnesses, would languish away in a brown box.

Occasionally, he would pull them out and have a flick through. It helped to cast a fresh pair of eyes over them in case something had been missed on previous case reviews. Invariably, nothing changed. They were statistics, nothing more than case file numbers.

"Ma'am, as I was about to say…" Scott glared at DCI Harvey, annoyed at how she kept interrupting him, "we are making inroads. The plastic tape that we believe was used to kill victim three this morning was still wrapped around the deceased's body. Forensics have that now. I've just come back from the school after being called out there by the caretaker. A derelict room in the old part of the school has been used recently. Now it may or may not be connected, but we're following up. And I'm fairly sure that the principal knows more than he's letting on…"

"So why isn't he in here being interviewed?" Harvey snapped back.

"I'm planning to, Ma'am…"

"Planning isn't good enough, Scott," she barked, rising to her feet. "I want a progress report from you first thing, understood?"

Scott nodded as she walked around his desk and made towards the door. "First thing…" she repeated.

―――――――

SOME WOULD HAVE FOLDED and questioned their ability

after DCI Harvey's verbal volley. Others would have walked around like a bear with a sore head all day, but Scott had been on the receiving end of worse. He was forever saying the wrong things to defuse confrontational situations whilst in training as a rookie. This had led to several of his trainers pulling him up on his communication style. It's one of the reasons that he'd gone on to learn NLP. He saw neuro linguistic programming as a way to better his ability to read others, understand human behavioural patterns, as well as improve his own depth of communication.

Scott took a deep breath before slowly releasing it to focus his thoughts. After straightening his Thomas Pink deep navy tie and repositioning his suit jacket, he headed off towards the drinks machine to grab a coffee shouting, "Briefing in five minutes!" to his team.

Leaning on the edge of Abby's desk, Scott sipped at the tepid, bitter coffee as he stared at the incident board that now had pictures of victim number three pinned to it. Three middle-aged men, all teachers, all dead.

"Listen up team. I spoke with Matt earlier. It's taken some time, but we can confirm that the rope found at Giles Rochester's property had the same fibre composition as the rope used on Johnson. I had a look around the school lawns to see if there was any missing from the boundary rope, but that's all intact. But I'll come back to that in a moment. Remind me if I forget, Abby."

"Guv, there's been a sighting of John Morecombe, the missing teacher. Hampshire police got back to me. Morecombe was nicked for speeding on the A31 east near Winchester. He was driving a hire car, heading east."

"Towards us…"

"Possible, Guv. That was two weeks ago. A week before that, he was arrested and bailed for being drunken and disorderly. Spent the night in the cells sleeping it off. He assaulted the door staff trying to throw him out. He threw a chair at them, apparently."

"Where's the car and Morecombe now?"

"Not been seen since. The car was never returned. I've circulated the car details to uniform here, so they can keep a look out, just in case he's coming back here."

Raj wafted a sheet of paper. "DNA analysis using the hair fibres and toothbrush from Rochester's property confirm that vic two is Giles Rochester, but we knew that anyway. Also, there were tiny fibres found on the compression marks on both Johnson and Rochester. In Johnson's case, two different sets of fibres were found under magnification. Fibres matching the boundary rope were present, however…" Raj paused as he referred to his sheet, "a second set of fibres were found on Johnson that matched those found in Rochester's neck skin."

All eyes were on Raj as he revealed more. It was during moments like this that Raj lapped up the attention. More often than not, he was given menial information gathering tasks to do that kept him occupied, and more importantly, silent, much to the delight of the team. For a thirty-one-year-old officer, Raj often found that he played the practical joker card a little too often, which meant he wasn't taken seriously as an officer or someone looking to push on in their career.

"The fibres are PP or polypropylene…as you'd find in plastic strapping tape."

"Okay, that's helpful. Thanks, Raj."

"What's PP?"

"It's a form of plastic, Sian," Scott replied. "In this case and judging from the width of the depressions left in the skin and how clear and sharp the edges are on the skin," Scott pointed out as he headed over to the incident board to point out the impressions identified in the close-up post-mortem pictures, "I'd say PP straps similar to those used as bindings around cartons and boxes.

"Unfortunately for us, it's a common packaging tape used around the globe, so not easy for us to follow up on. You can buy it anywhere, even on eBay. I guess there's the option to do a chemical composition analysis on it."

The news left the team with mixed feelings. Another dead end it appeared.

"The DCI is really pushing for some results, so we need to pull out all the stops. There's more to this case than meets the eye. The principal is without doubt hiding something, so, Mike, I want you to bring him in. Tell him he's helping us with our enquiries. I've just come from the school, and he's a little too laid-back for my liking. He seems angry about all the proposed changes put forward for the school. Our first two vics seemed to approve and side with Mary Harrison about future proposals. It's clear the school means a lot to Collier and he'd do anything to keep the status quo."

"Enough to commit murder?" Raj asked. Scott didn't have an answer.

Scott's phone vibrated in his trouser pocket. Ignoring it, he continued.

"Sounds like it, Guv," Mike said.

"Guv, you said to remind you."

"Yes, cheers, Abby. Two things. After I left Bennett, I came across an aviary of some sorts…behind Bennett's cottage. Amongst the birds, were a few white pigeons. Could be completely random and they're freely found in any park, but the fact that we have white feathers left with the victims is suspicious. I thought that they could have come from there. There was also more boundary rope behind his house. Now purely circumstantial again, but we still need to follow it up."

"Are you suggesting that Bennett may be involved?" Raj asked.

"I won't rule him out, but he doesn't seem capable of planning something like this. I can't think of a motive. Collier after all, gave him a break with a job. How many times have we seen ex-offenders struggle to get a job, *and* reoffend? The cage isn't locked, so anyone could access the birds. I've given Matt some samples," he said. "There are firms doing DNA profiling for animals, but results take five to seven working days. Clearly we haven't got that long, so he's going to try and push them to prioritise our analysis."

"Who would have thought you could do that," Raj remarked.

"Apparently, it's very common in racing pigeon circles because birds are so precious. They do all sorts of testing and screening like DNA parentage, genetic disorders and infectious diseases like cryptosporidium and pigeon circovirus. And before you ask, no I haven't got a sodding clue what they are, and nor do I wish to know."

A light ripple of laughter spread around the team.

"The other point I wanted to bring to your attention was the CCTV still image we've got of Rochester. I've had the image enhanced," he said, pinning a fresh blown-up image to the incident board.

He had their full attention as the team straightened up in their seats and took in the new image with a mixture of nodding heads and the odd raised brow.

Scott took his pen and used it as a pointer. "As you can see, Giles Rochester appears to be in a state of distress, but what you can see clearly now is a white line of some sorts around his neck. We can assume that he was driven there under duress, and that the line is some sort of ligature. From the way the ligature is placed and secured, it looks tight and that suggests someone was in the back holding it."

"So the persons unknown were hunched down in the rear passenger well to avoid detection?"

"Correct, Abby. They wanted to avoid being caught on camera. Unfortunately, there's no evidence or indication of who it is, but at least we can assume that Giles Rochester went to the car park with the person who most likely killed him."

Scott's phone bleeped again in his pocket. Pulling it out, he realised he'd missed a call and now a text from Cara. *She could wait.*

"Also, Bennett, the caretaker, showed me an abandoned room in the old part of the school. It's certainly been used recently, and there's evidence of something going on that I'm not comfortable with. I've got SOCO down there at the moment. Sian, can you check with the council to see what objections have been raised, if any, towards the new development?"

Scott locked his fingers behind his neck and stretched his back, the vertebrae cracking as they unlocked and released the stiffness that had been building for days. The burning sensation under his left shoulder blade still irritated him like a mosquito bite that needed scratching.

"This whole white feather thing has been playing on my mind. If we explore this coward thing further, then something may have happened in the army. A triggering event. I've been checking the backgrounds of the deceased. They all had a background in the army, including our victim from this morning. Collier was a prefect when he left Edmunston to join the army. All the deceased were recruited by Collier into the army after their days as school prefects, and then from the army back to Edmunston as teachers when Collier returned to Edmunston as deputy principal. They basically followed him."

The information raised a few eyebrows as the possibility of a new line of investigation opened up.

"Mike, with your military background and understanding, get working on that the moment you get back here with Collier. I need some answers by first thing tomorrow when I update the DCI. Abby and I will interview Collier."

Mike nodded as he rose, pulling his suit jacket off the back of his chair before proceeding to tuck in the bottom of his shirt. The garment had been exposing his large, overhanging, hairy stomach through the gaping spaces between each button.

The team turned back to their desks busy with a fresh to-do list. Scott headed back to his office so he could call Cara.

He sat down with a refreshing smile on his face as he unlocked his phone hoping to listen to a nice message from her. His moment of excitement fast evaporated. Cara's panicked voice faltered as she tried to explain over the tears. "Someone's outside the mortuary...they've been banging on the windows...I'm scared."

27

S cott sped the short distance from the station towards Brighton and Hove mortuary on the Lewes Road. He'd left Abby to deal with the imminent arrival of Collier, assuring her that he'd be back in time for the start of the interview. He'd thought about organising a patrol car to make its way there ahead of him, but figured he'd arrive just as quickly.

There'd been too many strange occurrences recently for Scott not to take Cara's distressed call seriously. What he couldn't figure out was whether the perpetrator had it in for him and was using Cara as bait. Just as likely was the theory that a disgruntled family member had a grievance with Cara over a case she'd dealt with. He dismissed the latter offhand as he'd never heard of such a thing occurring in his career.

As he pulled in through the gates of the cemetery and made his way towards the mortuary, he couldn't see evidence of anyone acting suspiciously in the grounds. The scene seemed similar to many prior occasions.

Scott pressed the buzzer several times without a response. At this time of day, the mortuary staff would have gone home but Cara often remained behind to write up her reports on post-mortems she'd carried out during the day. With no response to his repeated attempts on the buzzer, Scott became increasingly concerned as he stepped back and walked around the perimeter of the building looking for any signs of forced entry or criminal damage.

He tapped her contact in his phone in an attempt to reach her. A lengthy pause ensued before she finally answered. "Cara, I'm outside. Where are you?"

"I'm…I'm sorry. I'm coming to the door now," she replied in a shaky, stuttering voice.

The door flung open as he arrived back around the front, with Cara running out towards him visibly upset as she grabbed him in a tight embrace, burying her head deep into his chest with a deep, long sigh.

"Hey…hey…you okay? What's happened?" Scott asked as he lifted her head from his chest. She blinked tears from bloodshot eyes. Her thick, brown lashes stuck together in clumps as if she'd immersed them in a bucket of water. Her tears made wet tracks down her face and dripped from her wobbling chin. "Shit, what's happened, babes?"

Her shoulders heaved as she tried to control her breath. "I…I was so…so scared." The words fell from her mouth in staggered fits of breath. "I could hear someone banging at the main entrance. I came down and there was no one there. I thought it was kids. I…I went back to the office and carried on. Then it happened again, but when I went to the door again, no one was there, but the bushes over there were moving," she said, pointing over towards the hedge line that skirted close to the building. "I still thought it was kids." Cara began to cry again.

"Then someone banged loudly on the frosted glass around the side of the building. I went to have a look hoping if I saw kids, I could shout at them and threaten them with the police." Drawing deep breaths, she continued, "But it was a man. I could see his outline, a man, thumping on the windows with both hands. I shouted at him to stop, but he didn't. The banging got louder and heavier. Then he let out a loud scream...and that's when I just shit myself and ran to the office to call you.

"He then moved to other windows and banged on them too...I felt so trapped," she said, crying into Scott's chest again.

Scott glanced around. He saw nothing, nothing that would concern him. "Listen, I'll get uniform to pop over a few times tomorrow. Did you see anything on CCTV?"

Cara's whole body trembled with fear. "No...that's the worrying thing. The screen is blank, like something has been sprayed over it."

Scott had heard enough. This appeared to be a deliberate act of intimidation for some reason unknown to him. "Have you had any run-ins recently, whilst driving, with family members here, anything at all?"

Cara rubbed her eyes and shook her head slowly. She thought hard, searching her mind for anything, anything at all.

"Let's get you back to my place. It's safe there. We'll go by yours first so you can grab some clothes, okay?" he said, wiping her dark, wet limp hair from her face.

THE DRIVE to Montpelier Crescent was silent for the most part, broken only by intermittent sobs and Scott's questioning. Cara was still insistent that she had no idea as to the identity of the person, and more importantly, why the reaction. In her mind, she was hopeful that it was an isolated incident involving someone who at best was doing it for a prank or wind-up, or at worse, someone who was less then mentally balanced. It was something Scott couldn't agree with, especially after what appeared to be a deliberate act of obscuring the CCTV lens.

His suspicions grew not long after they'd parked in an available parking space close to her apartment. Montpelier Crescent was a sweeping arch of mid-19th century grade two listed buildings set back from a small, grass parkland opposite. Imposing three- and four-storey white structures commanded a distinct presence. Regency styling blended with Victorian grace, creating a desirable location. A mixture of cast iron first floor balconies, together with ornate stone cornices and large sash windows only added to the grandeur of the street.

Cara led the way as they went through the communal front door, but froze within feet of her door. An icy chill ran through her body, rooting her to the spot. Her pupils dilated. Her heart thumped rapidly. Her mouth fell open in disbelief. She turned to Scott, her eyes wide in fear.

Scott raised a finger to his lips as he looked beyond her to the door that was ajar, wood splinters scattered over the hallway carpet. He took slow, light steps past her before he turned and mouthed "stay here" to her. He slowly pushed the door open and peered in. There were no sounds of movement. He took one step at a time as he made his way down the hallway, taking a moment to peer into every room.

Once sure the apartment was clear, he gave Cara a shout to come in. She took tentative steps, the fingers of one hand covering her mouth in disbelief. Her concern turned to confusion as she realised that nothing had been disturbed, until she got to her bedroom, where Scott waited at the doorway. She scanned the room, her eyes drawn to the top drawer of a small four-drawer chest that sat in an alcove. It was half pulled out, the contents in disarray.

Cara was about to step forward when Scott put his arm out to stop her. She glanced at him in bewilderment, before peering back down the corridor trying to make some sense of the events.

"That's my underwear. It's on the floor," she said, looking at the assortment that lay scattered on the carpet.

"From what you've seen, has anything been taken?"

She hesitated for a moment as she ran her hand through her dark hair, throwing it back over her shoulder. "I don't think so. Why wasn't my TV taken or my iPad that I left on the sofa? My Kindle or the Michael Kors watch by my bed... nothing?" she asked, pointing to her underwear. "But some perv has rummaged through my underwear drawer...I don't get it."

"Listen to me, Cara," Scott said, holding her by the shoulders and spinning her around to face him. "This isn't your normal run-of-the-mill break-in. To me, this is getting personal. First your car, then the pig's head, then the morgue and now this. This is personal."

"Scott, I don't know…I just don't understand," she said, her eyes darting left to right as she trawled her memory. "Is someone after me, or trying to frighten me?"

"I'm not suggesting that but look at the events over the past week. Something is going on…your underwear is all over the floor for fuck's sake, and nothing appears to have been taken. That's not your normal burglary, babes."

Cara began to hyperventilate as fear returned to her body. She wrapped her arms across her chest, scared to move. "I don't know what I've done…what do I do, Scott?" she pleaded.

"Well, you're coming back with me. Don't go in the bedroom; it's a crime scene. I'll get Matt from forensics to send someone over to do a sweep. It's a long shot, but worth a try. If you need more clothes, we can stop at the shops on the way to mine."

Cara nodded, worry distorting her features. Her fine lines and soft skin replaced with puffy eyes and red, blotchy skin.

The events were more than a coincidence in Scott's eyes. Someone was out to put the frighteners on Cara or him. The question was who, as he glanced around the crescent waiting for Matt to answer his phone.

28

Matthew Edrington looked tired and frail. Dark circles framed eyes that furtively shifted, scouring the corridor for any signs of danger. Thankfully, he could blend in amongst the throng of pupils that snaked their way from the breakfast dining room back to their dorms. He was safe for now. Danger came when he was alone, his vulnerability exposed. Defenceless and weak, he was an easy target for the prefects.

Or so he thought. A hand reached into the back of his shirt collar pulling him backwards, the force taking him by surprise. His throat tightened.

They'd cornered him, pushing through into the doorway of an empty classroom. It seemed that his confidential discussion with his housemaster Edward Chapman had been anything but that.

They reminded him in their own inimitable way that snitches were lower than pond scum. Rollings pursed his lips and raised his hand back. He threw it forward as hard as he could before whipping it across Matthew's face. The crack of skin on skin echoed off the walls. Vibrations of pain exploded in all directions across his face. Rollings's palm was bright red, the same red mark that matched the one on Matthew's face. The boy stared at Rollings with his blue eyes wide in fear as he protectively lifted his hand to his fire-red cheek.

Rollings's flicked shaggy hair that hung low over his face to one side. There was no remorse in his expression as he stared at Matthew, just anger-filled eyes. A triumphant grin spread across his face as satisfaction coursed through him.

"You pathetic, limp-wristed prick," Hunter said through clenched teeth, his impish boy looks replaced by an unfazed menacing stare as his eyes locked onto Matthew. "Not only do you let our house down, you let yourself down. You're supposed to take this like a man, but you're not. You're a waste of space. Do us all a favour and go hang yourself like Johnson," he said with a sneer.

Rollings repeatedly slapped the cowering boy around the head in a frenzied flurry, laughing to himself. Matthew's ears were hot, red and stinging. He grappled with Ford as he desperately clung onto his blazer. It was hard for him to know where to focus his attention. Rollings was incessantly taunting the boy, whilst Ford attempted to rip the boy's blazer from his tight clutches. Other students turned a blind eye as some walked past looking the other way, whilst others doubled back and took alternate routes to avoid witnessing the drama unfold in front of their eyes.

There was an unspoken rule amongst pupils…avoid those prefects at all costs. They ruled the school through intimi-dation. Speaking out against them would only ensure that they too were on the receiving end of their 'personalised attention'.

Relief came in the form of Timothy Saunders who'd followed not long afterwards from the student dining room en route to his office. This was the second occasion where he'd had to step in to break up an assault on the same pupil. The prefects laughed at Saunders as he tried to step in between the two sides. They'd goaded him too, unafraid of his authority. Bravado and adrenaline fuelled their determination to stand their ground.

"This is wrong. This is so wrong. I will not tolerate behaviour like this. Any form of bullying is not tolerated in the school, and those found to be doing it will be severely punished, do I make myself clear?" Saunders threatened. "I'm going to report the lot of you to the principal."

His threat of disciplinary action was met with sniggers and further sarcastic taunts of "oooh, you're really scaring us now!"

Saunders could feel the anger crawling into his chest. His stomach twisted and flipped over, as he clenched his jaws, breathing in furiously through his nostrils. He certainly didn't have the commanding presence or the level of respect that many of the teaching staff enjoyed throughout the school. Enraged by their abrasive attitude, he ordered them to disperse whilst stepping between the prefects and Matthew, shielding the boy from them.

Saunders turned to face Matthew, glancing briefly back over his shoulder to make sure the prefects were dispersed. "Are you okay, lad?"

Matthew stood there, nervously shifting his weight from one foot to another, his shoulders rocking in unison. He still had one hand placed over his red, stinging cheek. He nodded once. His eyes slowly misted up, a lump of sadness stuck in his throat making it hard to swallow saliva.

"I'm not going to tolerate this, lad. Listen, I know how you must feel. It used to go on in my school as well. You have to be strong. You have to stand up to them or they'll continue to keep picking on you." Saunders leant forward a little, placing one hand on Matthew's thin, bony shoulder. "Don't make the same mistakes I made. I let people walk over me."

"But…but, sir, I have no one else to turn to. I've already gone and spoken to my housemaster. The prefects found out about it. If I tell anyone else, they'll…" Matthew's voice trailed off as his chin sank to his chest, his eyes gazing into the darkness of the black stone floor.

"Listen here, Edrington. I will speak to the principal. I won't stand by and have another child's life ruined by bullies. Besides, I thought school was supposed to be the happiest days of your life. Unfortunately, they weren't for me. I've got nothing but bad memories. But we don't want that for you now, do we? Leave it with me. If those boys bother you again, I want you to come and find me. Understand?"

Matthew shrugged before picking up his blazer from the floor and trudging off wearily, his shoulders heavy, slouched forward in defeat and resignation.

Saunders watched Edrington move away awkwardly, his thin, bony frame dwarfed inside a school uniform that now appeared a size too big. The months of mental, emotional and physical torment were clearly evident. The next job on his list was going to see Principal Collier.

SAUNDERS STORMED into Principal Collier's office without the normal consideration of knocking first. "A word, Principal Collier. I've just broken up yet another incident involving pupils of Stanmer House. How can you tolerate prefects picking on younger boys?" he asked, slapping an angry palm on Collier's desk.

Collier wasn't used to others challenging him in such a cavalier fashion. He rose abruptly from his chair, pushing it back, before striding around to Saunders. A tense stand-off followed as the two glared at each other, their eyes locked in a battle of wills, neither relenting or turning away.

"May I remind you, Mr Saunders, that the discipline within this school is my responsibility and that of the senior management team. I suggest you'd do well to focus on what you're here for…the catering manager of this institution," he replied in a firm, but measured tone that hinted of suppressed anger.

Saunders, his fists pressing into his sides, was incensed that Collier was clearly more concerned with titles, and the demarcation of jobs than the welfare of pupils. "Are you not listening to me? A pupil was just being bullied out there," he said, pointing back towards the open door. "And you're more concerned with whether I'm doing my fucking job."

"Mr Saunders, you're treading a fine line of insubordination…"

"Are you that detached from reality? You're happy to turn a blind eye to what I've just witnessed. It's not the first time I've seen this happen."

"There's no bullying in this school. What you have is conditioning..."

"Conditioning?" Saunders said, tripping over his words. "Are you for real? This isn't the army, or some secret sect. This is a school!"

"These men need to be tough. They think it's tough in here...hah! It's a ruthless world out there. They could be representing our nation on the battlefield, for our government in a far-flung country...do you think there's room for weakness in combat?" He sneered.

"They're boys," Saunders pleaded, "just boys, learning about life and themselves. This should be the happiest time of their lives, but what you're doing here is wrong! Do you hear me? It's wrong. You're ruining lives."

Collier erupted, his face reddening as he ripped off his glasses and went nose to nose with Saunders. "Get...out... of...my...office now...before you find yourself unemployed. Consider that your first and final warning!" His jawbone tensed as he clenched his teeth, his lips pursed tight, leaving nothing but a thin line that appeared as if it had been drawn on in biro.

Saunders shook his head as his chin touched his chest. A mixture of frustration, anger and sadness washed over him. He had tried, Matthew had confided in him, and now felt like he'd failed Edrington. "I won't let this rest, I'll...I'll contact the governors. You can't keep ruining their lives," he spluttered as he stormed out of the room leaving a defiant Collier pleased that he'd won that contest.

29

S cott had dropped Cara off early at the mortuary with strict instructions to dial 999 if anything happened that was out of the ordinary and concerning. She'd nodded slowly, her eyes firmly fixed on an imaginary object far off into the distance. He had noticed a different side to her that morning. Her usual exuberance and confidence replaced with a quiet, pensive and guarded mood. The events of the past few days were clearly starting to affect her more than she was willing to admit. He started to really feel for her. Beneath that strong, fun and dedicated persona, she was soft and fragile. Delicate enough to be wrapped in cotton wool.

They'd both had a restless night. Scott had jolted upright in bed after another of those dark nightmares. He'd not had many recently. Whether that was down to him coming to terms with the loss of his family, or having Cara in his life replacing the empty chasm, he wasn't sure. Nevertheless, it had left him exhausted and drenched in sweat with his heart bursting out of his chest.

Cara had spent the night tossing and turning in bed, her mind processing the events of the day, before giving up on sleep and heading downstairs to watch TV. Any chance of sleep had fast faded after Scott had startled her with a gasp as he bolted upright in bed. His eyes widened with fear as he searched in the darkness for what his mind had led him to believe was there in front of him…his family. He'd sat there, his knees pulled tight into his chest, his arms wrapped around them.

Salty tears streaked his cheeks as he gently rocked back and forth in her arms. She tried her hardest to calm and reassure him. She'd pulled his head tight to her warm chest. A repetitive soft calming "ssssh" and "it's okay, babes, I know you're hurting" soothed his pain. She couldn't think of anything else to say at such a difficult time in the dark of the night. Cara hadn't seen this side of him much, the gentle, vulnerable side that he left hidden from friends and colleagues.

Despite his pain, the resulting vulnerability was an endearing quality that drew her closer. Seeing it peeled back another layer and took her closer to his core, the real Scott. He was nothing more than a child in her arms until he'd finally fallen asleep again.

Curled up on the sofa wearing one of Scott's large T-shirts, her legs folded up beneath her, she'd channel-hopped in the futile attempt of finding something decent to watch. She had come to the conclusion that night-time TV was dreadful, and would be the perfect tonic for insomniacs. She'd finally settled on watching the *Time Team* doing an archaeological dig in Leicester at an old hall she'd never heard of. Cara could never quite take the presenter of the show seriously. She'd always associated him with the role of Baldrick in *Blackadder*, which only made her smile.

———————

SCOTT PUSHED through the double doors of the CID office keen to get an update from Abby's interview with Collier, but she was already flagging him down as he made his way to his office to throw off his jacket.

"Guv, Mike couldn't find Collier last night; he was nowhere to be found. He went back first thing this morning and tracked him down. You've got one pissed off principal waiting downstairs in the interview suite…he's not a happy man," she said, leaning back in her chair taking a sip from her mug of piping hot tea.

Scott paused for a moment before throwing his jacket back on. Interviewing Collier now would be a wise move considering the DCI wanted an update first thing. Perhaps he could squeeze something out of Collier that would get DCI Harvey off his back.

"Let him sweat for a while, Abby. Where's Mike now?" he asked, sniffing the air before deciding an odour was coming from Abby's direction.

"Where do you think?" she replied, rolling her eyes. "Filling his belly. He moaned about missing breakfast this morning. He's in the canteen getting a sausage and bacon butty."

Scott sniffed again, smelling perfume. "Did he get anywhere with the MOD enquiries?" he asked, taking a step closer to Abby before leaning in, much to her consternation, causing her to lean back as far as she could to keep her distance.

Abby was forced to push back her chair the closer Scott got, unsure about the invasion of her space and the curious look on Scott's face, not to mention the heavy waft of Hugo aftershave that shot up her nose.

"Not yet, Guv, getting through to the right department last night wasn't easy. The pen-pushers at the ministry have a unique knack of delay and distraction. They send you from one extension to another and keep you on hold whilst some garish music tests your patience. The hope is you eventually hang up.

"Our Mike isn't gifted with patience as you know," she said with a shrug and a raised brow as Scott continued to sniff the air around her, circling her chair. "He did finally get through to the right department but ended up going round in circles with some AO, and as an administrative officer, they didn't have the authority to release details of past service. He was going on about how only a grade six and seven had the authority to divulge such information."

Scott looked at Abby, a small smile breaking on one side of his mouth. "Are you wearing perfume?"

Abby looked sheepish. Suddenly the tea in her mug looked far more interesting than looking at Scott. Her cheeks flushed with embarrassment.

"You are, aren't you? You never wear perfume..." Scott played with his chin as he folded his arms, before wagging a finger in her direction. "Don't tell me. You're in lurve... with Jonathon. Things getting serious?" he teased.

Abby couldn't help but smile, a smile that said it all, but

nevertheless, she was reluctant to admit that Scott may be right. "I'm not. We're just getting on really well, that's all."

"Well enough to roll out the perfume, Miss Trent? You must be keen. Do I need to pick a hat?" he joked.

Abby was never one to publicise her private life. Her Facebook page only ever showed the occasional funny quote or pictures from the gym every few months. She certainly didn't fall into the prolific Facebooker category, and there was never any reference to her kids or personal life. Feeling a little exposed to Scott's fishing, she swiftly cleared her throat and changed the subject. "So as you can guess, Mike didn't really get anywhere."

"Don't tell me…a grade six or seven wasn't available?"

Abby nodded as she stared at the odd trail of steam that spiralled upwards from her cup, waiting for her flush to fade.

"We're expecting a call back this morning, Guv."

"Not good enough, Abby. Get Mike to chase them as soon as he gets back. We could be waiting hours for a call, and that's being optimistic."

Scott was disappointed with the news. He'd hoped to have had something to explore further with Collier in the interview, and feedback for Harvey. She'd be chasing him any minute for a progress report, and the last thing he wanted was to tell her that nothing new had been uncovered. For the time being, he needed to stay off her radar.

———

COLLIER SAT IMPATIENTLY with a hand wrapped around a

cup of tea, the fingers of his other hand strumming away in sequence on the table. He'd reluctantly agreed to accompany Mike to the station and had waived his opportunity to have a solicitor present. Mike had an imposing, heavy build and weathered face which often meant he got what he asked for and many dared not to question him.

Abby set the recorder up and covered the formalities as Scott sifted through his file. He noticed that as Abby went through the introductions for the tape, Collier didn't avert his gaze once towards Abby. *The guy has a serious hang-up about listening to women.*

"Mr Collier, did you enjoy your time in the armed services?"

Scott's question caused Collier to look up from his tea. His eyes flickered left and right as he processed the question. The direction of questioning took him by surprise. Abby hadn't picked up on it, but Scott had. Through years of experience and training, he'd become adept at picking up on eye accessing cues.

Through his training in neuro linguistic programming, he'd been taught to imagine that the brain is a computer and the eyes were the filing system. It had helped him to understand that when the brain was asked a question, or asked to recall a piece of data, the brain went on a search. A person's eyes would move in many directions depending upon the type of search and what they were thinking or recalling.

As an officer, it was essential to create an environment that would facilitate the extraction of information and evidence. Scott excelled and relished interviews more than most of his colleagues because of his fascination with human behaviour and the mind. He had found that using words more aligned to a person's way of processing information often helped him to glean more. He had put himself to the test on more than one occasion by asking questions in multiple ways to see which approach gave him the best results.

Collier had diverted his eyes ever so slightly up to his left, and that indicated he was accessing his stored visual memories. He then looked down towards the table to his left. Again Scott picked up on this small movement. *He's having a chat with himself.*

"Can I ask why you should need to know about my military service? I was led to believe that I was attending the station to help you with the death of my teaching staff."

"You are, Mr Collier. I'm just trying to build a timeline of those involved."

"I see."

"Clearly, well?"

Collier cleared his throat. "I had an excellent career in the forces. I wouldn't swap it for anything. You learn a lot about yourself, what you can handle…and how far you can push yourself," he said with a measured nod as his confidence returned.

Abby watched the exchange, choosing to let Scott lead.

"And did you see it as a hard thing to push yourself?"

"Not particularly," he replied, shaking his head confidently.

"You led soldiers if I'm not mistaken?" Scott asked.

"Yes, that's correct. Very well, I hasten to add."

"How did you find that?"

"It was an honour and a privilege to command a troop. To turn boys into men...fighting men. We don't have room for whingers and cowards."

"Cowards?" Scott repeated with a raised brow.

Collier didn't answer.

"Cowards...did you come across any in your military career?"

Collier sat back in his chair, crossed one leg over the other and locked his fingers together before resting them on his knee. He casually looked upwards towards his left and then right.

"Not that I recall."

Scott leant back and mirrored Collier by crossing his legs and locking his fingers over his knee. "You see, Mr Collier, I have a dilemma. I'm dealing with a triple murder investigation. Two of your staff have been murdered, a third retired teacher, also from your school, has been murdered, and that's no coincidence? Don't you agree?"

Collier looked down towards his left, deep in conversation with himself, before he looked up he said, "It certainly looks that way."

"Is there anything that happened during their military careers that could be connected to their deaths...or even prior to their careers in the military?" Scott paused for effect.

Abby furiously scribbled away in her notepad as he spoke.

Collier's eyes danced the Irish jig now. One moment they were down to his left, and then they were up to his right, before darting left to right. Scott had him scared.

Collier shook his head without a reply.

"For the tape, Mr Collier shook his head. Before their deaths, did you have any conversations with any of them? Did they say anything that may have suggested they were concerned, worried or fearful about their lives?"

Collier's glare remained firmly fixed to a small spot over Scott's shoulder. A slight adjustment in his eyes from centre to top left and then right went unnoticed by Abby.

Another shake of his head.

"Mr Collier, for the tape, can you say your answers, please."

"Not that I recall."

Liar.

"What can you tell us about John Morecombe?" Scott asked, changing direction.

"Excuse me?" Collier said, a deliberate mask of unfamiliarity painted on his face.

Scott smiled and glanced over to Abby. "Oh, I think you know exactly who we're talking about. Ex-teacher, John Morecombe. You sacked him about a year ago after he stood up to you about the bullying culture."

Collier raised a brow. "Ah, yes, we clearly had a difference of opinion. We came to the conclusion that it was in his best interests to seek a more appropriate position elsewhere."

"That's a diplomatic way of putting it," Abby said as she crossed her arms.

"Have you had any contact with him at all since his departure?"

Collier shook his head in response to Scott's question.

"No texts, phone calls, letters, nothing?"

Collier shook his head again. "Actually, now you come to mention it, I did get few letters of the hate mail variety."

"What did they say?"

Collier stared up towards the ceiling, strumming his fingers on his kneecap. "I can't remember to be precise, something along the lines of I won't get away with it." Collier chuckled to himself. "It didn't bother me, frankly. I've been called worse and threatened far worse than that. Staring down the barrel of a gun whilst on a tour of duty gives you a bit of a tough skin, Inspector."

"Where are they?"

"I threw them away a long time ago. He doesn't scare me," Collier replied as he stiffened his stance and pulled his shoulders back in defiance.

"We believe that he may be heading back towards Sussex or may already be here. Is there any reason he may do that?"

"I have no idea, Inspector. Maybe he's missing us all," Collier said, a smug smile dancing at the corners of his mouth.

Scott concluded the interview not long after and arranged for Collier to be taken back to Edmunston-Hunt.

"HE WAS as tight as a duck's arse." Abby sighed as they made their way back to the CID office.

"Far from it, Abby, he was lying. The victims and Collier had had conversations recently. I'm certain of that."

Abby shot Scott a confused glance. "How do you know that?"

Scott paused in the corridor just outside the doors of the office. "It's quite simple. When I was asking questions about cowards in the army, and whether he'd had conversations with the deceased recently, if you'd watched his eye movements, he just casually glanced up to the left and then right of his peripheral vision."

"I didn't see that, Guv."

"That's because you weren't looking for them. When someone does that, they look up to their left to remember a picture or a scene, and then they access a part of their brain when they look to the right which helps to create a lie or make up the scene in their head."

Abby looked perplexed, as she too was now looking up to her left and tracking back through her memory to picture the interview and what she missed.

"He lied about the cowards and he lied about not having conversations with the deceased." Scott had excitement in his voice as his mind raced. "He's connected to the three murders in some way, and he was running scared in there," he said, pointing back down the corridor.

30

DCI Jane Harvey stood by her window looking out over the front of the station onto John Street. Her attention hadn't been drawn to anything in particular, but her thoughts pulled her into a void of deep contemplation. To her left, a large office block offered an interesting distraction. It was the new premises of American Express. Encased in glass from street level to roof, she could see the many workers scurrying around from room to room, floor to floor unaware of how their lives were being played out for all to see like some voyeuristic attraction.

To her right stood, 'The Wedding Cake', the popular name for Amex House, the former HQ for American Express. The unique white concrete bands and dark blue rings of glass windows on each floor were how it acquired its name. The structure was a distinct landmark on the skyline of Brighton, and one that could be seen from any tall vantage point. Harvey reflected on what the landscape would look like once the building was demolished and replaced with flats and smaller offices.

Harvey was so deep in thought that she hadn't heard Scott knock on her open door. Her head snapped up at the loud banging. "Ma'am?"

Scott's arrival jolted her out of her reverie that saw her spin around on the heels. "Sorry, Scott. What have you got for me? The chief super is on my back," she said as she sat down with a heavy thud behind her desk, fiddling with her fingernails and waving him towards the chair opposite her. "Time flies when you're having fun, doesn't it?"

The randomness of both her behaviour and off-the-cuff remark took Scott off guard. The fact that she wasn't even looking at him was surprising.

"Following our last conversation, I had Collier, the principal, in for an interview. He is definitely implicated in some way. He is adamant he didn't know anything to suggest that victim's lives were in danger. But he's lying out of his back teeth. There's a connection between all of them. Whether that's linked to their days together in the army, or before that, is something we'll be working on." Scott paused for a moment when he realised the DCI wasn't paying attention to anything he was saying.

"Ma'am, tell me if I'm speaking out of turn, but you seem a little distracted. Is everything okay?"

Harvey looked up, dropping her head to one side, before looking reflectively in Scott's direction through narrowed eyes. "I may not be here for much longer, Scott."

"Sorry, Ma'am, I don't quite understand. Are you not well?"

Harvey shook her head dismissively. "The ACC thinks it's time I hang up my gloves. It seems my methods and approach don't fit in with the modern stance on policing. He's asked me to seriously consider taking retirement." She sighed.

"Has the ACC spoken to you directly?"

"No. His views were communicated via the chief super."

"And how do you feel about that?"

Harvey paused for a moment, unable to find the right words to express her frustration. "Well, between you, me and the four walls of this office, I've given my whole working life to the police, serving the community to the best of my capacity. Policing isn't what it used to be. Now it's about figures, meetings, pleasing crime commissioners, budgets and endless bureaucratic form filling. We were supposed to be impartial, but I'm not entirely sure we are these days," Harvey replied, as she swivelled in her chair to gaze back out of the window again.

The helplessness of the situation resonated with Scott. On the one hand, Harvey was a copper's copper, but she hardly fitted into the stereotypical image of a senior officer in the modern-day police force. She was cantankerous, argumentative, hated management meetings but was fiercely protective of her staff. She pretty much left him to get on with his job, which was a quality he did like in her, but she was hardly forward-thinking, progressive or dynamic, essential qualities the force were keen to identify.

"What are you going to do?"

"I've been asked to take some time out to consider my position."

Scott knew her position was untenable. They were effectively asking her to leave under her own steam with dignity or be booted out in humiliation.

Confused as to what would be the best option for CID, he considered with a slight tinge of guilt that perhaps fresh new blood wouldn't be such a bad thing. "Of course I wouldn't want you to go, Ma'am, I…we value your leadership, but I will support you in whatever decision you take."

Harvey didn't reply, her gaze firmly fixed through the window as she contemplated the situation.

Scott rose from his chair feeling less than comfortable with the stony silence in the room as he left Harvey with her thoughts. His slow walk back to CID, left him pondering whether or not Harvey was still going to be his commanding officer in the coming weeks.

———

THE MORNING WAS RACING AWAY from Scott. Even though the triple murder investigation was taking up much of his team's time, a bundle of other case files sat in his in tray waiting for reviews and instructions. He had no choice but to prioritise the workload, leaving many of the cases to take a back seat. That was the problem with modern-day detective work, far too much work, and not enough time.

Each case file took him a few hours to review. He'd closely review the action steps that his officers had taken on that case and identify if they had missed anything before leaving instructions over what action to take next. With more than a dozen files, he just didn't have the time to review them all now.

It always played on his mind. He felt personally responsible for the outcome of all the cases his team handled. Budgetary cuts across the force meant overtime wasn't an option, so they had to make do with the resources that they had available to them. Frustration tinged with guilt always sat heavily with him because there were victims and concerned loved ones waiting on any snippets of news. Their pain carried on every day, they couldn't walk away and close the door like Scott could at the end of his shift.

One other case plaguing him was that of a series of sexual assaults on students at Sussex University. A series of random attacks over the past three months had started to cause panic amongst the student population. Scott promised himself that as soon as his current murder investigation was wrapped up, he'd focus all his attention on catching the sexual predator loose on campus.

His stomach rumbled. He'd had nothing to eat since break-fast. A less than desirable grated cheese and lettuce baguette that he'd forgotten to eat yesterday would have to do as he flicked through the current case file.

Mike had already emailed him having finally got past the guardians at the Ministry of Defence. Their service records had all come back clean, no misconduct, no issues with tours of duty...nothing. Scott had hoped that their enquiries would have thrown something up, but he'd hit another brick wall. The team was working on identifying all known colleagues past and present of the victims in an effort to find a breakthrough. The school itself was under guard to protect staff and pupils, a job made easier after a trip to France had been hastily organised for the majority of the lower years, the sixth- formers remaining behind for exams.

Scott stood and stretched his arms high above his head. His shoulders cracked in approval. On the main floor, Abby was the sole member of his team still around and typing up the notes from their interview.

"Where's the others?"

"Unfortunately, Mike and Raj have officer safety training for the rest of the day, and Sian's about somewhere."

"OST...really? We're in the middle of a triple murder case, and they've been told to do officer safety...for fuck's sake."

Officer safety training was something that all officers went through annually, so there was little he could do about it. It was part of the force's policy of safeguarding their officers which he accepted was important. However, practising how to apprehend and secure suspects safely and quickly using handcuffs or batons, or how to handle public order incidents was something they all knew how to do competently. In his eyes, bureaucratic time-wasting like this was frustrating.

Matt Allen from forensics poked his head into the CID main office. His bright red chequered shirt stood out like a beacon against the blandness of the brown doors. "Ah, Scott, thought I'd find you here, mate. Can I have a quick word?"

Scott nodded towards his office just as Sian appeared. It didn't matter what the time of day or what the weather was doing, she was always impeccably turned out. A white, short-sleeved blouse and dark grey skirt gave her a smart, professional appearance. A look that Scott felt said a lot about her outlook and approach to work.

"Sian, do me a favour. Mike's not around, so can you look at the schooling of our three victims? Mike's already looked at their time together in the army, and turned up nothing. So let's go back even further. They all went through Edmunston-Hunt School, so have a look and see if anything else stands out. See if there's anyone else that they had associations with. Maybe we've missed something."

Sian nodded, as she chewed on the frame of her glasses. "Yes, Guv."

Scott closed his office door behind him as Matt helped himself to a chair and slouched back in it.

"Make yourself at home..." Scott said, pushing Matt's shoes off his desk.

"Oh, I was just getting comfortable."

"Not in here, you aren't, mate," Scott replied, running his hands over his face. "Tell me you've got some news...good news...any news..."

"Er, well now that you're unavailable, you're no longer the most eligible male in the station, so it means I can sidle into the top spot."

"I meant proper news," Scott hissed through pursed lips.

"Well, yes and no..."

Scott groaned. "Go on."

"Cara's flat..."

Scott leant forward, now interested, and alarmed as it dawned on him that he'd not once texted or called her today to make sure she was all right. *Shit.*

"We didn't pick up any identifiable prints from Cara's flat other than hers and yours I'm afraid." Matt paused still glancing down at the brown file on his lap. "But we did find traces of semen on her underwear...and the door handle of the bedroom."

Scott's eyes widened. "Don't look at me."

"Don't worry. I've checked your DNA profile already. It's not yours...yours was only on her lower bed sheet."

Scott looked suitably embarrassed and cleared his throat.

"The door was levered open with a flat instrument, probably a crowbar, pry bar or something of that nature. That's all we've come up with so far," Matt said, rising from his chair and heading back towards the door. "We're running checks now on the semen sample...I'll give you a shout as soon as I know more."

"Okay, keep me posted." Scott thanked Matt for his swift attention and discreet feedback. *Someone's got it in for her*, he thought as he punched out a quick text on his phone to her.

Hope you're okay. Sorry for not checking in sooner, bit manic here. S x

31

The day had dragged on. Another mind-numbing day of teaching young adults had taken its toll. Over recent years, Laurence Goddard found his patience being tested more frequently. In his eyes, getting delinquent adults in their twenties ready to sit their GCSE English exams was a thankless task. *Those idiots should have paid attention in school.* But then again it paid his bills.

Goddard had lost count of the number of times he'd discussed the concept of themes in *Of Mice and Men* or *Pride and Prejudice*. The room felt stuffy. His small office was situated off the main teaching room, with no windows or natural light. The faded white walls seemed to close in on him, crushing him from all four sides, squeezing the breath out of his chest.

His mind spun, his eyes strained to focus on his best friend Jack. Tonight it was just the pair of them. Jack helped to take away his pain, his fears, but they didn't stop the trembling in his fingers as he held his hand out in front of him.

The trembling in his hands had worsened in recent months. He'd kept meaning to make an appointment with his GP, but fear stole his courage every time. His chair squeaked as he leant forward pushing the untidy mess of files across his desk, an attempt on his part to create some space. But it wasn't really space he needed on his desk, but space in his mind, space to contemplate and make some sense of the confusion that reigned around him.

Sweat beaded from his forehead, zigzagging down his temples before racing into his long sideburns. The clamminess of the office and the lack of fresh air made the room feel like a sauna. His back felt damp, beads of sweat ran down the centre of his chest to his navel. He was a mess and he knew it, but there was nothing he could do…nothing anyone could do. They were all gone. If he lay low, he might be okay. If he watched his back, he might live.

His eyelids fluttered closed, the combination of tiredness and his friend Jack slowly taking him to a place where he could escape his demons. His mouth was bone dry and his breath reeked of alcohol. He'd had enough for today and wouldn't stay much longer before heading home.

Home…Did I really have a home? He'd already made the decision to go back and teach his wife another lesson. He'd enjoyed her futile attempts at fending him off. A few slaps and punches would be enough to beat her into submission again. He felt manly, more in control when he had her pinned down. At least that was one part of his life that he could control. At least he didn't have to pay for it, *she would put out whether she liked it or not*, he thought.

There was a pause of a few seconds between the door flying open and his mind registering commotion behind him. His body moved in slow motion as he turned in his chair unable to comprehend exactly what was happening. It wasn't long before he realised it was his turn.

His whole body and mind swayed as he stood up, the room spinning like a centrifugal force around him. He was defenceless; he was weak...too weak to even open his mouth. He lazily brought his arms up to his side to surrender in a comical way that would only have been seen in the old cops and robbers movies.

"Youuu fuckerrr," Goddard slurred, as his eyes rolled around desperately trying to lock on to the intruder in front of him. "Whooo do you think youuu fucking areee?" he said as his head dropped to one side.

The intruder, dressed from head to toe in black, stood there rigid and rippling with menace. His bravery had grown over the week. Fear once had gripped him, once had ruled his life in equal measures with anger, but not anymore.

"*Ignavus iners timidius tu mori debes.*"

"COME AGAIN?" Goddard replied, as his eyes narrowed in confusion.

"Did you think you could get away with it? Surely, you must have realised that I would come looking for you," the man said.

Goddard sluggishly lunged forward. His mind wanted to strike first, but his body was slow in getting the message. His fist lazily swung in the air towards the intruder. He was far off the mark; the momentum of his swinging arm rotated his body in a wide arc that sent him off-balance.

It was all the attacker needed as he reared up behind

Goddard. The flash of white plastic tape caught the light, each end wrapped several times in each hand. He pinned Goddard face down across his desk as he threw the tape over Goddard's head and dragged it down to his neck.

He pulled hard, the tape slowly cutting off Goddard's means of survival. Goddard attempted to steady himself with one hand, the other desperately grabbing and clawing at the tourniquet that slowly starved him of oxygen. He flailed his arms in a dire attempt to free himself. Folders and files were pushed and thrown off his desk, scattering paper across the floor. His teeth snarled as his lips pulled back. With jaws clamped tight, spittle seeped out between his stained, rotten teeth. Red blotches tainted his skin; white spots filled his vision as the world around him started to darken.

Triumph enveloped the attacker as he breathed in a satisfied sigh. This had been the easiest one so far. Goddard's body slumped and folded in on itself, falling to a contorted ball on the floor.

SCOTT WAS ABOUT to start an evening briefing when the call came through that a body had been found in one of the serviced offices on the Knoll Business Centre in Hove. Scott, Abby and Sian raced over to Hove, gathering details en-route about the incident. A cleaner had stumbled across the body and paramedics had confirmed the victim was deceased on arrival but still warm. The team was optimistic. The incident was fresh, and with SOCO and Cara en-route, the first few hours after a body were found were critical in any investigation.

The scene had already been secured by the time Scott arrived, the familiar blue and white police tape cordoning off the entrance to the business park as the outer cordon. Scott had called ahead to instruct uniformed officers to start searching the locality in case the perpetrator was still hovering. Scott had found that in some cases, a perpetrator would lurk about the crime scene, watching from a distance with a macabre curiosity as the emergency services arrived on scene, as if teasing them to *come and find me, catch me if you can.*

Knoll Business Centre, situated on the western outskirts of Hove, didn't have the glamour of modern serviced units. It was housed in an old 1900s boy's primary school set behind tall railings just off the Old Shoreham Road. The drab and dreary external brown brick façade replaced by modern bright, white interiors, polished wooden parquet floors and funky-coloured furniture.

Scott had noticed as he pulled up outside the business centre that traffic had started to crawl along the busy dual carriageway as drivers slowed in curiosity at the large police presence. He'd need to get some traffic units to manage traffic flow if an accident was to be avoided.

Emily Bates, who had found the victim, sat in the back of a patrol car visibly upset. She held a tissue to her mouth, her face puffy, her eyes red and swollen from her crying. Scott instructed Sian to take a statement from her, and Abby to talk to other business unit holders that might still be around. He also instructed her to get onto the caretaker of the centre to see if anything was noticed the CCTV he'd noticed at the entrance.

Local officers had directed him to Goddard's offices. Along the way, Scott had taken note of other businesses that occupied the centre. A cake making business proudly showed off its name across its double doors, *The dough knot* made him smile. He wondered how people had the ability to be so creative with business names.

Further along the corridor was a room with desks and terminals. The sign on the outside of the door indicated it was a flexible co-working lounge where individuals could rent a desk. Other signs indicated meeting rooms, light industrial units and studios scattered amongst the two quad-rangles that formed the centre.

An inner cordon of blue and white police tape signalled the location of the Goddard's unit. There was urgency in Scott's steps as he peered into Goddard's office. With the death being so recent, the next few hours were crucial, and hopefully CCTV would be his saviour. Two SOCOs were already present and starting their preliminary analysis, painstakingly photographing the scene, the victim and his surroundings.

Scott was hit with a warm blast of air from the stuffy room. High temperatures, sweat and the stench of alcohol led him to pinch his nose. Cramped conditions meant the SOCOs had little space to move around the room, let alone around the body. He could see the outline of a man slumped on the floor. The body was curled into a foetal position, his white shirt rippled across his back, still damp from sweat. The end of a red tie poked out from beneath the body, and Scott spotted a pair of thin-rimmed glasses that lay a few inches away from the man's head.

He wouldn't be able to inspect the body for the time being which frustrated him, but he could live with that. Another officer had informed him that the pathologist was on her way but had been held up in the evening rush hour traffic.

Cause of death would have to wait, but paramedics had confirmed evidence of a fresh ligature mark around the neck with localised minor bleeding.

"Guv," Abby said as she appeared over his shoulder.

"I've spoken to the caretaker. The unit was rented out to a Laurence Goddard. He ran a private tutoring business. He's been renting it for the past few years, and paid his rent on time," she said, glancing at her notebook. "He's getting me a copy of the CCTV footage. Apparently, there are cameras at every entrance."

Scott hummed in agreement but still cast an eye over the body. His thoughts over whether this death in suspicious circumstances was connected to his ongoing investigation were soon confirmed as he glanced over his shoulder and behind the door to see a row of certificates and framed photos, presumably of Goddard.

One particular photo caught his attention. A gold-framed photo hung there, identical to the one he'd seen in Edmunston-Hunt of the current serving teachers. This time it was of a bespectacled man with a large forehead from a receding hairline. The gold inscription beneath the photo read 'Laurence Goddard, English Teacher, Edmunston-Hunt School'.

32

The scenes-of-crime officer had been able to retrieve a wallet from a jacket that hung off the back of the chair. The photo ID on a driving licence seemed to correlate with the victim. Scott's next task was to get the body formally identified. He stood in a small close just off the Dyke Road. It was a street with modern town houses with bay-fronted windows, and Juliet balconies on the first floor. Low-level laurel bushes framed the front of each house neatly tucking in under the ground-floor window ledges.

Scott and Abby checked the address to confirm they were standing outside the correct property before Scott poked the doorbell. They could hear padded footsteps in the hallway, and then the flick of a switch, the light from the hallway peeking out from around the edges of the door.

A woman with brown, highlighted shoulder-length hair answered the door. She was wrapped in a pink, fluffy dressing gown which had small red hearts randomly dotted over it. Scott could see cream-coloured, silk pyjamas. It wasn't what she was wearing that caught his attention, but what appeared to be heavy bruising on her chin, cheek and around her left eye. She shielded her face with a hand, as she looked nervously between the two visitors on a doorstep.

"I'm Detective Inspector Baker and this is my colleague Detective Sergeant Trent. We are from Brighton CID," he said as both officers held up their warrant cards for inspection.

The woman's nervous eyes darted between the warrant cards and the officers. "What's this about?" her voice trembled as she wrapped her arms around her chest.

"Can you confirm your name for us, madam?" Abby asked.

She cleared her throat. "I'm…Samantha Goddard…can I ask what this is about?"

Scott and Abby exchanged a glance. "May we come in for a moment?"

Samantha Goddard waved them into a modern but narrow hallway. Birch laminate flooring offered a crisp, clean look to go alongside the light cream walls and white skirting and coving. She led them into a room on the left and offered them a seat. It was a warm comfortable lounge with modern contemporary low-back fabric sofas neatly angled, facing a large flat-screen TV fixed to the chimney breast.

Scott and Abby took the sofa whilst Samantha Goddard sat on the opposite sofa facing them. She rested her elbows on her knees and cupped her hands beneath her chin.

"We are here about Laurence Goddard. What's your relationship to him?" Scott said.

Samantha wrung her hands, her eyes darting between the two officers. She licked her lips nervously.

"He's…my husband."

Samantha felt panic rise inside as her thoughts swirled. *Were they here about her assault? Had a neighbour called out of concern? Maybe someone had heard her screams? What do I say if they ask me about my bruises?*

"And when did you last see him?"

"Erm…this morning before he left for work."

Abby scribbled notes but couldn't help but notice how the woman clenched her hands so tight that they paled a pasty white.

"And where does he work, Mrs Goddard?"

"He has a private tutoring business at the Knoll Business Centre."

Scott gave Abby the slightest of nods. "Mrs Goddard, there isn't an easy way of saying this, but I'm sorry to say that a body was found just a few hours ago, and we believe it's your husband. We found a driving licence in his name in a jacket, and a picture seems to resemble the victim. Of course, if you're willing, we would need you or another next of kin to formally identify that it is your husband."

Samantha Goddard fell silent, staring at an imaginary spot on the floor in front of her. Her eyes searched for answers; her brow furrowed. Silence filled the room.

Scott and Abby closely observed Samantha's reaction. Relatives of victims often reacted in different ways. Some cried hysterically, others displayed anger and some fell into a silent shock. Samantha Goddard fell into the last camp.

Scott nodded in the direction of the kitchen telling Abby to rustle up some tea. "Mrs Goddard, are you okay?"

"He's gone…" she said in bewilderment.

"At the moment, we believe it is your husband. And we're very sorry for your loss."

"He's gone…he's finally gone. I'm free," she said, her eyes darting around the floor as her mind processed the news.

Perplexed by her answer Scott probed further. "I'm sorry, Mrs Goddard. Can you clarify what you meant when you said 'I'm free'?"

"I'm…*free*," she said in slow, soft monotone slur. Her eyes levelled with Scott, pointing towards her bruised and battered face. "I'm free of this. He can't hurt me anymore."

"Are you telling me that Laurence Goddard assaulted you and caused those injuries?"

She nodded in reply as she looked down to hide her face.

Scott didn't know if her reticence was out of embarrassment or shame.

Abby appeared in the doorway of the lounge. "Guv, a quick word."

Scott made his excuses and joined Abby in the hallway and followed her into the kitchen. Abby picked up a newspaper from the kitchen table and handed it to Scott. *The Argus* front page from earlier in the week had reported on the death of Christopher Johnson. It wasn't the story that caught Scott's attention, but the fact that the picture of Johnson had been circled in red marker and a few small red crosses had been placed beneath it.

Scott looked back at Abby as she raised her eyebrows in response. "You might want to see this as well," she said, handing him a note.

It was a handwritten note.

My darling Christopher. I can't believe you've left me. I'm so heartbroken. S xx

"The handwriting looks pretty similar"

"That's what I was thinking, Guv."

With the note in hand, Scott walked back into the lounge and sat opposite Samantha Goddard. "Mrs Goddard, did you write this?" Scott asked, holding the note in front of her.

She briefly glanced up at the note, her eyes widened in surprise, before staring back down towards the floor. She nodded once.

"Who is Christopher?"

When she wasn't forthcoming with a reply, Scott decided to push. "Mrs Goddard?"

She opened her mouth but paused for a moment as she looked away, a tear escaping down her cheek. "Christopher Johnson…"

They had come to break some devastating news but had stumbled upon the writer of the note they'd recovered from the first murder, and pending her confirmation, probably the second murder.

"Mrs Goddard, I'll arrange for an officer to take you shortly to identify the body. After that, we'll need to talk to you at the station about this message," Scott said, waving the note.

THE TEAM BUZZED with the news of a small breakthrough in the case. Raj and Mike had returned from officer safety training, and together with Sian were listening to details from Abby.

"So do we think Samantha Goddard was also involved with Giles Rochester?" Raj asked.

"It's quite likely. I'm just about to go down and interview her, so will know shortly."

"Saucy tart, married and shagging two other blokes," Mike uttered under his breath.

His comment was swiftly admonished. "Any further wisecracks like that from you, Mike, and you'll have the guv to answer to," Abby said.

Mike raised a brow in defiance as Abby headed off to the interview suite, knowing full well he should have kept his mouth shut even if he'd meant it.

33

Samantha Goddard had been given time to dress before being taken to the mortuary where she'd confirmed the body was indeed her husband. The female officer accompanying her had reported to Scott that Mrs Goddard had expressed no emotion on seeing the body, or since.

Scott and Abby deliberated outside the interview suite. Abby leant up against the wall. She yawned and stretched as she looked up towards the ceiling. Clocking off time had come and gone a long time ago when her shift had ended at six p.m. It was shifts like this that wore her down. She had frantically called in favours from grandparents so the kids were looked after. With a fresh body and Samantha Goddard's admission to the note, it was going to be a long night. With her grey suit now crumpled, her brown hair hanging loosely, the hairband discarded a long time ago, she was in desperate need of a shower and her bed.

"Do you want to lead on this one, Abby?"

"Fine with me," she replied as she pushed the door open, stifling another yawn.

Now that Samantha Goddard had had an opportunity to wear something more appropriate, Abby saw a different woman. She had initially had her hair up in a bunch with no make-up when they had visited earlier in the evening. Now her hair was neatly combed down in a long bob to her shoulders with a subtle side parting. Golden highlights came off the parting offering a contrast to her light brown hair. She wore a light blue blouse with dark-coloured jeans. Abby couldn't help but notice that despite her bruises, she had a round pretty face with dark brown eyes.

"Once again, we're sorry for your loss. Samantha, your husband was attacked in his office. Had he been in trouble recently, or has he mentioned anything about being worried?"

Samantha sat upright in the chair facing them, her arms wrapped tightly around her chest. "No, he…we never talked much," she replied softly.

"Had he been in any trouble in the past that you know of?"

Samantha shook her head slowly, unable to offer anything of substance. Her eyes slowly moved from Abby to the table and back. Her eyes darted around the room, as she shrugged her shoulders in bewilderment.

"Can you describe your relationship with Laurence?" Abby asked.

Samantha paused as her mind fought to find the right words. "We didn't have a relationship. You call this a relationship?" she said, pointing to her bruised face. "After he left Edmunston, things were okay. He was excited about setting up his tutoring business. More recently he changed. He became moody. He'd come home late. He was always drunk. A drink was never far from his hand."

"And you can't explain why there was a change in his behaviour?"

"No. He became horrible. He was always angry, really angry, almost resentful. He'd shout a lot, drink alone, throw stuff around the house and then come upstairs and well…" Samantha's voice trailed off to whisper. "I tried to avoid him as much as I could. He was a horrible, nasty person by the end. I couldn't take it anymore. After he raped me, I just wanted it over. He can't hurt me anymore, and I'm pleased about that."

"Wanted it over enough to harm him?"

Samantha looked up, her brows furrowed. "No…no, of course not. Are you thinking that I had anything to do with this?" she protested.

Abby pushed. "Samantha, we have to explore every avenue, and you had enough cause to want him out of your life."

"Yes, I did want him out of my life, but that was it, just out of my life and gone…just gone, away, away from me, but certainly not dead. I didn't deserve to be his punchbag," she defended.

Abby nodded in sympathy as Scott watched Samantha. Her pain and anguish were clearly evident as Abby questioned her in depth.

"What was your relationship to Christopher Johnson?" Abby asked.

Samantha stared into a corner of the room, her eyes lost in despair and shock. "He loved me; we were lovers."

"How long were you in a relationship with him?"

Samantha smiled, as she thought about happier times with her lover: their walks across the Sussex Downs hand in hand, cosy meals in remote Sussex pubs where no one would know them, and of course their passionate lovemaking. "About two years."

"How did it start?" Scott asked.

"We had a school barbecue which we were invited to. Laurence as usual got drunk and made a fool of himself. He turned on me and pinned me by the throat to a tree. He was so angry. He said I was dressed like a tart; that I was desperate for it." Her eyes became damp. "Chris saw what was happening and stepped in. He organised a taxi to take Laurence home, whilst I stayed back. Chris took care of me, made sure I was all right. He was a handsome, caring man…"

"And you began a relationship after that point?" Scott asked.

Samantha nodded in silence.

"Were you having a relationship with Giles Rochester?"

"Yes."

"At the same time as your relationship with Christopher?" Abby prompted.

"Yes."

"Was there any particular reason that you began a relationship with Giles?"

Samantha turned to Abby. "He was a lovely, kind, caring man, too, I guess. A man with a big heart. There's nothing he wouldn't do for me. He had this cheeky confident smile, and well, I couldn't help myself. He was always there for me. I could call him whenever I felt down, and he'd always find a way of cheering me up. He hated the way Laurence treated me. On more than one occasion he wanted us to go public and begged me to leave Laurence."

"So you were having two relationships and your husband didn't know about either?" Abby probed.

"I don't think so. He was too wrapped up in his own world. If he'd found out he would have beaten me senseless. And not because I'd cheated on him, it would have been out of pride and control. I think he felt like I was his property."

"Were you not worried that Christopher and Giles would find out about each other considering they both knew each other?"

Samantha gazed intently at Abby, her mind numb. "I guess I'd never thought of that. I guess I was grateful that people cared enough to want to be with me." She shrugged.

"Why didn't you leave if he was so abusive towards you?" Abby asked.

Samantha shook her head, her mind searching for a valid reason as to why she stayed. Confusion clouded her thoughts. Her mind was a whirlwind of doubts, justifications and questions. *Why did I stay? Did I love him? Perhaps I was too scared to leave? Where would I have gone?*

"I wish I knew. I don't know why I stayed. I guess a part of me still loved him. He was my husband. He was stressed.

Don't they say that you always take your stress out on those closest to you?"

Abby interlocked her fingers in front of her and placed them on the desk between her and Samantha. From experience in the job, Abby knew that many partners involved in relationships with domestic violence realised it wasn't simply a matter of walking out the door. Leaving was a process.

It was difficult for many people to understand why a person would stay. Every case was different and there could be many reasons they stayed. Abby knew from her DV training that strong emotional and psychological forces kept the victim tied to the abuser. Sometimes basic situational realities like a lack of money keep the victim from leaving. They could convince themselves that their abusive partner would change because of their remorse and promises to stop the violence.

She'd even known in several harrowing cases that the victim had stayed out of fear because their partner had threatened to kill them if the abuse was reported to anyone.

Victims often felt fearful of change, many carried guilt that it was their fault the relationship had come to violence. They felt helpless and trapped, with nowhere to go. Many women were worried about the harm to their kids, or just plainly believed that the police wouldn't take their claims seriously…especially if the victims were males.

Sadly, in Abby's view, a domestic violence victim like Samantha could see an affair as an essential lifeline. Someone who could be an ally to her, who cared about her, and gave her purpose and made her feel good about herself. A lover who made her feel wanted…not neglected. The violence and the mental and physical abuse had driven Samantha to seek solace, support and love from those who offered it, just to validate her own self-worth and existence. With her fragile confidence and low self-esteem, she needed to confirm that she was loveable, desirable and wanted.

"Perhaps but beating you black and blue is a step too far in my book. It's common assault."

"Did you write these notes?" Scott asked, holding up several clear evidence bags with handwritten notes that they'd recovered from the properties of Johnson and Rochester.

Samantha gave the bags a cursory look before nodding. "Yes, I wrote those. I know what you're thinking. That I'm like some black widow that uses people, but you have to understand, I needed them, they needed me, they loved me, and I loved them. I've felt so empty inside for so many years, when they came along, they made me feel alive. They made me feel wanted. They gave me all the things Laurence couldn't give me. Perhaps I was being greedy."

"Where were you earlier this afternoon, Samantha?" asked Abby.

The question took her by surprise. "Are you still thinking I had something to do with this?" she asked with a raised voice. The first sign of emotion either officer had witnessed.

"Well you had a good reason. Your two lovers are dead. Your husband drove you away, and you've suffered abuse at his hands. Perhaps you were angry over everything you've lost?"

Samantha shook her head vehemently and denied any involvement in Laurence's death. "Yes, I hated what he'd done to me. He was a bastard to me, but I could never kill him, or anyone for that matter."

"Mrs Goddard?" Abby asked again.

After a lengthy, reflective pause, she spoke again. "Belinda Evans…yes, Belinda, my neighbour, can vouch for seeing me this afternoon. We chatted after Belinda had arrived at my door with a parcel that had been delivered to her house accidentally."

"Is there anything else that you can think of that may help us piece together why your husband was attacked?" Scott asked.

Samantha rested her chin in the palm of a hand as her mind tracked back looking for answers. *Had she seen anything? Had anyone been lurking around outside that looked out of place? Had there been any crank calls to the house? Had Laurence said anything out of the ordinary? Think! Think!* Her mind raced. It all seemed a blur. "Wait…yes, a few weeks ago he collapsed in bed drunk again. A few hours later I was woken by his restless sleep. He muttered something. He said, 'I'm sorry. They made me. It went too far'."

34

A week had passed since the investigation had begun. Scott and his team were no closer to identifying the killer. He had to admit that a few loose ends had been tied up, but he wasn't even touching the sides of the investigation. With pressure mounting from senior officers, there was a real risk of the investigation being passed over to a new senior investigating officer if results weren't imminent.

If there was one thing Scott hated more than anything else, it was failure. It wasn't a prospect he had dared to entertain. He would go above and beyond to get a result in whatever he did whether it was personal or professional. He would put in extra hours to get the job done, and he would push harder in his fitness regime if it meant he'd stay in peak condition. It even extended to when he sat his inspector exams. He had locked himself away in his bedroom for two weeks and learnt PACE, the Police and Criminal Evidence Act 1984, parrot-fashion in order to pass.

His sense of failure was never more poignant than the day

he'd lost his beloved family. His life was turned upside as he stood there helpless, witnessing his wife and daughter mowed down in a hit-and-run accident. He should have been able to protect them. It was his duty to protect those he loved most, and he'd failed. It was a heavy, dark burden that weighed him down every waking minute and haunted his dreams at night.

At the time of the accident, friends and colleagues rallied around to reassure him that he wasn't to blame. After all, it was an accident he couldn't have prevented. But they weren't inside his head; they couldn't see and feel the mental torture that ripped him to shreds. How could they? They meant well, but it didn't make things any easier.

The sense of guilt he felt was now his life sentence. It was the fear of failure that spurred him on.

The morning hadn't started the way he'd planned. A briefing for nine a.m. had been pencilled into his diary. DCI Harvey and Superintendent Meadows had insisted on Scott giving them an update first thing ahead of their meeting with Assistant Chief Constable Anne Grayling. The pressure was mounting, with both Scott and DCI Jane Harvey becoming decidedly more uncomfortable as the case progressed.

Chief Constable Lennon was clearly worried about how he and his force looked in front of his Masonic members who had a vested interest in Edmunston-Hunt School and were now asking discreet questions. And for this reason Lennon was demanding answers.

A surprise call from Mary Harrison, the deputy principal of Edmunston-Hunt, had meant a change to his plans as he made his way over to Ditchling to meet her. As far as he was aware, she'd been signed off with stress following recent events and was due back to work imminently. A curious voicemail message from her about a development with Matthew Edrington had piqued his interest.

Scott had pleaded with DCI Harvey to cover for him and spin any old yarn about being called away to deal with a development in the case. At this stage, he couldn't be certain if there was anything of value that Ms Harrison had to offer or whether it had any bearing on his ongoing investigations. It was the fact that she had mentioned Matthew that had compelled him to follow through.

The boy was troubled; Scott was sure of that. He'd witnessed the intimidation that Matthew had faced, and for that reason, he couldn't stand by. Maybe it was the paternalistic side of him, but the one thing he knew was that he hated to see any child suffer. His last big case involving the death of Libby Stevens still affected him and the team even though they didn't talk about it.

They were still human after all. They had feelings, and were deeply moved by Libby's death and the horrors that Sabina and Kelly, two girls who were trafficked and abused, had endured. They were crimes that had robbed young girls of their innocence and childhood. Scott couldn't wait until the crimes and the ruthless individuals behind them had their day in court.

Scott parked just inside the gates of the school as Ms Harrison had instructed. Her unusual request only fuelled his inquisitive mind and the nosiness that all coppers seemed to have inbuilt like a sixth sense. She'd specifically asked him to park out of sight of the main building. Then he was to make his way along the front perimeter of the school to the walled gardens on the right flank where she'd be waiting. In any other situation, Scott thought that the instructions could have been those shared between two clandestine lovers.

As he made his way through the gardens, he noticed that each plant, each shrub and each neatly pruned bush had a brass name plate on the floor in front it. Scott was hopeless when it came to matters of the garden. He couldn't tell a tulip from a crocus, or a daffodil from a dahlia, and found himself walking past an array of names that were lost on him. Wisteria, clematis, star jasmine, they were just plants to him. An infusion of floral scents that surrounded him.

Navigating around the lily pond that formed the central feature, Mary Harrison came into view, partially obscured behind a large tree that offered a darkened space beneath it. Not far behind her, stood the small figure of Matthew Edrington. Scott immediately noticed a darkened area beneath one of Matthew's eyes.

"Thank you for coming so quickly, Inspector," Mary Harrison said, glancing over her shoulder towards Matthew.

"Your message sounded important?" Scott replied. "Are you okay, Matthew?"

The boy stood quietly in the background, his big, doughy eyes bloodshot, a pained expression etched deeply on his face as he pursed his lips tightly. Matthew nodded once as he held his hands in a ball pressed firmly into his chest.

"As you know, I've been off, Inspector. I've found it incredibly stressful following the death of Mr Johnson. But needs must and I'm trying to get back into some sense of normality, but as you can imagine, that's a little hard to do when members of staff are dying around you."

Mary Harrison paused awkwardly when she realised that she'd probably said that a little too loud in front of a pupil as her eyes shifted towards Matthew, who had now inched closer to her. Beckoning Matthew, she placed a protective arm around the boy's frail thin shoulders and pulled him in towards her.

"Matthew came to see me yesterday and confided in me that he's being bullied…and I'm not talking about the usual name-calling or barging into you in the corridor type of thing. Quite frankly, I'm deeply upset by what he's been experiencing and the deliberate oversight by my colleagues. I just felt I needed to take this further. I'm afraid to say, Inspector, that from what I've heard since I've been here, the school has a reputation for bullying and shall we say *taking things further*."

Scott nodded slowly as he shoved his hands in his trouser pockets. A look of concern washed over his face as he looked down at Matthew. "Is this true, Matthew?"

The boy nodded hesitantly as he looked up towards Ms Harrison for reassurance, and a much-needed hug.

In the silence of the walled gardens, Matthew's faint voice was hard to hear as he slowly shuffled on the spot, his mind a melting pot of confusion, sadness and fear.

"I don't want anyone to get in trouble. I just want it to stop," he said, his voice slow and high-pitched.

"It's a very brave thing for you to come forward. Often the first step is the hardest, but I'm here to help you…we both are," Scott replied, glancing towards Mary Harrison who nodded reassuringly. "So how about you tell me what's been going on?"

35

M atthew Edrington cast a disconsolate figure as he sat between Scott and Mary Harrison on a stone bench. With his hands tucked firmly beneath his thighs and head bowed, Matthew nervously swung his feet back and forth as he stared at the ground looking decidedly unsure of himself.

"Tell the inspector everything you told me, Matthew. It's okay; I promise," Mary Harrison said with a reassuring tap on the boy's arm.

Scott had briefly seen Mary Harrison at the start of the investigation. He'd forgotten how her soft, well-spoken southern English accent felt calm and reassuring. Scott had to admit that her whole persona was appealing on several fronts. She would easily fall into the category of a typical English rose with her brunette hair, long and flowing with wispy ends that framed her thin face. A creamy-white, blemish-free complexion was offset by red cheeks and dark, warm brown eyes.

"Call me Scott," he offered.

For children, titles like inspector and even constable could be daunting, off-putting and create unhelpful barriers. Children needed to feel safe, and from previous experience, Scott knew that remaining silent and giving the child space to think and express their feelings and experiences was vital.

Matthew's gazed remained firmly fixed to the ground as the tips of his shoes flicked small stones that formed the path that weaved in and around the fixed planted areas.

To gently prompt Matthew, Scott asked, "How did you get that black eye?"

After a lengthy pause, Matthew said, "They did it...they pinned me to the wall and punched me."

"Well, why don't you tell me what they've been doing?" Scott asked.

For the time being he deliberately held back from asking who had hit him for fear that Matthew would clam up straight away if put on the spot.

"They've been picking on me. Wherever I turn...they're there. It started off with a bit of pushing as they walked past, then it went to pulling pages out of my books...and then when I said I'd tell our housemaster, they..."

Matthew clenched his jaws desperately fighting the urge to cry as he swung his legs furiously. His whole body ached with sadness and fear. He'd lived off adrenaline for months, his body on a heightened state of alert for the next attack.

He craved sleep, but fear kept him awake for hours every night, the bedcovers tightly pulled up under his chin, his senses ready to register any change in his environment. He'd heard it all, a creaky floorboard in the corridor, the soft sound of approaching footsteps and heavy breathing. Just thinking about it turned his stomach into knots and parched his mouth.

His first words seemed to be the catalyst to releasing months of pent-up frustration and sadness that had haunted him.

"They what?…" Scott asked gently.

Matthew looked out of the corner of his eyes towards Scott, it was just a brief second, but he felt he could trust the officer.

"They just picked on me all the time. First it was name-calling. They said I looked like a girl. They called me pussy, said I didn't deserve to grow up a man…" His voice trailed off.

"Go on, Matthew. You're doing really well," Ms Harrison reassured him.

"After sports lessons, they'd taunt me in the showers. They'd take photos of me and steal my towel, saying stuff like I'm going to get bum fucked because I was gay."

Scott listened to Matthew's story. The boy's plight touched a nerve in him. "Why would they say something like that?" Kids could be so cruel.

"Because of this," Matthew added, pointing to his ginger mop of hair. "I'm not an athlete. I'm not strong enough to play rugby. I can't compete against the others. I'm like the odd one out here, and because of that they picked on me. They'd come into my dorm and do things to me. I slept in a wet bed more times than I can remember…"

Scott glanced at Mary Harrison, sadness made her face heavy, her eyes moistened. "Listen, Matthew, I'm sorry you've been through so much. I only wish you'd spoken to someone earlier. It's not right that they've singled you out like this. No one should be bullied."

Matthew shrugged heavily as he slumped, his shoulders drooping forward. He shook his head. "It's not just me. It's been happening for years, since the school was founded. I'm not the first to go through this. It's my turn I guess. It was my turn to get black-balled." He sighed as if he'd been expecting this at some stage in his time at Edmunston-Hunt.

Scott turned towards Matthew, his eyes narrowed. "What do you mean black-balled?"

Matthew hesitated for a moment, his eyes darting from left to right as he sought answers to Scott's question. The events of that night haunted him. He'd been humiliated, his body abused and his mind torn apart. He replied in a soft, stuttering voice.

"They'd taken me from my bed to a room. It's in the old part of the building. I wanted to run, I really did, but I was too scared and they gripped my arms and dragged me there. I begged them to let me go, but they just laughed." Matthew began to cry, tears collecting on the tip of his nose. Like a slow dripping tap, each drop fell in to his lap.

"They tied me by my ankles and wrists. It hurt, Scott. The more I tried to get free, the more it hurt. They punched me and laughed. I wanted to run away, but even if I could, I had nowhere to go, nowhere to hide."

Mary Harrison placed her arm around Matthew once again, pulling him close protectively, like a mother would. In the absence of family, Mary fitted the role perfectly, Scott thought.

"They…they…then put hot shoe wax on my balls. It hurt so much Ms Harrison," Matthew said as he cried into her chest.

Mary Harrison pursed her lips and winced in sympathy at Matthew's last recollection. She stroked his hair, apologising, promising him that it was going to be okay.

Scott gently reassured the boy with a few taps on his shoulder. This was a clear case of assault in Scott's eyes. He was lost for words. As an officer that had seen and witnessed the most heinous of crimes, it was those involving children that affected him the most. His whole team was still coming to terms with what they'd uncovered in the child trafficking case, and here he was now listening to the premeditated intimidation and bullying of a small boy unable to stand up for himself.

Scott was furious that a boy under the care of an expensive boarding school had been let down by the system, and by people who were there to guide and protect him. The school was there to give him the best start in life, to put in place the skills, attributes and abilities that would shape Matthew's journey in life. However, the opposite was now the case. He'd been left a fragile, traumatised and frightened boy. And something Matthew had just mentioned got Scott thinking.

WALKING through the large front doors of Edmunston-Hunt School was becoming far too frequent. On each occasion, frustration had tinged his visit with the lack of cooperation, the tense atmosphere, and the sheer bloody-mindedness of Collier. On this occasion, it was no different. The school was eerily silent as his footsteps clicked on the tile floor and echoed around him. But to his surprise Mrs Hilary, Collier's sidekick and gatekeeper, appeared to be less than her usual cantankerous, bullish self. If anything, he'd swear that she was in a flap.

"Where's Collier?" Scott demanded as he strode up to her desk.

"I...I don't know. You see he hasn't turned up...I...I just don't know where he is," she stuttered as she nervously fiddled with her pearl choker.

"And you've checked his office?"

"Yes...of course I did," she replied defensively, as if Scott had asked something preposterous. "In all the time I've known Adrian...I mean Mr Collier, he's never not turned up. Even if he was unwell, he'd be here bright and early, his eyes full of life, his head held high, his big strong shoulders pinned back, looking perfectly turned out..." Mrs Hilary suddenly stopped mid-sentence as her cheeks flushed a deep red.

"And you have no idea where he is? Did you check with our officer outside?"

"Yes...No...No, he's not answering his phones. I was just about to go over to his residence to check up on him," she replied, hastily reaching for her handbag.

With his suspicions raised, Scott left her with the clear instruction to call him the minute she had found Collier or had further news on his whereabouts.

36

"Get me a black coffee will you, Raj?" Scott shouted across the floor as he marched into his office to throw his jacket over the spare chair. Frustration and anger in equal measures started to piss him off as he headed back out towards the incident board.

The pictures of the victims stared back at him. Crime scene photos, post-mortem photos and brief descriptions of the victims were spread out across the whiteboard. He still felt like the team was skirting around the edges of the investigation. Something was being overlooked, something glaringly obvious that once identified would break this case apart. Various elements just rolled over in his mind. *Cowards, white feather, black balling, bullying...why?*

"Okay, listen team, we need to break this case, and something I heard today makes me think that the school itself is a key factor in this case. To add to that, Collier has gone missing. Now we can't be certain if he's a potential suspect or a victim for that matter. His disappearance is out of character by all accounts. His car is still on the school grounds at his residence, so we can assume he's either disappeared on his own accord or has come to harm."

"You think he's been had too?" Raj asked.

Scott tightened his lips. "I wouldn't put it in quite those terms, but as I said, I don't know if he's a victim or suspect. He's run the school as if it was some sort of military academy. Collier seems too nonchalant about the deaths of his staff members and carried the belief that violent and ritualistic bullying is acceptable."

The team exchanged glances amongst each other as they absorbed Scott's last point.

"Who's being bullied? The staff?" Mike asked as he twiddled a pen through his chubby fingers and eyed up the Krispy Kreme doughnut that was sitting on a plate near Raj's coffee. He started to reach out for it, but was suitably deterred by a cold, possessive stare from Raj. Mike shrugged it off and thought he'd sneak it from under Raj's nose once the guv was gone.

"No, Mike. The pupils. From information I received this morning, bullying appears to have been an accepted practice as long as the school has been around. And that's got me thinking. How are we doing with chasing up past teachers, Sian?"

Sian cleared her throat as she rifled through a pile of papers on her desk. She neatly gathered a few sheets and placed them in front of her. Pushing her hair behind her ears, she began to summarise the information she'd found out so far.

"In the main, Guv, most of the ex-staff are ex-military."

"That figures," Mike said. "There's always a tendency for

the military to look after their own. It's like a kinship, a bond. Once you've been in the forces, you're never on your own. We all stick together."

"So what happened to you?" Sian smirked bravely, not normally so forthcoming with the sardonic digs.

Mike scowled as Sian raised a brow in defiance. The others smiled.

Sian continued, "The only other teacher I could find so far other than John Morecombe is Stephen Barrington. Interestingly, he's only the second teacher I've come across so far *without* a military background. He left three years back; he was only there two terms and resigned."

"Not long…" Scott pondered.

"Didn't even see out a whole academic year, Guv."

"Where is he now?"

"He's at Longhill High School in Rottingdean."

"Call the head and tell them we're coming over to see Barrington this afternoon. Abby, you and I will see him. Sian, keep working through your list. There may be one or two other teachers we're not aware of."

"Guv, forensics came back with more results on the plastic tape that was used on Goddard. There were traces of food-like substances that they analysed further. It was starchy in composition which they narrowed down to potato. That may not mean much at the moment, but there was an oil-based compound that was sent away for analysis. It came back as a refined spice-infused oil," Abby said.

"Can that be narrowed down in any way? Can we identify

who supplies it? Where it's distributed? What it's used for?"

"I should think so, Guv. We can get on to local catering suppliers and food manufacturers to see if they can shed any light?"

Scott murmured something to himself, his mind working overtime to join snippets of information.

"Okay, that could actually be really helpful. Mike, can you look into that whilst we're out and call me if anything interesting crops up. I've also had an email back from forensics. The DNA profile of the feathers I collected from Bennett's aviary match those placed on the victims."

"Is Bennett in the frame, Guv?"

"That's a possibility, but I've spoken with him at length and I really don't think he had the nous to pull off something like this. If anything, he's too much of an obvious suspect. He had access to the whole school, to boundary rope, to white feathers and...he's just weird. I called him yesterday and asked him to come in to help us with our enquiries. He's downstairs now, so Abby and I will see him."

With that, the team busily got stuck into their tasks as Abby joined Scott as he left the office.

BENNETT HAD BEEN SHOWN through to an interview suite. The dark grey floor and white walls of the room drained it of any character or warmth. It could have been described as functional, with a solitary square table and two plastic chairs either side. The Ritz it most certainly wasn't. The room felt stuffy and claustrophobic during lengthy interviews, and with no natural daylight, it was easy to succumb to fatigue and tiredness quickly.

After Abby had done the introductions and set up the tape recorder, Scott began. "Mr Bennett, thank you for coming in. This isn't a formal interview and you're not under arrest. We're recording this interview as standard procedure. You're free to leave at any stage should you wish to. I understand that you waived your right to legal representation, is that correct?"

Bennett nodded.

"Mr Bennett, you'll need to say your answers for the tape."

"Yes."

Scott went through some questions asking him about his role at Edmunston-Hunt, what he liked, didn't like, etcetera, to develop some rapport, before he probed a little further.

"Mr Bennett, how well do you get on with the staff at the school?"

Bennett held Scott's gaze for a brief moment with his standard deadpan expression. For a moment Scott thought he'd need to repeat the question in case Bennett hadn't heard.

Bennett shook his head and shrugged. "I don't really have much to do with them. I don't think most even know I exist. I'm there to clean up after them and make the place look tidy like."

Scott flicked through a brown file. "Mr Bennett, I understand that you did a stretch of twenty-seven months. ABH for glassing someone in a pub in Soho, London, plus a further four months for assaulting a police officer involved in your arrest. Do you get angry often?"

"No."

"So what happened in this situation?"

Bennett paused; his hands were firmly clasped on the table between them. He looked between Abby and Scott. "Because they kept saying I was thick, said I looked like a retard."

"Who did?"

"Dunno, some blokes in the pub. Then one tripped me up as I went to leave. I fell. I was mad. I hate it when I'm called thick."

"So you lashed out and attacked one of them."

Bennett nodded.

"Mr Bennett," Scott said as he nodded in the direction of the recorder.

"Yeah."

"Did anyone call you thick at the school? Pupils? Perhaps the teachers?"

"Nope."

"How well did you get on with the principal, Mr Collier?"

Bennett fixed his gaze on his locked hands and shrugged. "He was okay. He gave me a chance. No one else would. See, I can't fill in those forms the job centre gives us. I can't read or write."

"At all?" Scott questioned.

"Other than writing my name. Sees I left school at nine, didn't see the point. I had no dad; he fucked off before I could walk. Mum was a pisshead and a tart. Had lots of men come round and take her out and stay the night. She'd tell me to stay in my room all day, gave me a can of cider and a few fags and a packet of cheese and onion crisps to keep me quiet. I'd sleep most of the day cos Mum kept me up half the night with her men and the things they used to do."

Scott and Abby exchanged a brief glance.

"Your aviary, do you like birds?"

Bennett's faced softened as he eyes gazed off into the distance. "Yeah, they're lovely creatures. Won't harm a soul. They love me talking to them."

"Who else had access to them?" Scott asked.

Bennett thought for a moment. "Well, anyone really. I used to have the odd student come and see them. They liked feeding the birdseed."

"Any staff?"

Bennett shook his head. "I don't even think most of 'em know they're there."

"So to clarify, anyone on the site could and did have access to the aviary because it wasn't locked?"

"Yeah, why is that a problem? I don't want harm coming to my birds."

"Mr Bennett, you've been extremely helpful. I'll get an officer to show you out. Oh, just one last question. Has anyone come to you to borrow any of that boundary rope or ask for packaging tape?"

"No, but a few weeks ago, I found one of the black wheelie bins round the kitchen on its side, everything out of it. I thought it was foxes looking for scraps."

"What's your thoughts on Bennett?" Abby asked as they made their way out of Brighton.

Abby had offered to drive, but Scott was forever saying that his life insurance wasn't adequate enough when she was behind the wheel, much to Abby's consternation. Scott always found it easy to wind Abby up, especially on the topic of her driving. He'd often teased her saying that men were better drivers, which seemed to always hit a raw nerve with Abby.

"I don't think Bennett is our man. For starters, he's just said that he can't read or write. And when I asked him to write out a sentence in the interview, it looked like a three-year-old's scribble. He couldn't even hold the pen properly. The aviary isn't locked, so anyone could get in there and help themselves to feathers, and as for the rope, he's got loads of it by his back door, easy enough for someone to cut off a length without him noticing."

They'd only just passed the marina when Scott's phone rang. He clumsily fiddled around inside his jacket pocket before retrieving it and throwing it into Abby's lap. "See who that is…"

Cara's name popped up on the screen. "It's the scalpel queen," Abby replied teasingly.

"See what she wants will you?"

It crossed his mind that in recent days the case had taken up a lot of his time and energy. He'd neglected his relationship with Cara, something that she'd been keen to point out in several texts recently. He felt bad, their relationship was only just taking off, and here he was doing what most coppers did, putting their job above and beyond most things in their lives.

He recalled hearing the phrase 'Join the force, get a divorce,' when he first signed up, and never really understood its meaning until now. Shift work had a destabilising effect on home life, the earlies, lates and nights, bigger workloads, tighter budgets, staffing cuts, coupled with the stress and pressure of the rank often took their toll. It was a thankless task sometimes. The public rarely thanked the police. The public was quick to blame them for not doing enough, and the senior management jostled in the politics of policing.

A long-serving DS had once taken Scott under his wing and given him an insight into what was to come.

"I speak from experience of two marriages and one divorce," the old-timer had said. "Going to bed early, and getting up at five a.m., or getting in around midnight absolutely drained, or getting home around eight a.m. just wanting to hit the pillow and then getting ready to go out again around nine p.m. was very telling on family and social life," he'd pointed out to a youthful and exuberant Scott.

"Whoa, hold a minute. Calm down; take a few deep breaths. Who's there?" Abby said calmly tapping the dashboard.

37

Abby had kept the line open as Scott turned around and raced back to Cara's flat. On loudspeaker they could hear Cara's screams, a male voice shouting, the sound of glass breaking and loud thuds as bits of furniture were being thrown around. Abby had also called through for a local unit to get there immediately as there was a threat to life. Scott's mind raced. His pulse throbbed in his neck as images flashed through his mind. *Who was there? What did they want? What were they doing to his precious Cara?*

It felt like déjà vu…a loved one in need of his help and him powerless to do anything about it. This time he hoped he wasn't too late.

He was taking corners and traffic like a man possessed. Abby did her hardest to hold on to the door handle whilst exchanging nervous glances with Scott. She knew what would probably be going through his mind right now, and thought better of asking him to slow down. She tried her hardest to reassure him that everything would be okay, that other units were on the way, but knew her words were falling on deaf ears. Scott stared straight ahead, his lips pursed tight, his hands gripped the wheel like his life depended on it. In Scott's world, that was probably an accurate assumption.

Scott screeched to a halt in the middle of the road outside Cara's apartment just as the flashing blue lights and wail of police sirens approached him from the opposite end of the road. The sight of four police officers abandoning their cars and racing towards one of the properties was enough to raise the curiosity and interest of passers-by and residents as curtains twitched and front doors opened.

Wood splinters and the front door hanging off one hinge greeted them. Scott tensed, the hairs on the back of his neck prickling. Breathing rapidly and fearing the worst, they barged in, only to be confronted by a tall, unshaven white male who stepped out into the hallway, a knife in his right hand clearly visible to the officers. Scott fully expected the assailant to come towards them as the uniformed officers released their retractable batons and screamed "Put the knife down now!" Instead, the man's eyes widened in a mixture of fear and rage. He snarled at them, his jaws clenched tight before he turned and raced for the kitchen and the rear courtyard garden beyond.

Scott ran after him, followed hotfooted by the two uniformed officers. Abby tailed off as she went from room to room looking for Cara, shouting, "Cara, where are you?" The lounge was in disarray, ornaments and flower-pots lay scattered around the floor. Potpourri had been trodden into the carpet, daffodil stalks lay broken on the floor. A bottle had been thrown against the wall, leaving a shimmering shower of green glass across the carpet. The evidence all pointed towards a violent episode, but Cara wasn't there.

Abby turned into the next room and found Cara draped across the end of a bed, her hair knotted and untidy, her T-shirt ripped from the violent struggle that had taken place, her cream bra partially exposed, and what looked like the red impression of a bite mark on her shoulder. Abby noticed that the button on her jeans was undone, but from where she lay, the jeans hadn't been removed. Lying there dazed and confused, Cara glanced towards the doorway; her left cheek flushed bright red, the corner of her lip crimson with a trail of fresh blood.

Scott shoulder-charged the intruder, forcing him to collide with the kitchen table and lose his balance before falling head first into the rear patio doors. The fall and subsequent impact dazed the man sufficiently to give the officers enough time to wrestle the intruder on to his front and secure his hands behind his back. Scott knelt down to see if he recognised the scrote, perhaps he'd come across him previously, but the face didn't register with him.

More officers streamed through the door. The small apartment began to feel claustrophobic. That was the good thing about being a police officer. When an officer or a member of their family was in trouble, officers were quick to respond. From the looks of it, half of Brighton nick had arrived, including a dog handler with a very large and aggressive black German shepherd straining at the leash, barking and snarling at all the commotion.

Scott left his uniformed colleagues to deal with the intruder as he sought out Cara. He found her wrapped in a cardigan, with Abby offering her a protective arm around her shoulder. His initial reaction was to rush over to her and wrap her in his arms, but he was stopped in his tracks by her repeatedly saying, "I'm sorry…I'm sorry," as tears streamed from her puffy, red eyes.

"Hey, it's fine. It's really fine. You're safe now," Scott reassured her, as he knelt in front of her and glanced briefly towards Abby who rubbed Cara's back. "We need to get you checked out to make sure you're okay."

"I'm sorry, Scott. I'm so sorry."

"Listen, there's nothing to be sorry about. We can get the details later."

Cara leant forward, resting her elbows on her thighs. "You don't understand," she whispered softly through swollen lips. "I…I know him. He's my ex."

Scott dropped his hands and knelt back on his heels. "He's your ex?" he said, sounding confused. "I don't get it. What's he doing here and why now?"

"He wanted me back. He's been following me for weeks, stalking me, scaring me. All those things were down to him…" she said almost apologetically.

Abby shifted awkwardly, but Scott didn't even register Abby's reaction. His mind raced, trying to make sense of the last few moments as he glanced away.

"Scott, he damaged my car. He scared me at the office, the pig's head…it was all him. He was after me, not you. Even down to the break-in I had here. It's all him." Cara shivered, the shock setting in, her shoulders quaking. "He was the reason I left London, to get away from him. Listen to me, Scott…"

Scott appeared stone-faced, his eyes glazed as he looked

straight through her. *What was going on here? What else hasn't she told me?*

He was brought back into the room, "Scott...Scott."

"I don't understand...why did he want to track you down?"

"Because..." Cara paused for a moment knowing that what she was about to say would hurt Scott beyond belief. "Because he was a bully. I fell pregnant but knew I couldn't bring a child into the world with that monster as its dad. I... I had a termination."

38

The events of the prior evening had meant that their visit to see Stephen Barrington had been postponed. Scott had left shortly after Cara's revelation. The news had left him confused, his mind replaying the scene in Cara's apartment over and over again.

He wasn't sure why he had reacted to her news. As the evening had worn on, his confusion had been replaced with sadness and then with an overwhelming feeling of guilt. On reflection, he felt foolish, stupid, almost childlike for his reaction. The more he brooded over it and ignored her texts, the stronger the feeling grew. *Why can't I get a grip?*

The drive to Rottingdean was silent for most of the way. Scott hadn't mentioned anything else and Abby had left him with his thoughts, but she could tell that it still bothered him.

He repetitively tapped his fingers on the steering wheel, his lips drawn in a thin line with the occasional shake of his head. Scott struggled to deal with what Cara had revealed. It wasn't like him to walk away. He was awash with emotions. One moment it was sadness, then recalling Cara's confession would flood his body with hurt, before being replaced with guilt over his reaction.

Abby couldn't sit there any longer. "Pull over…"

"What?" Scott asked softly, not taking his eyes off a point in the distance that had him transfixed.

"Pull over," Abby repeated, pointing to an approaching lay-by.

"Why?"

"Just do it, please?"

Scott indicated and pulled in before turning in his seat to look at Abby. "What's the matter?"

"You're the matter!" she said forcibly, poking him in the arm. "I'm not being disrespectful, Guv. I'm talking to you as a friend, Abby to Scott. I know what you've been through, and any loss of a child is difficult and painful. It's something no parent should experience in their lifetime. I know I'd find it hard to continue if I lost one of my brats. But an outsider would think that it's you who's been assaulted."

"Abby, we're in the middle of a multiple murder investigation and you want to give me a pep talk? It's none of your business…my private life is none of your business," Scott said angrily.

"Pot and kettle spring to mind. I've lost count of the amount of times we've talked about my personal life. You've given me some great advice in the past. You've also taken the piss out of me over my poor choice of men…and admittedly, you've had a point. I've always been shit at choosing men." Abby shrugged in agreement. "But I was surprised by your reaction yesterday. She didn't hurt you on purpose, did she? She clearly lived in fear of that tosser, and decided on a clean break, a new life…a life that now involves you…you big clut! She clearly loves you…and whether you choose to admit it or not, you love her."

Scott remained silent, dropping his eyes to fiddle with the stitching on his steering wheel. A mixture of embarrassment and surprise robbed him of his usual confidence.

"Do you honestly think *any woman* takes the decision for a termination lightly? Terminating a life? She decided based on what she thought was right at that time in her life. Regardless of whether you or I think it's a right or wrong decision, she chose to do it based on her circumstances and the evidence available to her at *that* time. How can you punish her for that?"

Scott shook his head slowly. "I know…I know what you're saying…but…"

"There's no *buts*, Scott. Just zip it for a moment," she interrupted, pinching her thumb and finger together and pulling an imaginary zip across her lips. "How could she possibly bring something like that up so early in a relationship?… Any relationship? 'Oh, by the way, Scott, I've had a termination. Hope you don't mind.' Get real, Scott."

Abby's voice rose an octave. "The woman is hurting still. It's probably played on her mind since that day, and she's carried it with her afraid to tell anyone, especially a new fella in case that changes their feelings towards her. And with what you've been through, how the fuck could she possibly find the right words *and* time to tell you?"

Abby abruptly stopped and stared in silence at Scott, fearful that she'd gone too far with her lecture. More softly she said, "Listen, just think for a moment about how she's feeling. A new life, a great but *weird* job, a new bloke in her life who's vainer than her," she added trying to lighten the mood. "Things are finally looking good for her...and you. A fresh start. So are you really going to ruin that, or throw it away? Because I thought you were better than that. You're one of a few people I admire and want to be when I grow up. Grow a pair and deal with this the way it needs to be dealt with, huh?"

Scott sat there gazing out towards the coast feeling suitably chastised. He had to admit that everything Abby said was true but admitting it himself was another matter. He'd been an idiot, a red mist moment had clouded his judgement and he'd jumped to the wrong conclusion. He was feeling sorry for himself, when in reality it was Cara who was hurting, not him. Yes, he hurt from losing Becky. And, yes, he felt that anyone who willingly aborted a child's life was being selfish when to him a child's life was so precious. But rightly or wrongly, it was an individual decision, her decision.

Scott sighed heavily and held out his hand towards Abby, palm down. Abby gently slapped it. "Consider yourself told," she said with a reassuring smile.

"Thank you," were the only words Scott said before starting the car and continuing their journey. *What would I do without Abby? Friends like her are hard to find.*

LONGHILL HIGH SCHOOL was situated in the middle of a cluster of four small towns that merged into one another making it hard to determine when one town stopped and another started. The school bore some loose similarities with Edmunston-Hunt School. Both had a sizeable sports field in front with undisturbed views across the fields, and a large, impressive sprawling light brown brick and glass main building. But that's where the similarities ended. Edmunston-Hunt carried centuries of traditions and memories, it carried architectural grandeur and it smelt expensive. Longhill on the other hand looked functional, boxy and cumbersome.

"This looks a bit like my old school," Scott remarked as they parked and made their way over to the main building. "I remember my first day in year seven; I was crapping myself, the sights, the sounds and a whole bunch of new people around me. I used to literally break out in a sweat trying to find my way from classroom to classroom in my first week. God, it gives me the shivers just thinking about it now," he added, staring up at the fabric of the building.

Abby kept quiet. Her experiences of high school were different from Scott's. The deprived area she grew up in meant her school had a higher percentage of pupils that had been excluded from other schools. Teachers looked weary and disconsolate from the constant barrage of abuse and lack of discipline from pupils. School buildings bore the hallmarks of years of neglect. Paint curled and peeled off the walls from damp ingress, leaky roofs left damp puddles on the floor, and the heating system barely gave off more than a lukewarm ambient temperature in the coldest winter months.

Yes, her experience of school was much different. The fact

she'd made something of herself was testament to her determination, grit and resolve to crawl out of the urban ghetto she once called home.

After a short wait in reception, Stephen Barrington came through some opaque swing doors, and greeted them with a wide, chubby smile.

"Thank you for agreeing to see us, Mr Barrington. I'm Detective Inspector Baker and this is my colleague Detective Sergeant Trent," Scott announced as they produced their warrant cards. "We'd like to ask you a few questions in relation to an ongoing investigation that we're dealing with. We believe you may be able to give us some useful insights."

Stephen Barrington glanced briefly at their cards before ushering them to a meeting room off the main reception.

"Please take a seat," he said, guiding them towards a large oval teak table with silver legs that had six dark brown leather chairs loosely arranged around it. The soft leather squeaked as they took their seats, catching Abby by surprise. She looked slightly embarrassed, much to Scott's amusement.

Barrington was a heavy man, who clearly liked his food. His belly spilt out over the top of his trousers. His belt did a sterling and vital job of keeping his rotund belly in check. His white checked shirt strained at the buttons, and his collar disappeared into his thick double chin that accentuated his neck to the same thickness as his head. His hair was cropped short, grey to the sides, with a hint of brown still on the top. He took the full width of the chair as he leant back and placed his arms on the rests.

"How can I help, Inspector?"

"We're investigating the death of several teachers at Edmunston-Hunt School, and we understand that you were there for a short spell three years ago. Is that correct?"

Barrington's face went ashen. He had the look of someone who'd been hit by a truck. The expression and life drained from him, a reaction both officers picked up on. Barrington shifted uncomfortably in his chair and licked his dry lips.

"Mr Barrington, are you okay?" Abby asked.

"Yes…yes, I'm okay. I've not heard that name for a long time," he replied, wringing his hands nervously.

"You weren't there for long, two terms I believe," Abby said. "Any reason why it was such a short posting?"

"It was never meant to be. I was delighted to have secured my post there. Not many teachers can migrate from state education to the elite private sector. I felt like all my Christmases had come at once."

"So what changed?" Scott asked.

"Everything…"

39

B arrington let out a huge sigh and buried his head in his cupped hands. The memories weighed heavy on his shoulders. "I don't know where to start."

"What was your first impression of the school?" Scott asked.

Barrington's eyes glanced up towards the ceiling, a sure sign in Scott's opinion that the man was tracing back through some visual images and memories.

"I couldn't have been more proud. I felt like I'd reached the pinnacle in my teaching career. In case you don't know, teachers with military backgrounds are recruited in to the teaching staff," Barrington said. Scott nodded to confirm he was aware of this point already. "It was everything I could have ever wanted. It was a big school, with big budgets and exclusivity. To begin with everything was great. The support from other teachers was great, even if a little rigid. The mark of respect that pupils showed teaching staff was amazing…you'd never get that in a state comprehensive!"

"And then?" Abby prompted as she looked quickly at Scott.

"And then I got to see the real school, something I never saw when I was given a guided tour during my interview process. I can't put my finger on it, but it wasn't right. Something just didn't feel right. It was the culture of the school. The kids almost seemed like zombies, regimented, disciplined, even fearful at times. And that fear was the problem I soon realised. It was the discipline; there was this underbelly of fear and conformity. You did it their way or no way at all."

"Can you give me an example?"

"Yes, Inspector, that's not hard to do. I recall on one Saturday morning, my year group were required...no *told* actually, with less than thirty minutes' warning, that they needed to prepare for six laps of the school playing field. One lad, I can't recall his name, wasn't feeling well. Asthma I think. The school didn't care. It was seen as a weakness to not do as you were told, or not take part because of ill health."

"What happened to him?"

"That evening he was made to stand in the middle of the field from six p.m. until nine p.m. and forgo supper as a punishment. He wasn't allowed to move or sit down. Just stand there to attention. Bloody savage if you ask me."

"Did you not say anything?" Scott asked.

"I dared not; I'd not been there long. If I'm honest, I was scared to speak out. And now I feel like a bloody coward for not sticking up for the poor lad." Barrington dipped his head in shame, shaking it in disbelief.

"Did you notice any bullying amongst the pupils?" Scott said.

"All the time, I'm afraid. I wanted to stop it on more than one occasion, but several times the principal caught me as I was about to intervene, and he'd do this thing with his head. He'd shake it very slowly and deliberately, almost as if to say, don't intervene." Barrington mimicked the principal as he demonstrated it to the officers.

"Are you suggesting that you believe that bullying was an accepted and sanctioned norm in the school?" Scott asked leaning on the table, as Abby furiously jotted a few points in her notebook.

"I think so. It seemed like a tradition-type principle carried through time. It was so weird, like something that was acceptable back then...if you lived in the era of Oliver bloody Twist!"

"What do you think was the principal's role in all of this?"

"To be honest, Inspector, I think it was all his doing. He's a dinosaur from a bygone era. It was the way the school was run from the very beginning, even when he was a pupil there, and being an old fart, he's doggedly carried on those traditions...all is not well behind those grand walls, Inspector."

"Clearly not, Mr Barrington. As you know, we're examining the case of several deaths amongst the teaching staff. Do you have any idea why those particular teachers were targeted?"

Barrington averted his gaze to stare at a blank wall behind Scott, his eyes searching for anything that would help. "I don't know. I read about their deaths, and it's both tragic and alarming. But that school seems to be plagued and haunted by mysterious deaths."

Scott shot Abby a curious and excited glance. "Mysterious deaths? What do you mean?"

"I thought if you're digging into the school's past, then you would have come across a death of a pupil many years ago. Probably a good thirty years, if not more, but I can't be certain of the exact date."

"Anything you might know could be extremely helpful to our investigation, Mr Barrington, no matter how small a detail," Scott highlighted in an avid tone.

"Well, I heard from the caretaker, God knows how he knew, but there was talk of a group of prefects who ruled the school with an iron fist. I mean proper intimidation. Anyway, the image of the school was tarnished after the drowning of a pupil allegedly by the prefects. At the time, the school covered it up and said it was a tragic and unforeseen accident. It never became public knowledge; it was all made to go away. They said that he'd taken a midnight dip in the pool which was against regulations." Barrington paused to reflect on his memories. With a shake of his head, he continued, "Apparently, the boy was naked when pulled out by staff. They, the prefects, hid the boy's clothes and as far as I know, they're still hidden in the old music room."

Scott gave Abby the slightest of nods. She left the room to pass this information onto the rest of the team.

"Thank you, Mr Barrington, you've been extremely helpful. Can I ask you to keep this meeting confidential whilst we conduct further enquiries? I'll arrange for one of my officers to take a formal written statement from you later today."

SCOTT AND ABBY hastily made their way over to Edmunston-Hunt taking shortcuts around the back of Brighton to circumnavigate the traffic and speed up their journey to Ditchling. Abby had instructed Sian to meet them there, but to go ahead and start searching the music room for the missing garments.

Scott felt progress was in the air. "I can smell it," he'd said as he drove.

More good news had been relayed to them en-route. Mike had been calling around food manufacturers and food distributors. He had some interesting news for them from the oil traces found on the packaging tape used in one of the murders. Through his enquiries, Mike had narrowed down the use of the refined spice-infused oil to the production of a halal and nut-free tikka paste that was used to marinate chicken. It was specially prepared to meet the strict needs of Asians and those with nut allergies.

Further investigation had identified one particular Sussex-based catering supplier who distributed this paste to schools nationwide. The interesting point that Mike had discovered was that only three schools in the Sussex area used this paste, one of them being Edmunston-Hunt, the others being Ardingly College and Worth School, neither being in close proximity.

"Relay that information to Sian, will you Abby? I want her to have a look near the kitchens and storerooms, anywhere that tape could be used or has been used," Scott instructed.

40

Sian assumed she'd arrived long before Scott and Abby as she glanced around the grounds and saw no trace of Scott's car. She stood for a moment in awe looking up at the grand splendour of Edmunston-Hunt's façade. Its impressive red brickwork and windows set into stone surrounds felt historic. It felt like the building had been happily situated since time began and had stood firm and resolute through wars, storms and natural disasters. She thought that even an earthquake wouldn't shift this old pile of stone.

Unsure of the layout of the school, Sian followed the boundary of the building and assumed that the kitchens and storeroom would probably be around the back somewhere tucked out of view and the refuse area not far from there. She'd start with the bins first before heading inside and towards the old part of the building as instructed by Abby.

I get all the glamorous jobs, she mused when she found what looked like a coal bunker of some sorts with three walls and a tin roof. One side was fully exposed to facilitate the easy access to four large, black wheelie bins. She turned up her nose in protest as the waft of rotting scraps of food drifted over in her direction carried by the light breeze that swirled around her. The warmth of the sun no doubt accelerated the decomposition of the discarded food.

Lifting the first lid, she screamed as a swarm of flies escaped and flew straight at her. The shock forced her to take a few steps back and flail her arms around her head like a woman possessed. It no doubt looked comical from a distance.

"Disgusting creatures," she fumed as she composed herself once again. Peering into the first bin, her day wasn't getting any better. A slurry of decaying food greeted her. Hastily dropping the lid, she held the back of her wrist up to her nose in a desperate attempt to stem the assault of the smells creeping up her nostrils.

The next bin offered no respite, *more shit*. She breathed a sigh of relief as she opened the third bin, crushed and flattened cardboard boxes were stuffed into this one. Cartons that once contained fruit juices, boxes that had fresh chicken pieces and cereal packets were all piled upon one another. *Result.* Sian had found some packaging tape inside a box which once had chicken tikka paste from a manufacturer called Ashrafs. This c*ould be what we're looking for*.

As Sian sifted through the material, unbeknown to her, he waited…and watched. *They were getting a little too close for comfort.*

Having safely stored away the packaging tape in clear plastic evidence bags in the boot of her car, and still with no sign of Scott and Abby, Sian went into the main school and followed Scott's instructions in order to find the old part of the building. Pushing through a storeroom door, she found herself staring at a decaying, worn, dusty corridor.

Plaster puckered and crumbled from the walls as damp sapped the strength from them. The odd strip of parquet floor that once adorned this well-trodden and magnificent corridor, now lay loosely discarded and kicked to one side. In its place, an exposed, dusty, uneven concrete floor that felt like coarse sandpaper through the soles of her shoes. A heavy stench filled the air and clung like an invisible mist that closed in on her from all sides. Sian scrunched up her nose once again. The eeriness and silence haunted her, enough to send a shiver down her spine.

Sian found the door that Scott had described, the same door that creaked open once again, its lower swollen edge dragging on the uneven floor. Her eyes adjusted to the semi-darkness, dust from years of neglect drifting aimlessly in the air, dirt gathering in a fine layer like grey snow on the windowsills. The place felt creepy to Sian. She clenched her teeth trying hard to fight off the urge to shiver with fear. *Spiders...I hate spiders. Where there were cobwebs, there had to be spiders*, she convinced herself. She was only grateful Mike wasn't here or she'd never hear the end of it. The great lumbering oaf would have had a field day taking the piss out of her, and playing cruel tricks on her like shutting the door behind her, or throwing a spider at her. *Bastard.*

There wasn't much for her to look at. A few wooden crates lay stacked upon one another. Discarded tea lights sat upon the old mantelpiece above the fireplace. There were a few cupboards that she plucked up the courage to peer into by opening the doors just wide enough to shine the light from her phone in, before closing them with a sigh.

"TRY SIAN AGAIN WILL YOU, Abby? She probably expected us ages ago, Sod's fucking law we get stuck in roadworks," Scott fumed.

"I've tried twice already, Guv. It just goes straight to voice-mail, signal must be shite where she is. I've tried her on the job radio, too. It's just crackling. I'll try again when we're around that bend up ahead. We'll only be a few hundred yards from her then."

SIAN BECAME INCREASINGLY FRUSTRATED. She didn't want to stay here any longer than she needed, and as for any evidence of clothing, she'd turned up a big fat zilch after peering into cupboards, looking under the fire grate and turning over wooden crates. The silence in the room was briefly broken by something that she thought she'd heard.

"Hello? Guv, is that you?" Sian called out, before making her way out into the corridor. She looked up and down in both directions and saw nothing. *Probably a rat…oh, fuck, if I see a rat, I'm out of here.* "Hello, it's the police. Anyone here?" she said, raising her voice. The silence continued.

A loud, crackling static noise caused her to jump as her Airwave's job radio sprang into life. "For fuck's sake," she said through gritted teeth.

"Sian, it's Abby. Blimey, we've been trying to contact you for ages."

"Sorry, Sarge, must have been in a dead spot. Where are you?"

"We're on our way; we got stuck in roadworks. We're just approaching the gates of the school. How you getting on?"

"Nothing to report so far. I've looked around the music room, bit dark to see much, but there's nothing of interest that I can see, Sarge."

"Okay, well stay put and we'll be there in a few minutes. We've got a searchlight in the boot we can use. Hold tight."

The sound came again. Sian still couldn't place where it was coming from. It seemed to echo off the walls of the corridor. "Standby, Sarge, I can hear something." Sian crept forward placing one foot carefully and slowly in front of another. "Hello, it's the police. Anyone here? Identify your-self." The silence continued.

"Everything okay, Sian? We're just parking up; will be with you in two minutes."

He struck silently as she walked past a large instrument cupboard that sat against one wall of the corridor. She saw the dark figure from the corner of her eye, but he had a second or two on her, which gave him the element of surprise.

A sharp pain erupted from deep within her, spreading out over her back, shocking her limbs, leaving her arms lifeless and loosely hanging by her sides. The knife had travelled in deep beneath the bottom of her stab vest, rising up and under, penetrating her lower back. Sian crumpled to the floor, her face hitting the dusty concrete.

Her mind willed her to move, *get up, run, run you idiot*, but her body froze. Everything moved around her in slow motion. Shock left her motionless, a spectator. *Fuck, fuck,*

fuck. The pain had subsided, masked by the rush of adrenaline that now coursed through her veins.

Footsteps, she heard slow, steady footsteps. Someone stood by her face. *Black shoes, I can see black shoes and green trousers.* Her mind willed her to move her head, to look up, to identify her attacker. She tried, but there was no response. A spot of blood dripped onto the floor by his shoes. *My blood, my fucking blood. Help me, help me*, she pleaded in silence as she stared at his shoes.

He didn't move. He stood there for what seemed an eternity, but in reality was only a few seconds. Then it dawned on her, *he's going to kill me, that's why he's still here, he's going to kill me.* Panic washed over her, her heart thundering like a steam train on its inaugural trip, her lips drier than a desert. A gurgle emanated from her throat.

And then he was gone, walking away faster than he'd approached. Disappearing into the blackness that was his camouflage.

"Sian, are you there? Sian?" Abby called out over the radio.

From somewhere deep within, her fingers found their motion. It was the same hand that seemed to have locked itself around her radio before being struck. *I can't move it… I can't move it.* Her numb fingers searched out the top of the radio. Between the volume button and small rubber aerial was the red emergency button. Sian mustered all her strength, and pressed down clumsily with her index finger. *Nothing's happening…harder, work you fucker.* Her mind willed her on.

Her body felt loose, limp and void of all strength. *Press again, you can do it…I don't want to die…come on try, try again. Yes.* She now had clear uninterrupted access to the airwaves for thirty seconds. The control room kicked in, barking orders, trying to locate her whereabouts using GPS. The voice faded in and out, swirling around her like a rampant storm. Confusion clouded her thinking. Was it coming from the radio? Or was someone coming to her aid?

Drawing on all the strength she could muster, she yelled "help" in the vain hope they could hear her before darkness filled her vision and her eyes closed. The commotion of the control room trying to reach her and Abby's voice screaming fell on deaf ears. The sounds of heavy footsteps racing towards her and then the words, "Officer down... officer down," faded away as her world fell silent.

41

A deathly silence descended like a dark mist on a cold winter's night. For what felt like an eternity, Abby knelt on the cold, hard floor cradling Sian's head. Her body felt heavy and cold as the seconds passed and Sian's life ebbed away.

"Stay with me, Sian. You hear me…stay with me. Don't you go anywhere," Abby repeated, hoping her words were reaching and registering with Sian at some level.

Those few seconds of sanity were fast replaced with Scott requesting immediate backup and an ambulance. It was all hands to the pump. The control room diverted all available units from Brighton and Lewes to the area. Officers were being pulled off all non-essential jobs and were being diverted to Ditchling.

Torn between staying with Abby and Sian, Scott pondered pursuing the assailant. In his mind's eye, he knew he needed to stay with his officers but the assailant was here, somewhere around them, and vital seconds were being lost.

He knew it would be too late once units had made their way towards Ditchling. Even on blues, the journey would take at least fifteen minutes, and the nearest NPAS helicopter wouldn't be here much sooner.

His fists clenched, his breathing exhaling in rapid pants... *think...think.* He was already treading a fine line with his superiors, having been branded reckless and cavalier on more than one occasion. He'd been criticised for putting results over officer safety, a claim that he'd fiercely refuted. He never saw himself as such; he had preferred to describe himself as pragmatic and energetic.

Sensing the dilemma within her boss, Abby shouted, "Go... go, we'll be fine! Go get the fucker who did this."

Scott hesitated, his next decision would be the one that would be scrutinised the most. "You sure?" he said, glancing down at Sian's pale, lifeless face.

"Yes, we'll take the flack later...together if we have to."

Scott didn't need to be told twice. He turned and raced down the corridor, his loud footsteps rupturing the silence. Silence laced with terror and death. He felt shit. He struggled to think straight. In the back of his mind, a hazy, haunting image flashed up almost stopping him in his tracks. The lifeless figures of his family sprawled across the road, the car that had mowed them down disappearing into the distance. At the time, he'd been torn between duty and being there for his loved ones. History seemed to be repeating itself once again, as if some higher being was putting him to the test once more.

A fire raged in his belly. His eyes narrowed. "Not this time," he said through gritted teeth as he sped up, flying through several sets of double swing doors before shoulder-charging a fire exit door that propelled him outside. He stopped for a moment to gather his bearings as he rubbed his sore shoulder. He couldn't see anything and the only sounds he could hear were those of birds singing and chirping innocently in the trees that backed on the rear edge of the school.

He ran to the forest edge. He looked hard, his eyes searching amongst the dense woodland for any sign of movement. Was he too late? The helicopter would be here in a few minutes. The crew would scan the forest for any discernable heat sources that the dogs could be diverted towards. If the assailant had doubled back around to the front of the school, then there was a chance that uniformed units would pick him up.

"Fuck!" Scott cursed.

Scott raced back into the school to find Abby and Sian. Abby looked a disconsolate figure, her eyes were heavy with sadness as she glanced up, hopeful. He shook his head. "He got away. Sian?"

"Not good, Guv. Her pulse is weak. I don't think she's…we need paramedics now."

"They're minutes away. They're just coming off Coldean Lane. There's a fast response unit a minute or two away as well."

For a fleeting moment, a change in the wind direction carried the approaching tone of a siren.

———

SCOTT BARGED through Collier's door, seething, his anger threatening to spiral out of control and engulf him like a

violent whirlpool. If Scott was honest with himself, he was
to blame. The job always carried risks. Any enquiry an
officer went out on had the potential to turn nasty. They
never knew what would be around the next corner or who
would open the next door they knocked on. A seemingly
innocent visit to follow up on ongoing enquiries had the
potential to go horribly wrong no matter what level of risk
assessment was undertaken beforehand.

He knew all that. Christ, he'd drummed that into all his
officers, but now an enquiry had gone horribly wrong and it
was on his watch. He needed to find an outlet for his anger,
and Collier was in Scott's cross hairs. He panted, his
muscles edgy and tense. Adrenaline coursed through his
veins like a raging river in storm, spiking his fight or flight
response and he knew that he was moments away from
doing something that he'd later regret.

He didn't give a shit.

Scott's eyes darted around the room, searching for Collier.
To begin with, he was certain that Collier had bolted, done
his disappearing act. Then from the corner of the room
Scott heard the red leather chesterfield creak.

"Ah, Inspector…I wondered how long it would take until
you appeared at my door," came the measure toned of
Collier.

Scott could see just a few wispy strains of grey hair poke
up above the back of the chair. He paced over to Collier,
grabbed the back of the chair and spun it round so hard to
face him the chair trembled under the attack. Collier clung
onto the armrests as his eyes widened and his lips parted in
a gasp. Their eyes locked in a gladiatorial battle, invisible
messages of hate and taunting passed between them.

Collier's lips broke into a smile that did a poor job of masking defeat.

"Do you know I have an officer fighting for her life on *your* school premises, and you have the gall to sit here as if everything is okay?" Scott said through gritted teeth. Their faces were an inch or two apart as Scott gripped the man's suit lapels pulling him even closer. "At every opportunity, you've done your hardest to skirt around my enquiries, spinning me yarns and holding back on me. You're going to tell me everything, because if you don't, I'll throw you out of the window now so help me God."

Scott shook. With anger. And fear. Fear for Sian. If she died, he couldn't be held accountable for what he might do to Collier. Cold shivers raced down his spine like bolts of lightning. His hands trembled through a heady mixture of rolling emotions. But the fear worried him the most, the fear of going too far, even though he knew he'd already done that.

42

Collier looked a resigned and disconsolate figure. His eyes drooped as he looked down, afraid to look Scott in the eyes any longer. All around them, the wail of sirens echoed as emergency vehicles converged on the school. The fight had all but deserted the old man, his stiff, methodical persona crumbling in front of Scott's eyes. He didn't look like the firm, disciplinarian principal that Scott had known to this point. Collier looked tired, weary and helpless.

"There's no way back from this, Mr Collier. I think it's high time you were straight with me. You see, you and I both know that you've been holding back on me. You've side-stepped my questioning from the very beginning. This school is in lockdown now. The school's reputation has been damaged beyond belief and you've just spent your last day as the principal of Edmunston-Hunt School. You and I both know that the school governors will back a vote of no confidence in you...so that's it. It's over."

Collier's lips broke into a thin smile as he shook his head. "Checkmate, Inspector. It appears that my options are limited. This school has been my life," he said, waving his hand lazily in the air. "It's been my home, my castle and my establishment since I was a boy. I've protected it fiercely; I would have laid down my life for this school."

In Scott's view, Collier had already done that. He knew nothing about the world outside these four walls, and doubted that Collier had been past the gates of the school in a long time.

"Mr Collier, I'd love to sit here and reminisce, but I've got to track down a violent criminal and identify the person who's attempted to murder one of my team," Scott said sternly, a sense of urgency in his voice as he spoke.

There was a lengthy pause as Collier reflected. With a heavy sigh, his chest heaved. "This has always been a school that prided itself on discipline. *Keeping boys in line* is built into the fabric of the school and it's taken as a given. I saw it with my own eyes…and to be frank was on the receiving end of it when I was a young lad here. But it set me up for what I was about to experience in my military career. Even when I came back here as a teacher and housemaster, I knew it was still carrying on."

"Right under your nose…and you never did a thing? You turned a blind eye?" Scott asked.

Collier puckered his lips. "I guess so. It was the done thing." He shrugged.

"And the pupil who drowned? What happened?"

Collier nodded slowly. "Peter Jennings, the name has stuck with me. The prefects at the time took their initiations and discipline a little too far."

"Hardly a little too far," Scott remonstrated. Collier ignored the suggestion.

"It was they who were responsible for Jennings's death. They threw him into the pool, but they knew full well that the lad couldn't swim. They pushed him away every time he tried to get to the side. They laughed as he fought to survive. After he drowned," Collier continued, pausing for a moment, "we covered up the unfortunate incident. We blamed it on Jennings breaking school rules. An *unavoidable accident* was how it was described."

"I understand he was found naked, his clothes?"

"Hidden in the flue of the chimney in the old music room. It was a very dark period in the school's history, but we did well to manage the situation."

Scott was incredulous. Collier sounded as if he was pleased at the school's damage limitation strategy. He shook his head in disbelief, Collier seemed to operate in a parallel dimension where the boundaries of respect, decency, ethics and moral responsibility had been distorted beyond recognition, like a hall of mirrors at a fairground.

The heavy thunder of footsteps behind him broke the temporary silence. Scott glanced over his shoulder to see Mike and several uniformed officers at the door. Armed officers brandishing their Heckler & Koch carbines stood either side of Mike, their sights trained on Collier. At this stage, anyone was a suspect, and to arriving officers, Collier could easily have been the one carrying a weapon.

"Why Jennings?" Scott asked.

There was another lengthy pause. Collier was in no hurry.

In a perverse way, he appeared to be enjoying the attention he was receiving. "He was allegedly having an unhealthy relationship with another pupil."

Scott's brow furrowed as he glanced towards Mike who looked equally perplexed. "Unhealthy relationship?"

Collier cleared his throat loudly and shifted uncomfortably in his chair. "He was a poof, Inspector."

"Based on what evidence?"

"He was always seen with another boy. They both were frail, weak and effeminate, always shying away from playing rugby. They'd both find excuses not to participate and were always the last in inter-house cross-country competitions. Poor exam results, spent all their time together and so on. You get the drift."

"And on that set of weak assumptions, you questioned his sexuality?" Scott asked.

"Well...yes, but the prefects had seen them in a disgusting embrace."

"So the prefects were judge and jury?"

"It's behaviour that we don't tolerate in this school, Inspector," Collier replied as he glared at Scott.

It was all starting to become very clear to Scott. The weakest in the school were punished. Those unable to defend themselves became soft targets for the bullies. The lasting image of Matthew sobbing raced through Scott's mind. *How many others had suffered over the years?*

Scott crossed his arms. "And the prefects were?" Knowing full well what names would likely be put forward.

"Christopher Johnson, Giles Rochester, Alex Winterbottom…" Collier paused for a moment. "And Laurence Goddard."

Scott shook his head in frustration. "This could all have been stopped before it got this far. And what was the name of the boy that Peter Jennings was allegedly involved with?"

"Timothy Marchant, a weak individual with no backbone. Plump, round face, dark hair, large forehead. There was no place for his kind in my establishment."

"And what happened to Timothy?" Scott asked, ignoring Collier's last comment.

"The very next day we shipped him out of here. His father was a government official based at the British consulate in Turkey. But the lad stayed with his mother who resided here in this country. Kent, I believe. Tonbridge to be precise."

"More damage limitation?"

"Hmm, something like that. I'll give him credit. He showed his mettle in the end and didn't go quietly. He was angry, didn't want to go, but equally was too upset to stay. Dithering idiot. I would have wiped the scowl off his face had it been under different circumstances."

"And this was sanctioned by the governors as well?"

An expression of guilt crept over Collier's face as he diverted his gaze towards the window, the silence that ensued suggesting otherwise.

Scott leant in forcing Collier to press back into the chair.

His eyes shot daggers at the principal, every sinew in his body hated the man, but he was here to uphold the law.

"You'll be charged with withholding information, and perverting the course of justice. And that's just for starters. Get him out of here, but don't take him back yet."

43

Scott left Collier in the capable hands of Mike and the uniformed officers, whilst organising other officers to do a more detailed search of the old music room in the disused part of the school. The claustrophobic atmosphere of Collier's room had been replaced by the frenetic activity at the front of the school. Police vehicles littered the front drive, parked at curious angles where they'd stopped in their haste to bail out and assist. He could hear police dogs barking in the distance and fast radio chatter as information was coming in.

The school was in lockdown. Armed officers assisted their unarmed colleagues who were stationed on the front gate. Other officers roamed the grounds looking for any evidence of the assailant or his weapon.

An officer that Scott hadn't seen before interrupted his thoughts. "Sir, one of the dogs has picked up a scent heading into the forest behind the main building."

"And where are they now?" Scott asked, making his way towards the old part of the building.

"The scent seems to double back on itself, leaving the forest about a hundred and fifty yards further down, back in the direction of the school." The evidence suggested that the assailant was still in close proximity having attempted to throw them off his trail by heading into the forest.

Scott turned the corner and saw Abby standing there. Time seemed to momentarily freeze, the commotion around them fell away like in an old-fashioned black-and-white silent movie. Streaks of salty tears zigzagged down her pale cheeks. Her arms hung loosely by her sides, the top part of her light grey trousers stained dark crimson. Scott's eyes moved to her arms, the sleeves of her cream blouse heavily stained with blood.

Abby slowly took a few steps towards Scott, her eyes bright red and heavy with tears. She didn't need to say anything; she couldn't say anything. The words wouldn't come. She tried to tell Scott but her mouth stayed frozen in shock.

"Abby?" Scott asked, knowing in his gut the news wasn't good.

Abby shook her head and cried. "We lost her. Sian passed away on the way to the hospital. They tried to save her, but she'd suffered too much blood loss…"

Scott pulled Abby in close to him as she sobbed heavily into his chest. His mind raced, thoughts tumbling over one another. *Sian's dead…I shouldn't have let her go in alone… Was this my fault?…Shit…What the fuck has just happened? A* cold chill raced through his body. A mixture of shock, fear and sadness tossed his stomach over as a thin veil of sweat glistened on his forehead. Waves of nausea bounced around inside him as he fought to keep the bile down.

A DIRECT ORDER brought Scott back to the station immediately whilst other officers contained the scene, searching for the assailant. Forensics had the grisly task of combing the crime scene for evidence, and capturing a visual catalogue of the last few moments of Sian's life.

He'd left Abby with paramedics who were treating her for mild shock. Abby had witnessed scenes like this before, but nothing really prepared them for when it happened to one of their own.

Officers watched in silence as Scott made his way through the station towards DCI Harvey's office. A sombre mood cast a pall over the scene. Officers spoke in hushed tones, huddled in corners, and digested the information that trickled out in dribs and drabs. None of the usual station banter, mickey-taking or shouts echoed across the office. The subdued silence only amplified the rings from desk phones and mobiles that seemed to punctuate the air with piercing clarity.

The odd pat on his arm in sympathy was matched in equal measures with cold glances. He wasn't sure if they were stares of disbelief, shock or anger. Had he gone too far this time? Had his reckless actions led to an officer's death? Was the label of cavalier fitting? His mind swirled. The heat built under his collar as he wearily made his way up the stairs before turning into DCI Harvey's office.

DCI Jane Harvey sat at her desk, her fingers interlocked

and resting on the metal surface. The presence of Detective Superintendent John Meadows seated in one of the two chairs opposite her only added to the tension in the room. The intimidating man appeared to be fighting for composure. The DCI shot nervous glances between Meadows and Scott.

"Scott, take a seat," she said, nodding in the direction of the only spare chair in the room. "Firstly, I'm sorry about Sian. We're all devastated at the loss of such a young, promising officer."

Scott nodded slightly, knowing the sentiment was genuine, but a prelude to much worse.

"We'll need a full report from you about what's happened, and of course there will be an internal investigation to assess whether procedures were followed correctly. We need to ascertain if there was an error in any part of the chain of command that could have prevented her death."

"Basically, you're saying that you're trying to find out if I fucked up?" Scott said flippantly, instantly regretting his choice of words. "I'm sorry, Ma'am, Sir. I didn't mean that and I apologise for speaking out of turn," Scott added, frantically trying to stem the tirade of abuse he was about to get from Meadows whose face had turned an unhealthy shade of red.

"Let me remind you Detective Inspector Baker, DC Mason was a member of your team and a member of Sussex constabulary. We've lost a young officer. I've already had several calls from the chief constable, and I'm due to give him a further update in an hour before he holds a press conference. You're more than welcome to take the call for me should you wish," he said, goading Scott. "This is a sad day for Sussex Police, and I don't give a fuck how you feel. All I'm interested in is finding out exactly what happened and whether it could have been avoided. The chief constable has the unenviable task of contacting DC Mason's parents to inform them that their twenty-seven-year-old daughter has been killed in the line of duty."

Meadows rose from his chair shooting Scott with a tight-lipped grimace before turning to DCI Harvey and barking, "Sort it."

An uneasy silence settled in the room after Meadows stormed out.

"Scott, off the record, could this have been avoided?"

Scott thought hard for a moment, "I don't think so, Ma'am. I'd instructed Sian to follow a line of enquiry at the school. At no point did I think her life would be in danger. Had I thought that, then I certainly wouldn't have sent her alone. You have to believe me, Ma'am. Abby and I were to meet her, so she wouldn't have been alone. Unfortunately, we got stuck in traffic, so we were late getting there."

The DCI sighed heavily. She knew her hands were tied. She'd always known that Scott was a hard-working, dedicated officer and an excellent team leader. She implicitly trusted him and his past results were a testament to his intelligence, tenacity and sense of justice. However, the spotlight was firmly fixed on Scott, and indirectly on her. She fixed her gaze on Scott, uncomfortable with what she had to say next.

"Scott, I have no choice but to temporarily suspend you whilst a full investigation is conducted into the death of DC Sian Mason. You'll be relieved of your duties immediately and we'll appoint another officer to take over from you."

Scott sat in stunned disbelief. His whole world had just been flipped over on its axis. The investigation was standard procedure, but the suspension was harder to stomach.

"Ma'am, I appreciate you have to do this, and it's standard operating procedure, but I've done nothing wrong. I'm getting closer to wrapping up this case. I've got motive, and I've now got a name, the potential suspect."

"Scott, you know the rules. Any information you've got regarding this case can be passed on to the next SIO. Whoever's assigned as the senior investigating officer can review your information and evidence and decide whether it needs a follow-up."

Desperation crawled from his gut up his throat, threatening to choke him. He'd spent the last eight days working tirelessly with his team to get a result. Chancing his luck, he asked, "Ma'am, just give me until the end of the shift. Let me get a result. Let me do this for Sian, please?"

DCI Harvey shook her head vigorously. "Scott you know I can't do this! Both of our careers depend on this."

"Ma'am, don't you think I know that?" Scott asked, nodding to the corner of the room, where a grey-coloured box sat on the floor half-filled with a few files, personal photographs and certificates. "Is that because of me?"

DCI Jane Harvey gazed at the box for a few seconds. "No. It's been a long time coming. They've been on at me for months to take retirement, to step down. I'm not stupid. I know I'm old school, and a bit set in my ways. I'm hardly the poster girl for modern-day policing, am I?" Harvey paused for a moment, and swallowed hard. "So I'm retiring with immediate effect. Someone more *their type* will take over the reins. Someone whose thinking and leadership is more in line with what they expect."

"They're kicking you out?" Scott asked.

"Well, I wouldn't exactly put it in those terms. It's more like a gentle shove to the edge of the cliff, with a ball of concrete attached to my ankles," she said sarcastically.

"Then give me just a few more hours to wrap this case. I've got a name and I've got a hunch. Just cover for me a few more hours, that's all. Let's both walk out of here with our heads held high, and one last good result under our belts. Please?"

DCI Harvey shook her head slowly. She knew the right thing to do would be to stick to the rules, but she'd never been one for rules. Perhaps that had been the reason for her downfall and subsequent managed exit from the force. She glanced at the ceiling, her internal dialogue racing around her mind. She blew out a deep whistle of air.

"Shit, I'm going to regret this. You've got a few more hours. Prove them wrong, Scott. And do this for Sian."

WITH HIS TEAM dwindling by the minute, Raj was the only one holding the fort as Scott burst through the doors of the CID room. Raj cast a sad and lonely figure as he sat there reeling from the news and staring at a blank computer screen.

"Raj, how are you holding up?" Scott asked, placing a hand on Raj's shoulder.

Raj jolted. "Sorry, Guv I didn't even know you were there. Must have been away with the fairies."

"I know. Listen, I'm only here for a few more hours, and then I'm on suspension pending a full investigation. So I need you to hold the fort with Mike until Abby's back tomorrow."

Raj's eyes widened and his mouth opened. "Sorry to hear that, Guv. If there's anything I can do to help, you know you can just ask."

"I know, and I appreciate it. But I'm in enough trouble as it is. The last thing I need is you getting into trouble, too. Actually come to think of it, there is something you can do for me. Have a look through the Edmunston-Hunt School website and look at the gallery section. See if you can find class photographs or year photographs going back about twenty to twenty-two years."

"No probs, what am I looking for?"

"I'm looking for a name. Peter Jennings. He was fifteen when he drowned at the school. If you find it, ping it through to me in the office."

Scott thumped down in his chair, his body aching. He couldn't really account for the last few hours. When he closed his eyes, today just appeared like a blur. His tight shoulders pinched his neck muscles and his legs felt leaden. He glanced around his office, hoping that this wasn't the last time he'd be sitting in his chair. He grabbed his phone and dialled Cara's number. In all the melee of today and the past few days he'd barely had the opportunity or inclination to call her. Feeling a little sheepish, he waited for her to answer.

"Scott, you okay, babes? Just heard about Sian. I'm so, so sorry," she said, her voice shaky with emotion.

Scott felt numb. He'd been running on adrenaline for the past few hours, and was now coming back down with an almighty bang.

"I've had better days. Think we're all still in shock about Sian. And…I've been suspended pending an investigation."

"Well, just remember it's not personal. They have to follow procedure. Listen, how about you come over afterwards? We can talk; we need to talk. I've missed you. I know you're busy but I can't stand the thought of you going through this alone."

Scott agreed. "I've missed you too, and I'm sorry for every-thing. I'll see you later."

He hung up not entirely sure exactly what would happen over the next few hours, but a hunch started to crystallise into a plan. The screen on his computer bleeped to signal an incoming email from Raj.

Good man! Raj had managed to take a screenshot of an old black-and-white photograph that showed two lines of students posing for a house photograph. The second row stood on an elevated platform. Beneath the photograph were the names of all the boys in a list, row by row. Scott scanned the names and found Peter Jennings. He looked just as Collier had described: thin, slight-framed, pale skin, red hair and freckles.

If anything, Scott noticed that Peter Jennings had similar characteristics to Matthew Edrington. Scott continued staring at the list of names as they appeared in the photo. Beside Peter's name was Timothy Marchant's. In fact, on closer inspection as he enlarged the photo, they were standing very close to each other, their shoulders overlapping more so than with any other pupils in photograph. Timothy Marchant was slightly chubbier, had a round face, dark hair and a large forehead with small eyes. But a charming, large radiant smile lit his face that stood out amongst the crowd.

The printer in the corner of his office whirred into action as the blown-up image rolled off. His next stop would have been the geeks in the high-tech unit, but they'd know about his suspension. Heading over to Sussex HQ in Lewes would be risky, too. He only had one option left...Sussex University would have to do.

44

Simon Barrett waited by the visitors' car park as Scott pulled up. "Inspector Baker, good to see you again. I wasn't expecting to hear from you again so soon, but it's a welcome surprise," he said, extending his hand.

"Yes, sorry for calling you out of the blue and so late in the afternoon, but my investigation is moving quickly, and the next few hours are critical."

"I'm sure, Inspector. I gathered that from the urgency in your tone when you called me."

"As I said on the phone, I need an image adjusted. We do have the capability to do it in-house, but I couldn't get it turned around in less than twenty-four hours, and I really need it now."

They walked through the corridors of the university towards the Centre for Photography and Visual Culture. "I've spoken to one of the lecturers there and he's assured me that they have specialist facilities and multiple edit suites with Adobe Premiere Pro alongside a Pro-tools suite. They'll have the Photoshop thingy you asked for," Simon said, cycling his hand as he tried to convey the terminology that had been explained to him by his colleague.

As they swung through some frosted glass doors, the fabric of faculty building reflected its use. Crisp clean lines and modern whitewashed brick walls created a fresh and exciting atmosphere. Small clusters of prints set out in symmetrical patterns dotted the walls at random intervals, like they would in a modern art gallery in London. Scott's shoes squeaked on the highly polished, dark red tile floors that offered a contrast to the lightness of the walls.

They turned into a small studio situated off the main corridor. The high-tech atmosphere surprised Scott. Several large LCD screens sat on stands above a long desk full of laptops, boxes that had a bewildering display of dials, switches and buttons. It looked like something from NASA launch control.

A middle-aged man, thin, with lanky, dark hair and thick, black box-framed glasses swivelled around in his chair, but didn't bother to get up. He seemed friendly enough as he gave Scott a nod whilst Simon did the introductions.

"Craig, this is Detective Inspector Baker from Brighton CID. He needs our...well, *your* help on a rather urgent matter. Can I leave him in your capable hands?"

After thanking Simon, Craig offered Scott the seat next to him. "Simon said you needed some Photoshopping?"

"That's correct," Scott replied, handing over the blown-up image. "I need to age this image if possible," Scott requested.

"I would have thought you'd have access to more sophisticated age progression software than our Photoshop?"

"We do but the turnaround is a bit slow with bureaucracy, paperwork, cost centres and all that stuff. You know how it is…" Scott said, trying to sound convincing. "It's that boy there that I want aged." He pointed with a tip of a pen.

"That shouldn't be a problem."

"Does this type of thing take long?"

"Depends on how much detail you need, the degree of accuracy and of course the quality of the original," Craig said, pushing his glasses onto his forehead so he could get a closer look at the quality of the image. "It's not great I'm afraid. It's an old picture. It's grainy, and more pixelated because it's been blown up."

Scott nodded. "Anything is better than nothing to be honest."

Craig seemed to have everything within arm's reach, and Scott wondered if it had been set up deliberately like this for convenience and laziness. He watched as Craig lifted the lid on a scanner next to him, placed the photo face down on the glass, closed the lid and pressed the black start button all in one deft, slick movement.

The image started to appear on a screen behind them. He smiled slightly as yet again Craig swivelled around another forty-five degrees to face the screen. Craig had certainly set up his studio in a way that reduced his physical exertions to the barest minimum.

Scott watched in fascination as Craig used a piece of software to outline the boy in question and then remove him from the picture, leaving a square hole. The sound of rapid mouse clicks made it hard for Scott to follow exactly what was being done, and he had to admit that Craig had lost him.

"I'm just cutting out the image, so we can work on just that. I'll save it first before opening it up in Photoshop."

Craig flicked through a few screens before the image reappeared in Adobe Photoshop surrounded by rows of editing features and tools. "Do you know much about Photoshop?"

"I've heard of it. I think I've even got it on my laptop at home, but I've never used it. I'm already lost just watching what you've done so far," replied Scott.

Craig let out small laugh. "Yeah, it has that effect on people. I'm going to blow up the image, which will make it a bit grainy to begin with, but that will get sorted as I work on it. Then I'll refine the edges as we go. How does that sound?"

Scott nodded in agreement.

"Age?"

"Sorry?"

"What age do you want him to be?" Craig clarified.

"Hmm, good question. Can we try later thirties?"

"Thirty-seven, thirty-eight?"

"Sounds good for starters."

"I'm going to add some puffiness to his face, a few wrinkles. What about hair?" Craig asked as he clicked furiously with the mouse, using one editing tool after another.

"Keep it dark, the same with maybe a little bit of creep?"

"So full head, but larger forehead," Craig verified, before he selected the brush option to work on the eyebrows.

The heat of all the equipment in the room made it increasingly stuffy. Scott felt his eyes getting heavier and stifled a few yawns through gritted teeth in the hope that Craig wouldn't notice.

"How's this looking?"

"Could you elongate the nose? It's quite a young, boyish, thick nose at the moment and doesn't suit the rest of the face."

"Sure, no problem."

"Beard, moustache, earring, glasses, scars, spots?" Craig asked.

"Not sure to be honest. Leave them off for the time being."

"Once I've got the image the way you want it, I can knock up a few more with a beard, without and some specs too?"

"That would be great. Could you email those to me if that's okay as I'll need to shoot soon."

An older face formed on the screen which piqued Scott's interest. "On second thoughts, can you add a beard in?"

Craig nodded and delivered the request in a few extra clicks. "Bushy, long, tight, neatly trimmed, colour?"

Scott's skin began to prickle as his eyes narrowed from the confusing number of choices. "Tight, trimmed and the same colour as his hair."

With a few final rapid clicks, Craig leant back to admire and show off his handiwork. "There you go. That's probably as best as I can get it with the little time we've got. Does that help?"

"One hundred per cent."

45

Why did traffic always appear to move slower when he needed to get somewhere? Scott fumed as he turned right into Coldean Lane and raced back towards Ditchling. Every learner driver, red traffic light, bus and slow-moving lorry seemed to be in his way deliberately testing his patience.

Scott called Mike's number, the ringing tone filling his car on loudspeaker. "Come on, come on, pick up, Mike," Scott barked at the Bluetooth. The evening sun hung low in the horizon, leaving a long eerie tale of red eyes glowing as traffic snaked up the hill and past the university's hall of residence.

The visit to Sussex University had been more fruitful than he had imagined. Whilst he'd sat behind Craig and watched in awe as he manipulated the image, Scott's excitement had expanded within his chest, threatening to overflow. At first he'd racked his brain to think of all the times, places and situations he'd been where he might have seen that face. At first, a vague reference flitted across his consciousness, and then he'd been able to figure out exactly where he'd seen it.

His revelation had not only opened up a new line of enquiry, but it had helped lock various pieces of the jigsaw together. Revenge was a plausible motive for the murders, but still left the unanswered question as to why Latin inscriptions and white feathers had been left at all of the crime scenes. *Were they a clue? A calling card?*

Sure Simon had said that the English interpretation of the inscriptions was in reference to cowards, but the why was becoming clearer. There was the belief that bullies felt powerful in numbers, but get any one of them alone, and their personalities changed. Most bullies were weak individuals in Scott's opinion. They lacked self-confidence, had low self-esteem and more often than not lacked intelligence. Rather than have these faults exposed or exploited, it was easier to hide behind a wall of violence, fear and intimidation.

"Guv?"

"Mike, are you still at the school?"

"Yes, Guv. Why? What's up?"

"We still got Collier?"

"Yes, we've got him detained. I hadn't heard back from you so uniform were just about taking him back to the station. Guv, I heard the news about you being taken off the case. Pardon my French, but what the fuck's that about?"

"I can't explain at the moment, Mike, but you must listen to me. It's really urgent. Do not let Collier out of your sight. Yes, he is a suspect and we've charged him, but I also think he is now a potential target. I believe his life is in danger.

I'm on my way and I'm just a few minutes away. I also reckon that the person who attacked Sian is still on the grounds of the school, and Collier could be the next target.

"The man we need to find is Timothy Saunders. He's the catering manager for the school. Keep your eyes peeled, and get uniform to check and double-check everything, search the grounds, search the school, his home…find him."

"Will do, Guv. See you in a bit."

"Mike, how are you bearing up? We've all had a massive shock."

"I'm okay, Guv. Yes, it's hard. I've been in shit like this before, but we've got a job to do."

On the face of it, Mike's response could have appeared cold and insensitive. But Mike had often spoken about his time served in the military. Losing a colleague was something he'd experienced on more than one occasion. Whilst serving in Afghanistan, he'd fought alongside soldiers who had lost their lives in horrific and unimaginable ways. Soldiers just a few feet away from him had died in daily attacks by Taliban insurgents.

He'd witnessed one young soldier lose the back of his head after taking a bullet through his eye from a sniper over five hundred yards away. Another rifleman had lost his left leg below the knee after stepping on an IED and Mike had spent the next fifteen minutes with both hands over the stump of the soldier's leg trying to stem the blood loss from the tangled and frayed mess of veins, arteries, shattered bone fragments and torn tissue. The soldier never made it back to the safety of Camp Bastion. He died in the field despite Mike's efforts.

What hit him the hardest was losing his best mate Jon Jo, a Welsh rifleman. A cheeky, brave and fearless soldier, who always found a way to make the platoon laugh. He was fit, into his weight training and did regular hikes up Pen Y Fan, the highest peak in southern Wales, just for fun. It was probably the reason he'd initially survived after taking a direct hit from a suicide bomber who'd raced towards the checkpoint they were manning in Helmand province. Mike had momentarily frozen unable to comprehend the loss before he'd snapped back into work mode and defended the ensuing attack.

Experiences like those had left Mike able to function when others struggled. He'd become emotionally detached and resilient from the horrors of losing colleagues on the battle-field and losing Sian.

46

An NPAS helicopter hovered overhead as Scott approached the school. Its bright searchlight flickering in the darkened sky. Its powerful beam widening as it illuminated the grounds of the school. A powerful thermal imaging camera helped to identify any heat sources not visible to officers on the ground. The on-board camera system and the video downlink capability beamed back real-time information to the control room.

The grounds were awash with officers undertaking controlled sweeping arcs, their torchlights dancing erratically in the darkness of the evening. The rhythmic high-pitched whirring from the helicopter engine as its four blades cut through the air interrupted the strange, morbid stillness that hung in the air.

Mike stood beside a police van when Scott drove up alongside and parked up. "Any sightings, Mike?" Scott asked.

"Nothing as yet, Guv, well, nothing concrete. The dog picked up a scent coming out of the forest and back into the school but it seems to end in and around the entrance to the school kitchens and where the school food bins are. The dog was going back and forth. One minute it picked up a scent, and the next lost it. The handler thinks that something's been put down on the ground to confuse the dog."

"Anything else from Collier?" Scott asked, peering into the side window of the van. Collier sat solemnly between two uniformed officers, a third officer who was armed sat opposite them. Collier held his head high and stared straight ahead, choosing not to exchange a glance with Scott.

"No, Guv, I've kept him here until you arrived. Even though I'm not sure why we've kept him here. Surely, if he's in danger then we need to get him away from here pronto?"

"One simple word, Mike…bait. Whilst Collier is here, our man still has unfinished business. If Collier is the last target on his list, he'd want to get to Collier, and that means he'll still be close by."

"He'd be stupid to try and get to him," Mike said, nodding towards the van. "We've got half the force here."

"I know, but until I got back, I needed Collier here. For all we know, he could be watching us right now. He knows this place better than we do. It's safe to say that if he wanted to get to Collier he would have done so by now. Get Collier back to the station, and as much as I hate to say this, make sure he's well protected."

"Want me to go with them?"

"No, you stay with me. We're going to look for Saunders."

"He can't have many places to hide out, Guv. The grounds are swarming with uniformed. We've got the helo up, a dog unit here and the roads leading to the school are cordoned off."

"Well, the old music room is being combed over by SOCO. The corridors and rooms are being searched. So where else would he feel comfortable or safe, Mike?"

Mike wasn't sure from Scott's tone if he was asking a question or prompting him.

Before Mike had a chance to answer, Scott headed off towards the back of the building. Mike jogged the few steps to catch up, his heavy frame trying hard to keep up.

SCOTT STEPPED through a white uPVC door that led to the kitchens. A mixture of smells that were reminiscent of being back at school greeted his nostrils. It was a warming mix of meaty aromas that reminded him of the school meat pie or shepherd's pie. Then wafts of sweetness from a different part of the kitchen drew him in, the smell of chocolate chip sponge and custard sprang to mind. The overpowering and sanitising odour of cleaning fluids that clung in the air and drifted along the school corridors long after lunchtime was over erased all pleasant childhood memories from his mind.

A distinctive strong smell that assaulted his nostrils differentiated this kitchen from those in Scott's memories. "Pepper and chilli powder."

"And a lot of it too," Mike added, his nose itching as the first signs of an impending sneeze started to gather momentum. "Uniformed have…have…swept this area already, Guv. Back outside is where the dog kept losing the scent," he managed to get out before a thunderous sneeze broke the silence.

"Bless you. What does that tell you, Mike?"

"That I need a tissue. Sorry, dunno, that he's trying hard to lose us," he sniffed loudly.

"Exactly…and that means?"

Mike looked confused, second guessing Scott's meaning. "He doesn't want to be found?"

"That's certainly true, but more importantly, it means we're close. We're close to him and he doesn't like that. Look around you, Mike. The metal work surfaces are spotless, the shelves neatly stacked, but the floor is covered in footprints, and a pungent mix of spices. Admittedly, some of the prints will be the work of uniform traipsing through here, but he's not going to go far. This is an area of the school he's most comfortable with. It's his territory."

"So you think he'd come back here?"

"Probably. Just in the way that Saunders wouldn't go into a classroom or interfere with teachers, teachers wouldn't come in here and interfere, so he'd feel safe here."

"Right, I get you, Guv," Mike nodded, looking around.

"On the face of it, he's just disappeared, but as it stands, he's not in the school building as far as we know. Nothing showed up on the heat sensors in the forest or grounds. Uniform are sweeping the surrounding area, *but* we know he's back here somewhere."

Scott paused. He crossed his arms and looked at the floor, his eyes darting from one set of footprints to another. *Where are you, you bastard?* Heavy imprints from

Magnum police boots criss-crossed the dark, shiny red tile floor. Dotted in amongst them were paw prints from the search dog. The dog had probably lost some of the scent due to the pepper and chilli powder mix. Nothing stood out; nothing made sense. Then he spotted it. Scott remained motionless as his eyes tracked them. A different set of footprints.

The prints headed off towards a corner of the kitchen furthest away from the door. "Mike, check these out," Scott remarked as he gingerly stepped around the prints and traced then in the direction they were heading.

"Saunders?"

"No idea, but it's likely if we can't place them with anyone else. And as far as we know, no one else has been in here."

"Kids?"

"Too big for kids."

The footsteps stopped by a large, industrial double door fridge-freezer that was pushed up against the far wall. Scott glanced around the sides of the unit, then behind it, before kneeling down.

"This has been moved, Mike. Look, there are rubber marks on the floor. Give me a hand."

Mike and Scott leant into the side of the unit expecting that due to its size it would barely move. They were both taken by surprise and exchanged curious looks when the unit smoothly glided with little effort. Scott knelt down again and peered underneath to see the unit resting on a set of roller gliders.

Pushing the unit aside, the men noticed the footprints

carried on and up to the wall. Again they both shot each other a glance before scanning the wall. There was no discernable or designated doorway. However, they could make out a thin line that had been cut into the wall towards the bottom.

"Just enough to crawl through?"

Scott agreed as he stuck a finger into the finger hole that had been drilled into the wall. Giving it a hard tug, a small section of the wall came away revealing a large dark space behind.

"Fairly easy for someone to crawl into and then pull the fridge back towards the wall…crafty," Mike murmured as he knelt down and peered into the darkened space. From within the blackness, Mike could just make out the outline of a corridor that disappeared into the distance. He reached for his phone and switched on his backlight to offer more illumination. "It goes on a bit, Guv. Judging from the stud wall partitioning, it looks like an old corridor that's been sealed up."

"Well, the building is old enough. I wouldn't be surprised if there's a warren of hidden walkways and corridors beneath the school and behind these walls."

Mike lifted a hand to pause Scott, before sticking his head further into the gap. He waited for a few moments before withdrawing. "Think I can hear something, Guv. Could just be rats, or the big rat we're after?"

"Only one way to find out. Call it in and get backup," Scott replied, squeezing past Mike and crawling through the dusty dark hole.

Mike followed whilst relaying their findings and position to the ops room. The corridor was wide enough for just one person to walk through so Mike followed behind, the lights on their phones barely strong enough to illuminate their way. The corridor smelt damp and musky, years of no ventilation and natural light had left an eerie, cold feeling as they walked slowly, feeling their way. Their hands were cold and moist from the dampness that clung in the air and weaved its way into the fabric of their clothes.

A rustling up ahead stopped them in their tracks. Scott strained hard in the darkness to focus and identify the source of the noise. Mike stood poised on Scott's shoulder ready to barge past in his normal heavy-handed manner. They waved their useless phones in the bleakness that surrounded them. A glimmer of brightness bounced back at them. Then it happened again as they inched further. An outline loomed ahead. The outline of a man.

47

"This is the police! Identify yourself!" Scott instructed as his narrowed eyes searched the darkness.

The silhouetted figure remained still and silent. He stood his ground, the glint of his blade bouncing off the walls as the light hit it.

"This is the police, identify yourself now!" Scott shouted, lips curled in a sneer. "We're armed officers! Put the knife down!"

"Now, now, Inspector, we both know you're bluffing. CID officers don't carry arms unless they're specially trained."

Yes, he was bluffing, and had been called out on it, but what took Scott and Mike by surprise was the reference to inspector. *Saunders?* Most people just cooperated or became further agitated when commanded to do something by the police, but not only was his command being challenged, but the dark figure appeared to know his identity.

"Make yourself known to us now, Saunders?" Scott barked again.

"Inspector, Inspector, that's not how we do things around here. There's a pecking order. You have to toe the line, *oh, the wonderful line*." A hint of sarcasm tinged his cold, measured tone.

"Put the knife down before it's too late. Let's talk about this and see how we can help you."

The figure started to retreat back ever so slowly, the darkness swallowing him up.

"Bit late for that don't you think, Inspector? You have an uncanny knack of sticking around and that doesn't help me."

Before Scott could say anything else, the figure melted into the emptiness, his retreating footsteps the only giveaway of his escape.

"Proceed with caution," Scott whispered as they followed in pursuit, slow to begin with as they watched their footing in the semi-darkness.

Their laboured breathing drowned out the footsteps of the man they pursued. Each heavy step they took on the bare wooden floor was amplified tenfold in the confines of the corridor as the pace picked up. Scott had lost his bearings, unsure what direction they were heading in and what would greet them at the end. Each cautious turn delayed them further as they travelled deeper into the warren of passageways.

In the back of Scott's mind, he knew that confronting and pursuing an armed suspect required tact, backup and caution. The very same elements he'd discarded as he'd gone after his man. He knew he'd put his life at risk as well as Mike's. But adrenaline coursed through his veins, spurring him on. His desire for a result and justice over-shadowed any logical argument for stopping the pursuit now.

A glimmer of light punctured the darkness. A soft glow that radiated out from a doorway up ahead. Scott put out his arm to slow Mike down before he placed a finger to his lips to indicate the need for silence. The glow flickered and danced on the walls of the corridor.

Alarm bells rang in Scott's mind as he pressed his back to the wall of the corridor and peered around the corner through the doorway before entering. The overpowering smell of fuel hung in the air like a deadly assassin.

Scott glanced around the room, dimly illuminated from an assortment of tea light candles that been placed around the perimeter. His eyes darted over towards the fireplace mantelpiece where several Molotov cocktails rested, primed with fuel soaked rags. Fear raced through his body as his heartbeat accelerated. Scott's mouth dried as he realised the volatility of the environment, then anger boiled up inside him as he realised that they had been lured into a trap. He knew that fumes from the fuel could be ignited at any moment. He could have seconds or minutes before the whole room went up like a Guy Fawkes Night bonfire.

Shit, as Scott looked around nervously, small pieces of paper had been pinned to the walls, all bearing the same Latin inscriptions. He couldn't be certain from this distance, but they looked identical to the ones that had been placed at each crime scene.

That murdering piece of shit, Saunders, stood behind a solitary wooden chair that had been placed in the centre of the room. Its worn seat still pooling a liquid that Scott assumed was more fuel. Several lengths of rope lay loosely around the chair's legs, handcuffs hung from the armrests ready to receive their captive. A green plastic fuel can and a box of matches sat close by.

The whole damn place was soaked in petrol.

"Saunders, it doesn't have to come to this. We can end this peacefully and all come out of this alive," Scott said, in a useless attempt to reason with a psychopath.

Saunders sniggered, enjoying the futility of the predicament that Mike and Scott found themselves in. Seeing grown men squirm and panic excited him. A soothing sense of satisfaction raced through his body, tingling his spine and relaxing his muscles. He inhaled deeply through his nose as he closed his eyes to enjoy the moment.

"It's a little too late for that don't you think, Inspector?" he replied, pointing the knife in their direction.

In the dull light, Scott could clearly see a dark coating that enveloped the blade. *Blood. Sian's blood?*. He fisted his hands at his sides. They twitched and itched in a desperate need to squeeze the life from this prick's body. Scott needed to keep Saunders talking whilst he analysed the situation. In a matter of minutes, reinforcements would be arriving, and if the situation went horribly wrong, the fire-ball created by the Molotov cocktails would race down the corridor like a raging bull taking out everything in its path as it sought an avenue to escape.

Scott elbowed Mike. "Get out of here, Mike. Get *everyone* out of here," he repeated, widening his eyes as fear and anger took over.

"Guv, I'm not…"

"It's an order, Mike. Get…the fuck…out of here. Now!"

Mike struggled with the need to be compliant versus his military ingrained instincts to stay, defend and fight. He glanced back and forth between Saunders and Scott. He was tetchy. Part of his mind calculated whether he could cover the six feet that stood between him and Saunders before Saunders could react. He reasoned with himself. Back in his military days, he wouldn't have thought twice about it, but Civvy Street had taken its toll. He was slower and admittedly, significantly heavier.

Mike stared at Scott as they exchanged silent thoughts. He felt a sense of duty to stand by his senior officer, but at the same time realised the need to avert a bigger catastrophe by warning the advancing officers of the danger that lay ahead. Mike started to take a few tentative steps backwards, retreating from the room, his eyes firmly fixed on Saunders. Every fibre of his body willed him to stay by Scott. The wrench of pulling himself away from the situation sat heavy with him.

"That's a good boy; you run along like the good inspector's told you. Save yourself because the inspector has a nasty habit of letting down those that matter…don't you, Inspector?" Saunders sneered again with a cold steely glare. "This isn't your battle, Inspector. I'll make you a deal. I'll exchange you for Collier."

"It doesn't work that way. Listen, I know what happened. I know about what happened to Peter Jennings."

48

"You know nothing!" Saunders screamed wildly, as his face turned from placid and relaxed to red with rage. "You know nothing!" he screamed again as he flailed his arms. "You'll never know what it feels like to lose someone you love."

"I do, Timothy. I do, trust me," Scott said softly. "I know what they did to Peter, but taking lives in revenge isn't the way to resolve the situation."

"They killed him. They punished him. They bullied him."

"Is that why you were so protective of Matthew, because he was being bullied? Because you felt his pain?"

"He's just a soft soul. He's done no harm, but that's the problem with this fucking place. It's wrong; the weakest don't survive," Saunders cried, his eyes heavy, tears escaping down his cheeks and into his beard.

Fearful of an imminent explosion, Scott pleaded with Saunders to leave with him now. Everything he said seemed to wash over Saunders, his behaviour becoming more erratic, volatile and unpredictable, just like the situation.

"Do you know how hard it was living a secret life?"

"No, why don't you tell me, Timothy?"

Saunders sobbed, as snot trails run over his lips. "I've known since I was a young boy that I was different. I dreaded coming here knowing I was different."

"And then you met Peter? Someone who felt the same way you did?"

Saunders nodded helplessly, the fight leaving him deflated. "I could handle what they threw at me…but Peter couldn't. He became the soft target. Johnson, Rochester, Winterbottom, Goddard…used him as their punchbag. They were scum. They were cowards and deserved to die. And yet they could do no wrong. Collier loved them, loved how hard and manly they were." His eyes narrowed, his lips thin and teeth clenched as he spat out his words with fury.

"Why now? Why after all these years?"

Saunders curled up his lip slightly, feeling pleased with himself. "It's taken me this long to get close to them. I've been planning this moment for most of my life. I wanted to see them up close. I wanted to live around them and see how they went about their lives without a care in the world. And they did. Goddard was the only one shitting himself, and rightly so. And what did he do? He got pissed and beat the crap out of his wife!"

As Saunders spoke, Scott had slowly inched further away from him towards the door.

"Do you think I wanted to be a chef…or a bloody catering

manager? I've wasted years learning how to cook. NVQs for this, NVQs for that. Going from one restaurant to another, one school to another, 'til I landed this job. Doing so allowed me to blend into the background and bide my time."

"And Collier? Why him? He wasn't involved?"

"Yes, he was. It was entirely his fault!" Saunders screamed again, his hands on either side of his head. "It was always him. He was the housemaster. It was his prefects. Then he brought them back as teachers. It was always Collier, and now you've spoiled the main event. Just like a guy on a bonfire, Collier's seat was all ready for him...'til you spoiled it, Inspector. And now you must pay the price...or give me Collier."

Saunders rocked on his heels, his eyes closed, mumbling incoherently. He shook his head from side to side.

"Taking your life doesn't solve anything. You're better than them. Give it up now, Saunders."

Saunders raised a finger to his lips. "I've done what I came here to do. I've nothing to live for. My time will come again, another life, another being." He reached into his pocket and pulled out a lighter, then proceeded to taunt Scott with it. "Justice will prevail; the weak will die. Justice will prevail; the weak will die," he chanted repeatedly.

"No!" Scott screamed. "Don't do this!"

Scott's word fell on deaf ears. Saunders opened his eyes and stared at Scott coldly. The emotion had drained from the man's expression. He looked solemnly in Scott's direction before a small smile broke across his face. The scratch of the wheel on flint was the last thing Scott heard before he was thrown back by a searing surge of orange heat. The blast threw him clean back out into the corridor. He scrambled to his feet. His face felt hot. His skin stung. His eyes burnt. He stumbled to the side of the door as he glanced back in, holding up a hand to shield his face from the intense heat that prickled his skin.

A yellow and orange ball of flames consumed Saunders's body. A human fireball. No cries or screams pierced the air. The man didn't even drop to the floor in an attempt to extinguish the flames or escape the skin-melting heat. Saunders's body stood motionless as it disappeared into a golden inferno. The chair in front of him roared, the wood crackling and creaking as the fire took hold and engulfed the room. Saunders's face melted, his skin peeling off like hot candle wax from a candle, his clothes offering the perfect kindling to encourage the flames.

Scott didn't have time to hang around. There was nothing he could do now other than save himself. He knew that once the Molotov cocktails exploded, the ensuing flashover and fireball could be moments away. That would be catastrophic for him as the fireball only had one way to travel and that was back down the corridor. He stumbled and fell from one side of the corridor to the other as he desperately tried to retrace his steps. He wasn't sure if the smoke that wrapped around him or his injuries slowed him down, but the passageway seemed to go on forever.

He fell to his knees. Smoke choked his lungs robbing him of air. His chest burnt; his eyes stung. He seemed to be in the middle of a thick acrid sea of black, choking smoke. He could feel the heat rearing up behind him. *Fire.* He needed to get away. He probed his surroundings but confusion tightened its grip on him. Darkness swooped around him

like a hungry vulture waiting to pounce on its weak prey.
He coughed hard through his parched mouth. Disorientated
and unsure which way to turn, he fell forward succumbing
to the smoke.

The corridor fell silent.

49

Mike kicked through the ashes. Blackened walls left a chilling reminder of the fireball that had ripped through the room. The choking, acrid smell of fuel hung invisibly in the air, stinging his nostrils. Sweat beaded on his forehead from the heat that lingered. He watched with his hands stuffed in his trouser pockets as firemen around him doused the burning embers. Columns of steam rose from the charred wood, spiralling upwards gracefully, swirling around innocently in the still air.

It was nothing he hadn't seen before. Burnt out Afghan houses and those who had once lived in them exposed him to the horrors of war. Parents, children, young and old, none of it mattered. Fire was indiscriminate; it took anyone who stood in its path.

He stared at the charred, blackened body of Saunders lying in the middle of the room. *Fuck that smell of burnt flesh.* He's seen enough charred bodies to feel unfazed by them now. It was an acrid, moist smell in your nose with a hint of earth and bubbling fat. It didn't smell like meat, but you

knew it was human and it was haunting. Mike remembered
one of his unit commanders talking about it. *It was a smell
that writes itself into your brain and cannot be erased.*

The coroner's van would be here soon to remove the body.
From where Saunders lay and what was left of him, it
would have been impossible to distinguish any discernable
features, yet alone if it was male or female. Mike shook his
head in bewilderment.

———————

HOT DAMP AIR clung around his mouth. Suffocated him. He
lifted his heavy hand in front of his eyes and gazed at the
white gauze dressing wrapped around his left hand. He
blinked hard as tears from his stinging eyes escaped and
carved white trails through the black soot that covered his
face. He coughed hard, mucus rising to the back of his
throat. He needed air, fresh air, but a paramedic had pinned
a face mask firmly over his mouth. He pulled it away to
take lungfuls of air which made him cough even more
violently. His hand stung as his fingers bent around the
face mask.

"I guess you like living on the edge," DCI Harvey said. She
was perched on a chair alongside Scott in the back of an
ambulance.

He tried to talk but winced when nothing came out. His
throat stung from smoke inhalation. He glanced over to the
DCI and shook his head in resignation. In a faint crackly
tone he said, "Well, I'm definitely on suspension now."

He felt exhausted, his mind desperately processing the
events of the last few hours. *What the fuck just happened?*

The ambulance rocked a bit as the large hulking figure of Mike clambered in. "You had a lucky escape, Guv. You okay?"

Scott blinked furiously, desperately trying to shake the fuzziness that prevented him from thinking clearly. "Saunders?"

Mike shook his head. "I've seen more meat on a barbecued spare rib."

DCI Harvey and Scott both shot him a disparaging look, which Mike met with one of his nonchalant shrugs as if to suggest, *what's the big deal?*

The DCI tapped Scott on the shoulder. "The good news is you'll survive. You've got a few superficial burns to your left hand, a bit on your face. You've lost a bit of your eyebrows, but nothing an eyebrow pencil won't sort out." Mike fought to contain a laugh that threatened to get him in even more trouble. "And you've got a bit of smoke inhalation. They're taking you to the hospital for a check-up."

"Abby?"

"Abby is doing okay. We'll be offering her a counsellor if she needs one, but our Abby is made of strong stuff. She'll pull through this. We've all been affected by Sian's death, not just CID, not just Brighton either but the whole of Sussex constabulary. It's going to take a long time for all of us to come to terms with it." DCI Harvey sighed.

Harvey's words brought forward the reality of his situation. He'd lost a good member of his team. A young, vibrant, intelligent officer who he had no doubt would have gone on to bigger and better things. He was her commanding officer. It was his responsibility to ensure her safety as well as the safety of others on his team, and somehow he felt that rightly or wrongly, he had failed. *Failed yet again to protect those around me.* No doubt the internal investigation would determine what part he had to play in her death. Were procedures followed correctly? Had a suitable risk assessment being conducted and more importantly could her death have been avoided?

50

S cott had to endure an overnight stay for observation at the Royal Sussex County Hospital. He'd been surrounded by geriatrics and the infirm who seem to have had their own inter-ward competition for who could cough the loudest and who could shout 'nurse' the most times during the night. His only consolation after a poor night's sleep had been a visit from Abby the following morning. She had been a welcomed visitor. They'd sat together in the day room sipping some rather unpleasant hospital tea from some chipped china mugs whilst talking through the events of the last twenty-four hours.

The DCI had been right. On the face of it, Abby appeared to be strong and coping well. It may have just been a front, a defence mechanism to get her through the trauma. They still had Sian's impending funeral. It would be a particularly difficult moment to deal with, and Scott really didn't know how he'd be able to face Sian's parents and family. Scott knew the eyes of the force would be looking at him. Judging him. He would no doubt face some difficult questions from friends and colleagues, and that was something he wasn't prepared for. He didn't have the answers. He wished he did.

THE FRESH SEA air felt cool and cleansing as they walked along the beach. The waves crackled over the stones as seagulls floated effortlessly, dipping and diving opportunists ready to swoop down and grab a discarded chip or half-eaten sandwich.

Scott and Cara walked hand in hand. An uncomfortable and awkward silence marred the majority of the walk. Neither knew what to say and neither were willing to start the conversation, afraid of where it might end up.

Scott stopped a short distance from the Brighton i360, the city's new attraction, a one-hundred-and-sixty-two-feet high observation tower with a viewing capsule. On a clear day, it offered spectacular views towards the marina and beyond towards the white cliffs of the infamous suicide spot Beachy Head in the east, and to Worthing Pier and Portslade in the west. It was an unmistakable modern feature on the Brighton landscape.

Cara stepped round to face Scott reaching out to hold each of his hands as she rubbed the backs of them with her thumbs. "Scott, listen to me. Babes, I'm really sorry. I know you're angry with me and I don't blame you. I put you…and us, in danger. But now you know why I had to leave London. Jason was a violent bastard.

"It all started off really well. He was really kind, very caring and generous. Then he started staying out later and later. He started drinking and coming home and being really aggressive towards me. I was being criticised about my job. He tormented me about it, saying it was creepy, that there must be something wrong with me. One minute it was my weight, the next it was what I wore, or what I cooked for him. He always found something to have a go about. He hit me a few times. Stupid me, I didn't leave. I was too scared. And…then I fell pregnant.

"And trust me, I really wanted a baby. I have always wanted children, but the thought of bringing up a child in that abusive environment…I knew it wasn't safe for me or the baby. It wasn't fair."

"So why didn't you just leave, and still have the baby?"

"Jason would have always been in my life because of the baby. As long as I had his baby, he had an influence in my life; he had a way of controlling me. He'd told me on plenty of occasions that if I left him, he'd track me down." Cara grabbed Scott's jacket and looked pleadingly into his eyes. "Scott, you've got to believe me. I've always wanted a family. I've always wanted children, but it had to be with the right person."

Scott turned away and looked out towards the sea, his eyes drawn to the emptiness of a vast ocean. "But you kept this from me. Meanwhile, we had all this shit going on and it was all down to him. I thought we had no secrets." He shook his head as he stared down at the ground unable to look her in the eyes.

"I'm sorry for keeping you in the dark and not telling you sooner. When an amazing relationship like this creeps up on you, coupled with what you've already been through, I genuinely didn't know how to tell you. I couldn't just say 'Hi, I love being your girlfriend, and oh, by the way, I was once pregnant but didn't want the baby so I had an abortion!'"

Scott shot her an angry glance, and shook his head in frustration. "I didn't mean it that way."

"Sorry, Scott. I didn't mean to be flippant. I fell in love with you, Scott, and the deeper I fell in love with you the harder it became to tell you. I know how much you've struggled every single day since losing your family, and I know just how much Becky meant to you. I was worried that you might think I didn't take the life of a child seriously, because if I did, I wouldn't have had a termination. I know I'm not making a lot of sense," Cara said, rubbing her temples with her thumbs and squeezing eyes tight. "I hope you understand my reasons at the time. I guess I ran away. I tried to get as far away as possible. To start a new life."

Scott's mind raced. He hated deceit; he despised lies. But he loved Cara, too. She'd brought brightness and happiness back into his life.

"I can't say that I'm completely okay about this. I do understand your reasons for leaving and your decision. God knows, I've seen the fallout from so many abusive relationships in my job, and you did something that a lot of women are unable to do, and that's to walk away.

"In my eyes, every child's life is so precious, whether born or unborn. And when my child was taken away from me, I guess I found it hard to comprehend why anyone would deliberately terminate a life. I guess that's why I was so confused towards you."

"I know. I don't blame you for being funny towards me. I just want you to appreciate the circumstances I was in that led me to making that decision. I love you, Scott Baker. Please find it in your heart to forgive me," Cara said through moist eyes as her bottom lip trembled.

Scott closed his eyes as they rested on each other's foreheads, their noses touching in a flutter of Eskimo kisses. Cara had filled a void in his life and for that he was grateful. She was right; everyone makes mistakes. It was his own internal demons that he was battling and if he was honest with himself, Cara's situation was a distraction for him to deflect the anger that boiled inside of him.

"No more secrets," he whispered.

"I promise."

———

PLEASE JOIN my reader's group for your free starter library:

www.jay.nadal.com

NEXT IN THE SERIES – CAPTIVE

CURRENT BOOK LIST

Hop over to my website for a current list of books:

www.jaynadal.com

ABOUT THE AUTHOR

I've always had a strong passion for whodunnits, crime series and books. The more I immersed myself in it, the stronger the fascination grew.

In my spare time you'll find me in the gym, trying to squeeze in a read or enjoying walks in the forest...It's amazing what you think of when you give yourself some space.

Oh, and I'm an avid people-watcher. I just love to watch the interaction between people, their mannerisms, their way of expressing their thoughts...Weird I know.

I hope you enjoy the stories that I craft for you.

Author of:

The DI Scott Baker Crime Series

The DI Karen Heath Crime Series

The Thomas Cade PI Series

Printed in Great Britain
by Amazon

83564839R00212